my brother's wedding

Andaleeb Wajid is the author of *Kite Strings*, *Blinkers Off* and *More than Just Biryani*. Her stories have been published in *Good Housekeeping* and she has written extensively for the children's supplement of *Deccan Herald*, 'Open Sesame'. Andaleeb worked as a technical writer and then did a stint in corporate communications before she quit to concentrate on a full-time writing career. She lives in Bengaluru with her family.

my brother's wedding

ANDALEEB WAJID

RUPA

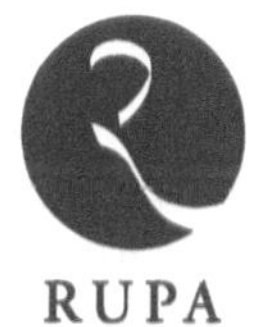

Published by
Rupa Publications India Pvt. Ltd 2013
7/16, Ansari Road, Daryaganj
New Delhi 110002

Sales centres:
Allahabad Bengaluru Chennai
Hyderabad Jaipur Kathmandu
Kolkata Mumbai

This is a work of fiction. Names, characters, places and incidents are either the product of the author's imagination or are used fictitiously, and any resemblance to any actual persons, living or dead, events or locales is entirely coincidental.

ISBN: 978-81-291-2399-2

10 9 8 7 6 5 4 3 2

Typeset in Dante MT Std by Saanavi Graphics, Noida

For my sons, Saboor and Azhaan

1

Ooh la la! It's my brother's wedding. As if I care.

POSTED BY THE OTHER T, 01-01-12

My brother is getting married finally. No, no, it's not what it sounds like. The thing is, my sister and my mother had a most harrowing time trying to find a suitable girl for him. Yes, my brother Y, the hugely successful software engineer who turned all of twenty-seven last month, is depending on my *mother* and my *sister* to find a girl for him. As if that wasn't enough, he won't be meeting her until *after* they're married, although I suppose he's feeling lucky that Q (my sister) snapped a quick picture on her iPhone for him when they went to 'see' her.

I started this blog as a way to rant at everyone in my family who is making my life hell, just because my brother is getting married. At times I think that if I had been a student living abroad, I wouldn't have bothered calling home unless I wanted to and I would have been pretty happy. But no, I'm nineteen, and I live right here in India with my family, trying to figure out Chaucer and Milton and pondering over my research paper when I am ambushed by my mother.

Ever since Q got married, she likes to come into my room, stare into space and rattle out random facts which she thinks I ought to remember. My poor mother misses Q a lot. They were/are like soul sisters. Completing each other's sentences and going shopping together and all that crap.

This blog is about my brother's wedding. I'm going to try and make it very entertaining as I plan to describe everything that happens in a typical Muslim wedding in detail. But I'm not using real names. There will be revenge, disownment and quick annihilation if the roots of this blog are ever traced to me. Of course, it's the revenge I'm worried about the most, especially if it comes from Q. So, I've decided to use the letters of the alphabet as initials of real people and, of course, it won't be their actual initials. That would be too easy to guess and would defeat the very purpose of this blog.

The wedding date has been set for June with an engagement in March and I am already fed up of people talking about it. It's all everyone does these days. They're excited about Y's wedding because there hasn't been a wedding in the family for a couple of years now. There's so much eye-rolling I do these days that it seems the expression of exasperation will become a permanent feature of my face. Despite all that, there have been a lot of interesting things happening at home, especially in these past few days.

Like the time when my mother and sister went to see the first girl for my brother.

2

'Step aside. I need the mirror,' Rabia said calmly as she applied mascara with skilful strokes of the brush.

'But you have a mirror! In your own room!' Saba said even though it was completely futile to argue with her sister. She moved away from the mirror where she'd been trying to squeeze out another blackhead that had popped up on her nose.

'The light here is better,' Rabia murmured and then dusted her eyelids with eye shadow. With a quick sweep of a thin brush she drew a line close to her eyelashes which made her look exotic and diva-like instantly. Saba tried not to look at her enviously.

Ammi had been calling out to her for the last ten minutes but that hadn't deterred Rabia. With a last touch of gloss at the centre of her lips, she stepped back to see her image in the mirror. Finally, with a sigh, she covered her hair with a rich and glossy brown scarf, wrapping it around her head until it resembled a perched bird's nest at the back of her head. The effect was amazing.

Finally, Ammi came and stood at the door of Saba's room.

'Are you ready yet?' she asked, taking in Rabia's appearance. Rabia nodded and slipped her feet into a pair of high heels.

'Done,' she said smiling elegantly at her mother who looked flustered. There were times her mother couldn't imagine how she had given birth to this sophisticated creature who walked into a room, bringing with her a startling cloud of Dune perfume, looking as though she owned the room and everybody inside it. This was one of those times.

'Come, let's go.'

As an afterthought their mother turned to her and said, 'Saba, don't forget to make tea for your father. I know you're busy studying (at which her sister rolled her eyes), but you know he likes to have his tea at five in the evening.'

'Abbu's not going?' Saba asked, confused momentarily. Surely Rabia wouldn't drive them down there? She was an atrocious driver. Dogs ran in the opposite direction when they saw her at the wheel and she was known for making sudden swerves like a lunatic. Her husband had already had to replace two cars because of her enthusiasm. Actually, Rabia just loved to sit at the wheel and *look* stunning. Saba always felt that Rabia walked around thinking that there were invisible fashion photographers clicking pictures of her every angle and profile.

'No, I've invited Shahid to drive us down there today. He's coming with his mother now. I don't know why your father won't hire a driver like others,' Ammi said, walking away looking distracted.

'Why Shahid, mom?' Rabia asked, sounding distressed as they made their way towards the hall. Everyone knew that the two of them couldn't stand each other. Shahid was Abbu's cousin's son and he was a couple of years younger than Rabia. Ammi and his mother had hit it off really well when Ammi had got married to Abbu and they used to joke that they would get their kids married to each other. Thankfully that had not happened. Shahid and Rabia would have simply killed each other.

They had been playmates when they were young, but Rabia's insistence that she be the queen in whatever game they played (even when there was no need for a queen) had been the beginning of their many fights. These fights had escalated into a cold war by the time they were teenagers and had billowed down only after Rabia got married. Now they were merely polite strangers who nodded at each other at family gatherings.

'Who else could I call?' Ammi said as she tied her scarf around her head haphazardly. Saba followed them outside, feeling curious. This was the first time Ammi and Rabia were going to 'see' a girl for her brother Zohaib and she wondered what would happen. Since she was unmarried, she couldn't go with them and they didn't even have a precedent of sorts for her to understand what actually happened when people went to see a girl. Rabia's marriage had not been orchestrated by the many 'brokers' and other such well-meaning people who fixed marriages in their community. In typical Bollywood fashion, her husband Rafiq had seen her at the wedding of a common friend and been instantly smitten by her. He had managed to track down who she was and where she lived, and had immediately sent off a proposal to their house.

The fact that they were from a different community had upset their parents quite a bit initially. But they relented because he was rich and good looking and in the end he was still a Muslim, right? (Saba couldn't understand why they harped so much about communities, but her opinion didn't matter, according to her mother.)

'You could have called. . .' Rabia trailed off. Shahid and his mother had already arrived and were sitting in the car outside the house and he honked loudly making Rabia mutter something under her breath. Saba waved at him and he waved back, smiling. She wished he had come earlier so they could have talked. He seemed to be the only one who knew how she felt about being Rabia's younger sibling, constantly in her shadow.

He spotted Rabia and their mother and his expression changed a little. He continued smiling but Saba sensed that the warmth was reserved for Ammi.

'Come on! Let's go!' Ammi said as she got in the back to talk to Nausheen aunty. Shahid shot poisonous looks at Rabia because the only place left for her was in front, with him. She opened the door delicately and sat inside, behaving as though she was placed inside a fragile glass ball which would shatter if she moved too quickly.

Instead of starting the car, Shahid got out and strode purposefully towards Saba, much to everyone's surprise. Ammi called out to him, 'Shahid! We're late already! They will be expecting us to be there at 5 p.m. and it's already 4.30 and we have to travel to the other side of town, beta!'

Shahid turned and nodded but still continued walking and stopped in front of Saba.

'Hey! How are the studies going?' he asked, tugging at her braid.

'Don't do that,' she said, pushing it back, making a face.

'I needed to talk to a sane person before I sit in the car with her,' he said, and Saba felt a bit affronted.

'She's not *that* bad!' she defended her sister and he lifted an eyebrow.

'Really?'

'No, you're right,' Saba admitted immediately and Shahid laughed.

'And what's with the hairdo man? She looks. . .'

'Amazing, right? And so sophisticated and elegant! I could never carry it off,' she said, enviously.

'Well, thank God for that!' he said and pinched her cheek affectionately before heading back to the car.

Saba smiled at his back as he drove off looking furious at having been interrupted in his work and asked to chauffeur three women around the city. But most probably he was furious because he would have to spend time with Rabia.

Saba returned to her room and rearranged the books on the study desk. Then she went up to the mirror and stared at her reflection for a little while. She wondered what the girl whom they were going to see was going to be like. Or rather, the girl whom they would eventually choose for her brother. Obviously she was going to be pretty and fair. Those were the first prerequisites. But what was *she* going to be like? Would she sniff disdainfully at books and watch soaps with her mother? Had she heard of Harry Potter? Would she come shopping with her and make it a girl's day out instead of behaving like she was suffering punishment like her sister and mother did?

Who knew?

3

First, but not the last

Posted by The Other T, 17-01-12

It wasn't very long ago that my mother and sister first went shopping for a bride. Oops! I meant, looking for a suitable bride. When they came back after seeing this girl, naturally I'd been very curious. What happened at these meetings? My cousin T and his mother had dropped them off and had gone away without coming inside because it was late, so I couldn't even corner T and ask him.

Q was untying her hijab and looked annoyed. Ammi looked a little upset and Abbu was staring at them grimly.

'So, what happened?' I asked and Ammi, who had been sitting at the dining table, looked at me, almost startled.

'She was hideous,' Q said and I winced. Unless someone looked like her (read tall, stunningly curvaceous with sculpted cheekbones) or looked like Kareena Kapoor, she called them hideous.

I turned to Ammi hoping to get a better report. Ammi, however, was looking far off into space and hadn't heard my question or Q's reply.

'Does this mean we have to ask the broker to show us some more girls?' my father sighed. When put like that, it sounds rather. . .umm. . .racy, you know? But when you're used to hearing about seeing girls and liking them and not liking them, all this just glosses over you like water over moisturized skin.

Ammi didn't answer him either.

'What do you call those fat men who wear diapers and roll around on the ground?' she asked.

'Sumo wrestlers,' Q, Abbu and I answered together. Ammi often couldn't recall the name of certain things, but she would use her vivid imagination to describe them. It was up to us to understand what she was saying. After so many years, we could now second guess her most of the time, but it wasn't without hilarious results. Err, hello? Sumo wrestlers?

'Yes! She looked like a sumo wrestler,' she said triumphantly and then her face fell when she saw Abbu's expression.

'Don't be so free to criticize others' daughters,' he muttered.

'But it's the truth! She was very fat. Around three times the size of Y,' Ammi stated.

At the mention of his name, my brother appeared from nowhere, which made me wonder if he'd been lingering nearby, hoping to hear the news about his fate. Silly, no? If he'd been a girl, my parents wouldn't even have bothered to inform him that they were getting him married. They'd just assume that he would have heard the news. But he was a boy and very much in control of his fate.

'So, it's a no then?' I asked, making the mistake of looking at Q.

'Obviously it's a no!' she said in a withering voice.

'I wish they hadn't plied us with so much food,' Ammi said, pulling at the fringe of the pallu of her saree.

My ears pricked up.

'Well, I don't have to feel guilty because I didn't eat anything,' Q proclaimed, brushing her hands lightly as she got up. She went and stood before the antique mirror on the wall facing the dining room and flicked something imaginary from her hair.

'I'd better get going. My husband will be home soon.' She turned to Y and said, 'Drop me home.'

Y made a face at her turned back. He looked rather disappointed with the turn of events and that again surprised me. He's had hundreds of girlfriends already. No; actually, I think he's had about four girlfriends till now. I've taken their calls for him in the days before mobile phones made it possible to have personal conversations surreptitiously. I've spoken to those breathy-voiced girls. So why is he in such a hurry to get married? That too the arranged marriage route, depending on Ammi and Q? Beats me.

'Chicken tikka, samosas, kheer. . .and what is that dark jungle cake you people like so much?' Ammi asked, looking at each one of us, as though mentally urging us to understand what she was trying to say.

'Black forest cake,' Q sighed. I was instantly attentive.

'Did they serve you all that there?' I asked, and Ammi nodded, looking sad.

'It's such a pity we had to eat all that food and then. . .we're going to have to tell them we're not interested.'

'But if you'd liked the girl you would have gladly eaten everything?' I asked, puzzled.

'No-o.' Ammi stretched out the word into two syllables. 'But at least then there would have been some chance of repaying their hospitality.'

'I'm leaving!' Q said and instantly we were all alert. Q visited us thrice a week, but each time we had to behave as though it was a special occasion and when she left, we had to make a great deal out of it. She'd sulk and refuse to talk to Ammi for days otherwise.

So we all stood respectfully at the door as Q swept out, her shiny purple Valentino bag clutched under her arm. At the door she slipped her feet into tottering high heels and reached the car where Y was already waiting for her. She turned around in an exaggerated motion that made sure her shoulder and side profile were in a straight line as she waved at us and called out, 'Let me know if there are any other girls.'

Ammi nodded but didn't look too happy. As soon as Q left, she looked withdrawn and sad.

Abbu, who was still at the dining table, muttered when Ammi came to sit back over there, 'I hope she doesn't get it into her head to start looking for girls on her own.'

'Why do you always have to sound like that when you're talking about her?' Ammi asked him.

'Like what?' Abbu sounded belligerent.

'Like you can't stand the poor girl,' Ammi got up. 'And what if she does find a girl for her brother? She has *excellent* taste.'

'Yeah right,' I thought. I kept quiet, however, as I watched the exchange of words between my mother and father over Q. Q *did* have excellent taste. When it came to clothes. Or rather, *her* own clothes. I remembered the Eid a couple of years ago before her marriage. It was an odd coincidence that the tailor had stitched *my* clothes in *her* size. Or that whenever she went shopping with Ammi for clothes, I ended up getting the drab and boring colours.

The annoying part was that Q thought that no one was onto her. Fact was, everyone was onto her and her manipulative ways. They just didn't know what to do about it.

4

Once again. And again. And again.

POSTED BY THE OTHER T, 25-01-12

Some families have insanely good looking people. You look at the kids and wonder what the parents did right to have such beautiful children. Or, you look at the parents and think that, 'Wow! These two are going to be the proud parents of some very good looking children.' What happens when people look at my parents and me is that they nod in understanding. It makes sense. But when they see Q and Y, they go goggle-eyed.

You see, my brother Y was named after this gorgeous chocolate faced Pakistani singer whom my mother had a massive crush on. She feels embarrassed to admit it now of course. Oddly enough, as though the charisma of the name rubbed off on him, my brother turned out to be definitely more handsome than he had a right to be. I can vouch for the number of girls who would call, hoping to hear his voice. And I'm sure they flung the receiver down in disgust when they heard my adolescent prattle on the other end.

A few days after the first debacle, Ammi got a call about another family. Y became excited instantly and I wondered why. Guys with his looks would have no problem finding a girl of *their* own choice. And if he went ahead and did that cardinal sin of a love marriage, I was sure my parents would relent eventually.

Nevertheless, the whole thing started again, with Q coming over and Ammi getting ready. This time Q had insisted that Ammi hire a driver temporarily for the day.

'Why can't Abbu drive you guys?' I'd asked when they were leaving.

'Well, it won't look nice,' Ammi said, as she adjusted her saree pleats and then wore her burkha. Q had stopped wearing a burkha after she got married. She now only wore the hijab or the head scarf that she wrapped around her head in innovative ways, designed to get the most attention. Her husband's family were of a different community that didn't harp so much on what she wore and whether she wore the burkha or not, but Ammi was uncomfortable appearing in public without a burkha.

So, as a concession to my mother's sentiments, Q wore the hijab. I personally thought she wore it because she knew how striking she looked in it, which kind of defeated the reason why one was supposed to wear it in the first place. Anyway, Q looked at me with the usual contempt in her eyes, the look reserved for earthworms and cockroaches.

'Get your head out of books and see the world around you. Do you think we will have any respect if Abbu drives us there?' she hissed.

I shrugged, not really understanding or caring. It had taken me a lot of practice to get that shrug right because it irritated her. At first I used to quail whenever she spoke in that tone to me, but with T's help, I was able to figure out Q eventually.

So they went to this new place to check out the girl and came back in a huff. Apparently, the girl was pretty but their *house* was dreadful.

The next time, the girl and the house were passably nice, but the girl's mother was very fat.

At yet another place, the girl was too homely.

And then there was the girl who didn't know how to wear makeup. ('Dreadful, hideous golden eye shadow! Made her look like a lizard!'—Q's unkind words)

Listening to Q's excuses and Ammi backing her up made me sick. They were being too choosy and picking on very minor issues.

'Can't I come?' I asked once, and that immediately started off a maelstrom of arguments. Abbu thought it was okay if I went. Ammi was horrified. 'What will we say when they ask who she is?' she asked.

'You'll tell them that I'm your daughter,' I said, making a face. Luckily, I had mentioned this at a time when Q wasn't around.

'My *unmarried* daughter!' Ammi proclaimed.

I still haven't been able to figure this one out. If getting married gets you all these privileges, like going to someone else's house and seeing *their* daughter, it should be a whole lot easier than this.

5

As a rule, Zohaib was never nervous. He'd grinned through his board exams, smiled through college interviews and charmed his way into his job. He was the epitome of what every mother wanted in her son, and all the married female relatives (who had crushes on him too) would point him out to their grubby sons and tell them to be like him or at least try and grow up to be like him.

Two years ago, at twenty-five, he had been the most eligible bachelor in Bengaluru with proposals coming in from every possible place. Women who wished they'd been born twenty years later would shyly ask Zohaib's mother at weddings if they had started looking for a girl for him, because they just happened to have a young and nubile daughter who would be perfect for him. Ammi had to fend off each of these women, because Zohaib had made it clear that he had no plans of getting married until he'd settled in his job.

He'd recently started working at Exodus Infosystems in the Application Development Management team and was barely managing to get a toehold there, so he did not want the added encumbrance of a wife and kids. He wanted to be the person his team leader could send to any part of the world on a project and he wanted to be able to go without having to consult anyone. So marriage had been out of the question. But a guy with his looks couldn't get too far without half the female population panting around his workstation, and he eventually gave in and had a fling with one of his colleagues.

It was a secret fling, because he just wasn't in the mood to hash it out with his mother or his sisters. While Rabia could be condescending and annoying, it was Saba he feared, because for some reason, she knew him better than anyone else in the family. It was almost as though she could read his mind; one day after an extremely steamy session with said colleague, he'd gone home to find Saba staring at his flushed face as though she could read everything plainly.

She was only seventeen but behaved as though she bore the weight of the world on her shoulders. The difference between having a girlfriend in college and having one in office was increasingly becoming clear to him. When he realized that the whole clandestine set up was affecting his work, he broke off with the girl. Or tried to.

He still shuddered at the thought of Meenakshi. It was a good thing that she got transferred to Mumbai last year, because she'd plainly decided to make his life hell. She *was* the ex from hell actually.

Nevertheless, when other girls in the office started eyeing him once he was free of her, he was more wary and decided that he'd rather concentrate on his work. At least more than three miffed girls decided that he was probably gay. He'd been affronted at first, but let them continue thinking that.

Zohaib checked his watch again. It was 5 p.m. and Abbu had said that those people would be coming shortly.

'Now is not the time to get nervous buddy,' he talked to himself and looked around to see if anyone had heard him.

Thankfully, no one was around. He was sitting in the living room, trying hard to downplay his normally glamorous features like his hair, which he'd hidden under a pristine white skull cap. It was not a decoy, he told himself, and he was not deceiving them into believing that he read namaz regularly because he *did* read namaz. Just not as regularly as he ought to. He'd also worn a crisp white shirt that his father had got for him sometime back, but one he'd never worn because it reminded him of his school uniform. He'd paired it with khakis that were creased perfectly, and he looked down at them, inspecting them for any stray threads or lint that might spoil the whole good boy effect.

He let out a sigh, wondering what a girl felt like when people went over to see her. But then, all she had to do was sit on a chair, close her eyes and look pretty. He, on the other hand, was expected to hold a conversation with these people, make eye contact and yet look respectful. He was supposed to look worthy enough so that these people would want to entrust their daughter into his hands. He resisted the urge to get up and check his reflection in the mirror.

After six proposals had gone awry with Ammi and Rabia rejecting them like they were flicking flies off mithais, Zohaib had started panicking. Would he *never* get married? Last week however, a broker had called and said that the girl's side wanted to check him out first and only then could they go to see her. Rabia had thought that was rather unreasonable, but Abbu had said okay.

'What do you know how these things work?' he had asked her, trying hard to suppress his impatience.

'Well, I'm a married woman and. . .' Rabia had started, but Abbu had cut her off again.

'Your marriage was different. This is not going to work like that,' he had said and turned away, leaving Ammi to soothe Rabia's hurt ego.

The bell rang and Zohaib looked up, almost startled. He couldn't go and answer the door. Not because he had mehndi on his feet, but because he was sure it wouldn't do for him to open the door. He turned around and saw that Abbu was walking towards the door with purposeful strides. As he passed Zohaib, he said, 'Sit straight. And don't worry so much.'

Ammi came out of the kitchen and stood there, wiping her hands on her pallu. Saba followed her curiously and both of them hurried back in when Abbu beckoned them to go inside the kitchen. Saba put out her tongue at Zohaib and then ran back inside where she had been helping Ammi get everything ready. Rabia hadn't come today as she knew that there was little chance of her meeting new people and showing herself off to them. Or rather, when she knew that she might have to toil in the kitchen with Ammi.

Zohaib sat erect and watched as Abbu led a group of five men towards the hall. He felt as though there were sticks poking his ribs and his spine, pitching him forward. He assessed the men who came and sat down, and he stood up to say 'Salam' to them. Two of them were in their thirties and the other three were very old. He took a deep breath. And then it began.

6

Showing off Y

Posted by The Other T, 31-01-12

Today, some people came to 'see' Y. I was surprised to hear that it happens even with boys! Apparently, the girl's side will see him and then decide if he's worthy or not, and *then* they'll let Ammi see the girl. I thought it was a pretty cool idea, and if the situation were reversed, I'd definitely have wanted Y, my father and maybe my cousin T to see the man I'd be getting married to.

Ammi and I were in the kitchen arranging the trays of snacks. One held a platter of samosas that Ammi had made a little while ago. Another had a few pastries that Abbu had brought over from Sweet Chariot and there was a last tray with teacups arranged on them.

Ammi looked frenzied as she washed the good china and wiped it dry, whipped things off the stove, transferred them to plates and attended to a hundred other things as well. No prizes for guessing why Q hadn't graced the occasion with her presence today.

'Your grandmother used to say that there should be two of each.'

When I looked at her mystified, she glanced at me for barely a second while straining the tea into a kettle. 'I meant I should have had another son.'

'Why?' I was slightly hurt.

'I'd have had an extra pair of hands to help me,' she said.

At that, I stopped slicing the almonds for the firni and put the knife down. What did she mean? I had to submit an essay tomorrow on the important theories of literary criticism, but I was in the kitchen with her, helping her make all these things.

'Oh not you!' she brushed her hands in the air dismissively. 'I meant outside. Moral support for Y.'

I went back to slicing the almonds without a word.

'Hey!'

I looked up surprised. It was T! When had he come? I hadn't heard the doorbell ring. I smiled at him as he leaned forward and helped himself to a few of the almonds. Ammi looked at him and her face broke into a huge smile.

'Oh thank God you came, beta! I was so worried about. . .'

He held his hand up in the air to stop her from speaking and she shook her head and went back to pouring the tea in the cups.

'I thought I'll come and make myself useful,' he said, coming to stand beside me. I had finished with the almonds and was sprinkling them on top of the firni. My heart felt lighter and I was just glad about everything. He seemed to have that effect on people. He winked at me as he rearranged one of the teacups on the tray.

'So which should I take first and go?' he asked. Ammi pointed to the tray with the samosas and he went out. There was nothing more for me to do, but I couldn't go to my room either because of the men sitting outside.

T came back to the kitchen after some time and took the other trays. 'Looks like it's going well,' he commented to me as he took the tea and went back to the hall.

After the men had left, Y came to the kitchen and stood there, breathing heavily.

'I don't know how you girls go through this,' he said to no one in particular. 'Once is seriously enough for me. How many questions they asked!'

T had followed him inside. He slapped his back and Y slumped forward and straightened himself.

'Watch it dude!' he mumbled as he brushed something off his trousers.

As I left the kitchen, I heard Ammi telling T that it would be his turn soon, and he said something like 'No way!' before laughing over something with Y.

It's 10 p.m., I haven't written a word for my essay and my teacher is nothing less than a fire-breathing dragon. Maybe I'll bunk college tomorrow, but then Ammi would make me do all the housework with her.

T stayed for dinner and it was wonderful. I could see where Ammi was coming from when she said that she should have had two sons. If one could be like Y, beautiful but surly at most times, especially when it came to younger sisters, one could have been like T. Sweet, funny, considerate and charming.

7

It was 11 p.m. by the time Shahid left. Dinner was enjoyable, particularly since Rabia was not there. He was a little concerned about Zohaib though. In fact, after dinner, the two of them had gone to his room where Zohaib had paced constantly, wondering whether things would work out.

'Why are you so worried, bro?' Shahid asked after Zohaib muttered something for the tenth time.

'Nothing,' Zohaib said and ran a hand over his face.

Shahid had idolized Zohaib when they had been young and even though there had been other cousins, the two of them had always stuck together like friends.

'You can tell me what it is,' Shahid said, his face serious. Zohaib turned to look at him, and then sat down at his desk with a huff.

'Why are you in such a hurry to get married? Is something wrong?' Shahid asked when Zohaib didn't speak.

Zohaib opened his laptop and switched it on, and Shahid got up with a sigh.

'You know you can tell me whatever it is,' Shahid said, putting his hand on Zohaib's shoulder. 'Give me a call whenever you need to talk,' he said and walked out.

Shahid stretched, rotated his shoulders and looked at the time and then after debating with himself over something, he stood in front of Saba's door downstairs. He knocked on the door and stood back, waiting for her to open it. When she didn't, he knocked again and then turned the handle. It wasn't locked.

'I just thought I'd say b. . .' the words died in his throat when he saw that she was asleep with her head on her desk. Her computer was on and the light from the monitor flickered weakly, illuminating her head as she slept.

Shahid felt himself grow still. He walked up towards her and lifted her head gently and somehow managed to turn her around so he could carry her in his arms. He laid her down on the bed and then extricated his arm from under her back. She curled to one side, pushing her knees to her chest like a foetus, and Shahid looked around for something to cover her with. He found a blanket near the foot of the bed, shook it open and covered her.

He could feel his heart expand in his chest as he watched a strand of hair trail on her cheek. He brushed it away, although he knew he had just needed an excuse to touch her again. He skimmed her cheek lightly with the back of his fingers and she murmured something. His jaw clenched and he pulled his hand back and then, feeling foolish, he backed up. He turned and switched off the monitor, looked at Saba's sleeping form once again, and left before he did something idiotic.

The alarm was ringing incessantly and Saba woke up, rubbing her eyes.

'Shit! I was supposed to write. . .' she looked around in surprise. She had been sitting at the desk to write her essay after she had put up a new post on her blog. When had she fallen asleep on the bed? And managed to cuddle under the blanket as well? She reached for her mobile phone and pressed the snooze button to silence the ringing. Was it morning already?

Feeling disoriented, she slept some more, wishing she didn't have to go to college. But Rabia was going to come home to dissect whatever had happened the previous day and Saba was sure she didn't want to be around for that. Rolling over, she swiftly typed a message on her phone and hit send. A few seconds later her phone beeped and she typed again. This continued for a few more minutes even as she stood up with her phone and walked towards her bathroom, texting, and then she finally dropped the phone on a table and went inside.

When she came outside and checked her phone, there were no messages on it. She'd first texted her friend Riya to find out if she had done the essay. Of course Riya hadn't. Apparently she'd been hoping that Saba would have done it so she could take some 'inspiration' from her. Then she had texted Anindita who headed the drama club in college, asking her if she had scheduled any rehearsals for the day. They had been practising for the intercollegiate drama festival that was going to be held the following month. If there were no rehearsals, she could safely skip college and maybe head out to Riya's house and come back in the evening, pretending she had attended college.

She wiped her face with a towel and only then remembered something. Her face whipped to the computer, to see if it had been on standby. She walked towards it and saw that only the monitor was switched off. The computer was still humming. She switched on the monitor and then her breath caught as she realized what she'd been doing before she'd fallen asleep. Her face blanched as she realized it must have been Zohaib who had come in and put her to sleep on the bed. Had he read the blog? How had she thought that she could escape being caught? Even though she'd used only initials, it was blatantly evident to whoever had read it that *she'd* written it. After all, she had described everything perfectly.

When she emerged from her room that day, ostensibly to go to college, she looked around fearfully for her brother. He'd left for work already. Maybe she could avoid him for as long as possible. Maybe he'd forget about it.

Much later, she was in the auto when a text from Anindita arrived. They did have rehearsals that day. Saba wasn't acting in the play but she had scripted it and Anindita, who was directing it, wanted Saba to attend all the rehearsals even though her input was hardly required.

'Great!' she muttered as the auto stopped outside the college gate.

It had been a tiring day and at the end of it, she was glad to go home even though she might have to face Rabia there. Or worse, Zohaib. But, neither Rabia had come home nor did Zohaib seem angry with her. At dinner, he was distracted and didn't speak much, his eyes lighting up only when Abbu informed him that he'd been okayed by the girl's family and that Ammi was to go and see this girl soon.

'Your mother is going with Nausheen and a few other aunts,' Abbu continued. Both Saba and Zohaib looked up in surprise.

'Yes, Rabia is not going this time. She's not well.'

Maybe things would work out finally. Just as Zohaib pushed back his chair, Saba spoke, 'Thanks for covering me with the blanket last night,' she said breaking the roti with more concentration than was required.

Zohaib didn't stop and lambast her for writing a blog that ridiculed his wedding. He shrugged and standing behind the chair, pushed it back in place.

'No idea what you're talking about,' he said and loped off.

Saba stared at his retreating figure, feeling uneasy and queasy at the same time. So he hadn't read the blog. She had to be more careful from now on. But, who had put her on the bed?

8

The Bawdy Aunts

Posted by The Other T, 04-02-12

Ammi and some aunts had gone to see a girl yesterday and they came back with a positive report. Finally they had found someone they all liked! Everyone gushed about her long hair and how pretty and fair she was. They all spoke together, cutting each other's sentences short, looking more excited than even Y.

Y came back from work and merely looked relieved when they said that they liked the girl.

'When is the wedding?' he asked and all conversation came to a stop. Someone giggled and one aunt pinched another and all of them erupted into laughter.

'What's the hurry?' Ammi asked, trying to ignore the ribald jokes being whispered in the room.

'Nothing, I just. . .fine. . .no, leave it,' Y said and stalked off to his room. I looked at him, wondering why he was so desperate to get married. I got up to follow him when an aunt pulled me down.

They started talking about how it was time for me to get married as soon as Y was out of the way, and I looked at them horrified. Marriage? I was only nineteen! And I was still in college, just in my fourth semester.

I tried to get up, but they wouldn't let me. 'Sit, sit!' someone said and clamped her hands on my wrist. I sat there suffering their jokes and silly talk, wishing I would get a phone call, so I could leave. Finally, Aunt M got up and wore her burkha. 'It's time I headed home,' she said. 'I won't get an auto otherwise.'

'Why? T isn't coming to pick you up?' Ammi asked.

'I don't know. He said he might,' Aunt M replied.

'Then call and ask him,' someone suggested, and Aunt M dialled his number from her mobile.

'He's coming,' she smiled, sitting down.

I've had bad days and I've had worse days, but this one hour of sitting with the aunts somehow managed to top the charts for 'unpalatable things' in my life. My head was buzzing with different thoughts about the play, about my upcoming exams, my notes which my friend had borrowed, and these women here wanted me to discuss jewellery with them. Had they mistaken me for Q?

'Get her a ghagra for Y's wedding,' an aunt said, and I turned to protest, but someone else quickly stepped in.

'No, no! She's not Q! *Look* at her! She doesn't have the height to carry it off. But her complexion is quite clear, and if you get the ghagra in a dark colour, she could look pretty. You put her in a nice ghagra and some woman at the wedding will definitely notice her and send a proposal immediately.' A round of giggles followed.

I looked from one aunt to the other as they discussed my features and whether I would get a good match like Y. Okay people. I'm still sitting here. Like right *next* to you. Will you stop discussing my attributes while I'm around? Argh! I had to clench my teeth and smile at everyone as though it was perfectly normal and finally, when the doorbell rang, I got up and ran.

I opened the door and saw T standing there, texting and frowning. He looked up briefly, smiled for a fraction and then looked back down, his fingers moving furiously over his phone as he stepped inside.

'Hey!' he said, but didn't look up.

'Don't go inside!' I warned him, 'All the bawdy aunts are sitting there and they'll make mincemeat of you.' He laughed at my description of the aunts.

'Who is it?' someone called out and T went towards the living room where all the women were seated and instead of escaping to my room, I followed him inside.

Just as I'd predicted, the aunts pounced on him when he sat down on the sofa.

'When are you going to start looking for him, M?' someone asked.

'I know a girl who would be just perfect for him!' one aunt said, waving her hands in the air dramatically. 'She's my neighbour's granddaughter. She's just finished her II PUC. She'll be perfect for him. Shall I ask?' she spoke rapidly, eyes shining with excitement. Probably because if she could pull it off, she'd tell the happy couple that she'd been the one to get them together—for the rest of their lives.

Aunt M looked from one aunt to the other, a little perplexed. Luckily, T stepped in. 'No, no, aunty. Not yet. I'm only twenty-four,' he said.

'He must be having girlfriend and all, no?' another aunt poked her fat elbows into T's ribs. T took a deep breath, and everyone else seemed to hold theirs. Including me.

But instead of answering, he got up and went towards Y's room. Thankfully, the aunts didn't notice me leaving as they were busy discussing whether T had a girlfriend or not. Aunt M was positive he didn't, while some aunt said that that's what all the mothers liked to think.

'Hey!' I called out, and he stopped. He raised his eyebrows and waited for me to catch up with him.

'What's up?' he asked, and I narrowed my eyes.

'Why didn't you answer? You have a girlfriend?' I asked. He shook his head and smiled, as though at a private joke.

'Why are *you* looking relieved?' he asked, and I cleared my throat.

'Relieved? No way. Doesn't make a difference to me,' I replied, crossing my arms in front of my chest.

He nodded and turned to Y's room and knocked on the door. 'Okay then. I'll get going. Catch up with you later, bhai,' I said moving away, and I saw his face darken.

He opened his mouth as though to say something but thought better of it and walked inside Y's room. Pah! I'll never understand guys.

9

Rabia stretched expansively and put her feet down from the bed, angling them so that they connected with a pair of soft fur slippers. She continued stretching a little more and contorted her face for ten minutes doing facial exercises. At twenty-six, she was a year younger than Zohaib and strived to look even younger than her sister. She'd have been successful but for her diva-like demeanour.

Then, she padded to the bathroom and emerged half an hour later, wrapped in a fluffy towel. Rafiq was leaving for office and he poked his head inside the room, his eyes widening in appreciation. Rabia ignored him and sat down before the mirror, clad only in her towel and moisturized her face and neck liberally.

'Do we have time for a quickie?' he asked, standing behind her and pressing his lips to her shoulder.

She moved her shoulder back to push him off. 'I *just* had a bath,' she said. Rafiq was not deterred. He kneaded her shoulders from behind and inched his hand down towards the knot of her towel. She slapped his hand away. 'Not now, Rafiq! And aren't you getting late for office?'

'Well, I'm the boss, so who cares!' he said. He turned Rabia around so she faced him and pulled at the knot until it gave away and bent down to kiss her. Rabia was reluctant at first, but in minutes they both fell together on the bed in a jumble of legs and arms and a damp towel.

'You're going to have to change your shirt,' Rabia whispered as Rafiq trailed his finger down the side of her face.

When he didn't answer, Rabia smiled. She *almost* loved him at these moments when he looked as though she had stunned him by simply existing. She moved to kiss the corner of his mouth when he suddenly spoke.

'It's been two years since we got married. Let's have a baby.'

Rabia pulled back as though she'd been stung by a poisonous bee. She sat up, gathering her towel and holding it to her chest.

'Where did that come from?' she asked sharply.

'Well,' Rafiq spoke, getting up slowly as he unbuttoned his shirt which had become wet. 'My cousin Arman got married last year and they already have a baby. All the couples our age are having kids. What are *we* waiting for?' he asked her.

Rabia felt herself grow cold. She'd always assumed there was plenty of time before she got pregnant, and she fixed a glare at Rafiq. 'I'm not ready yet,' she answered, getting up.

'Get ready then,' Rafiq said, holding her wrist to stop her from re-entering the bathroom. 'Keep a fresh set of clothes for me on the bed, okay?' he said and went inside to take a shower.

'Get them yourself,' Rabia muttered as she sat down at the dressing table, clad only in her towel, and picked up the latest issue of *Vogue*. She couldn't even bring herself to flip the pages because the words and images were crowding in her head. A baby! And why was he suddenly behaving so aggressively?

These past few months she'd been busy searching for a bride for Zohaib and hadn't paid enough attention to Rafiq. However, she hadn't gone to see the last girl, not because she was sick, but because she was annoyed with her father. He kept making obtuse suggestions that she didn't know their customs just because she'd been married off in another community. But imagine her surprise when Ammi called to tell her that they had selected the girl without *her* approval! Ammi had pacified her saying that they would go to see the girl with her again, probably in a couple of days.

When the sound of the water stopped, Rabia busied herself with reading the magazine.

'Rabia! Towel!' Rafiq called out. She didn't get up. When he called out again, she put the magazine on the dresser with a huff, stalked off towards the bathroom and whipped out her towel and handed it to him.

'This one's. . .'

'Yes, I know. It's wet,' she completed and got inside the bathroom before he could say anything further. Rafiq was not there when she emerged a few minutes later. She slipped into her clothes, towelled her hair dry and stood at the mirror staring at her reflection, first from the front and then sideways, wondering how she would look with a baby bump and shuddered involuntarily.

10

Riya yawned and covered her mouth with her hand. The lecturer who taught them metaphysical poetry was, unfortunately, doing a bad job of it and Saba looked at her over the heads of fifteen other students, feeling irritated.

She scribbled something on her notebook and pushed it towards Riya who looked at it and raised her eyebrows.

Why is she making Andrew Marvell into such a pansy? He's the guy who wrote 'To his Coy Mistress'!

Riya scribbled back and passed the notebook to Saba.

Who the fuck cares?

I do.

Then tell her you'll take the class.

I just might.

Saba felt her heart constrict and her mouth go dry when a shadow fell on her book.

'Can I look at that notebook please?' Ms Archana spoke softly.

Before Riya or Saba could react, she had leaned forward, dispensing a view of her crisp saree pleats and pulled the notebook towards her. Riya didn't even have the time to shut the notebook. She picked it up, read what the two of them had written and a frown line creased her forehead.

'You think you know more about Andrew Marvell?' she asked, her voice noticeably louder.

'I. . .uh. . .' Saba faltered, blushing furiously.

'I have an idea,' the teacher spoke swiftly. Turning to the class, she announced, 'Saba here is going to give us a presentation on Andrew Marvell after lunch.'

The silence in the class could aptly be described as deathly. One girl spoke, 'But Ma'am, we're having practice for the Western dance competition for our fest today.'

Another girl added, 'And we don't have classes in the afternoon. All of us had planned on some practice or the other, Ma'am.'

'Well, I'm sorry. Saba will be giving a fifteen minute presentation on the life of Andrew Marvell and his work. Without using PowerPoint, please. I want you to do it the old school way.'

The class was relieved. Fifteen minutes was okay. It would zip off and they would be free to do what they wanted. But Ms Archana spoke again.

'And Riya will be teaching Andrew Marvell's "To his Coy Mistress' after Saba's presentation.'

'But. . .' Riya looked horrified. 'I. . .'

The bell rang and yet, no one moved. Ms Archana walked away and, before leaving, turned to face the class. 'I want everyone in this classroom after lunch. I'm taking the attendance for this hour at that time. So if you're not here then, you know that your attendance for this hour won't be counted.'

'Bitch!' Riya exhaled as the teacher left. Immediately the class was murmuring and the sounds grew louder.

'What the hell were you two up to? You've gotten all of us into trouble!' Simran spoke. She was the one who had been worried about the Western dance competition. 'Our choreographer is finally coming today. What do we do now?'

They had to quieten down eventually, because the teacher for their next lecture had entered the classroom, holding the attendance register.

'I'm seriously not in the mood to study literary criticism today,' Saba muttered as the class settled down.

'Shut up, or we'll be in more trouble,' Riya said. Saba scowled at her but turned to face the teacher who had started talking about Jacques Derrida and his theory of deconstruction.

'Derrida or bloody daridra,' Riya whispered, and Saba tried to contain a giggle. They couldn't possibly afford to get caught again.

At lunch, the two of them were again accosted by the girls who were furious about having been robbed of their precious free hour.

'I promised my boyfriend that we'll have the practice during the free hour today, so he got us two tickets for a movie, like *right* after college. What do I tell him now?' a girl called Samaira demanded.

'Don't go!' Riya retorted.

'What?' she asked, her hands on her hips.

'I'm sorry, but I'll try and make it up to you guys somehow,' Saba spoke. Some of the noise died down slowly although most of the girls were still angry.

'Arre baba! Don't come for the class, na? Simple,' Riya explained, shrugging her shoulders.

'What? And miss attendance? Why do you think I sat for an hour today, listening to her boring monologue?' someone asked.

'Okay! I'll go and speak to her. I'll apologize, I'll prostrate before her and ask her to let you guys off,' Saba said dramatically.

'But. . .'

'No, Riya. It's not fair that the whole class gets punished.'

Together Saba and Riya sought Ms Archana out in the staff room and although they stood at the periphery, hoping she would come outside and talk to them, she continued sitting inside.

'What is it girls? Speak up!' Ms Archana demanded from her seat, without even looking at them.

'We were wondering. . .'

She pushed her spectacles to the top of her head and spoke clearly. 'I didn't know we were doing such a good job, ladies,' she addressed the staff room. Fortunately, only three other teachers were there.

'These girls here think that they can teach better than us! Saba, for example, claims she knows more about Andrew Marvell than me! And Riya's vocabulary is so colourful that I thought the two of them should be given a chance to showcase their skills to their classmates.'

Saba hung her head and lifted it fractionally. She glanced at one of the other teachers who looked at her sympathetically.

'I'll do anything you want, Ma'am. Just let the class go after lunch, please,' Saba spoke softly.

Ms Archana rested her chin on her steepled fingers.

'Ten pages. Both sides. By this afternoon before you leave for home. Neatly written, not typed. Both of you.'

Saba looked relieved instantly. 'Ten pages about what Ma'am?'

'I want you to write ten pages about what you want to do with your lives, and where you will see yourselves five years from now.'

'Ten pages!' Riya exploded as they left the staff room. 'Bloody hell! What will I fill up ten pages with?'

'Shh!' Saba whispered as they made their way downstairs. They hailed Simran who was sitting under a tree explaining something animatedly to a captive audience.

'You guys are free,' Saba called out and a loud cheer rose. 'Go and give your attendance to her now.' There was a scramble as everyone rushed towards the staff room.

'Which would you prefer? Writing something or teaching an uninterested class?' Saba asked Riya as they sat down after college got over that day, writing their ten pages.

'Whatever!'

It was four-thirty by the time they had finished. They left college and were looking around for an auto when Saba spotted a car that looked familiar.

'Tell me it's your Greek god of a brother,' Riya muttered as Saba waved and the car stopped near the pavement.

'Uh, no! It's my cousin Shahid,' Saba said, smiling at him brilliantly. She was able to instantly banish the thought of what a fiasco the day had been when she saw him getting out.

'Ooh!' Riya exclaimed.

Saba turned to look at Riya in surprise. 'What?'

'He'll do very well too,' Riya breathed.

'He'll do very well for what?' Saba asked puzzled.

Riya sighed, 'Eye candy, darling. What else?'

11

Just a rant

Posted by The Other T, 08-02-12

Let me state this at the beginning. This post has nothing to do with my brother's wedding. I'm just pissed off and I need a place to rant. Usually, the person who always listens to my rants is my friend (let's say her name is X), but this time I can't do it because I want to rant *about* her.

I've known X for exactly two years since I joined college. But it has always felt like I've known her forever. But today we got caught in class over some silly thing and we both had to write ten pages of absolute drivel. So what happened was that it was way past our usual time to leave college. We came out, and who should we see cruising by? My cousin T! (Is it just me, or is he like everywhere these days?)

Anyway, I stopped his car and thought we could get him to give us a lift. But the *way* X acted around him! She simpered and flirted and did all the silly things she swore she'd *never* do over a guy. That too, over T! He's not even as good looking as my brother Y. But she saw him step out of the car and was immediately in lust with him.

I don't know why this is pissing me off so much. I sat shotgun, but she kept sending me hundreds of texts *about* him from the back of the car! My fingers are burning after having borne the brunt of deleting all those texts.

Does he have a girlfriend?

How many girlfriends has he had?

Where does he live?

Is this his car? Do you think he's had sex with some girl at the back where I'm sitting?

I'm melting just thinking of that although it's kinda disgusting too.

He's so hot!

I love his stubble, man! I want to eat him up!

What kind of questions are these? I have no idea about anything that she asked. I don't even know if he's had a girlfriend. And T is hot? Excuse me while I wear some glasses and come back to take a proper look. And anyway, she's asking the wrong person about his private life. We've practically grown up together and he's always been protective of me whenever we were with other cousins. He'd never let anyone bully me and get away with it, especially Q.

So, to think of him in this context is kinda eww, you know? But what's worse is that now she's got me started, my mind is full of just these things. I'm getting all sorts of weird thoughts about T and I hate X for having spoilt my perception of him.

Also, T flirted back with her. That was simply too much. He offered to take us for coffee somewhere and although I'd hoped to head straight home, X agreed immediately. We got down at a Barista and the two of us sat opposite him and ordered cappuccinos. I don't know why he was in such a chatty mood, because after coffee he ordered chocolate cake and offered to share it with her. Uh, hello? He's never met her before and. . .and. . .I just don't know why this whole thing made me so angry. Then he went to pay the bill, and X clutched my arm excitedly, asking, 'Do you think he's interested in me?'

What-do-I know? (spoken through clenched teeth.) It's a good thing there's no college tomorrow, so I don't have to see her. And I don't want to see T anytime soon either. Really.

Since that rant is out of my system, I think I can get around to talking about Y and his famed wedding now. They've set the date for June and I don't know why he was looking annoyed that it's almost five months away. There's an engagement in March at the girl's house. Also, Q went with Ammi and Aunt M to see the girl again and Q took her photo for Y. Q did not look too happy with the girl and when I saw the picture, I knew why. The girl was too pretty.

Why is Q so insecure? She's so gorgeous and can carry off any outfit with ease and she has a one helluva handsome husband and a house of her own, *without* a mother-in-law. But she sees another pretty face and gets all her war paint out. This girl was startlingly pretty. In the picture, her eyes were closed as is the custom. But she had a faint smile and that lent a charm to her face. She had an oval face, framed by chocolate brown hair and simply flawless complexion.

Y barely looked at her photo and went off. Immediately he returned and asked Q to email him the picture and then he looked at it for sometime as though deciding whether she added up to some mental calculation of his.

Nevertheless, the word is out that my brother is spoken for and many heartbroken women have probably lamented that they couldn't ensnare him. For their daughters, I mean. He, on the other hand, is looking more relaxed and relieved for some reason.

As per tradition, the boy's side takes laddoos to the girl's side on the engagement and Abbu has promised that he will get the halwais home so they make the laddoos in front of us. I am definitely not going to miss that. The boy's side also takes jewellery and a number of clothes, some footwear, makeup and all that stuff to the girl's side on the engagement. Ammi has said that she and Q will begin shopping soon. I managed to tag along with them when they bought the ghagra for the bride, and that's another story altogether.

12

Colour me pink

Posted by The Other T, 12-02-12

When Q suggested that we buy the bride a pink lehenga for the engagement, I was shocked. Pink was one colour that Q had always dissuaded me from wearing because it was *her* favourite colour. She looked marvellous in it and she didn't want anyone else to look prettier than her. Not that I minded, I tell you. Pink is a rather drab and lifeless colour! Give me red any day. Or sunshine yellow. Or moss green.

So, getting back to the point, we had to buy a ghagra for the bride. Traditionally, the boy's side brings the bride's outfit for the engagement and even the wedding. That's something that I can't get my head around. What if the boy's side didn't have any fashion sense? What if they bought something totally atrocious like iridescent yellow with fat flashy sequins? The girl would still have to wear it.

So, is this girl lucky that my sister is on the buying committee? Probably. See, Q never goes wrong when it comes to clothes. Unless they're mine.

In the brightly lit showroom on Commercial Street, Q walked in looking awesome as usual. She'd perched her sunglasses on top of her hijab, multiplying her style quotient ten times over. The salesmen stood upright all at once when she entered, as though someone had given them booster shots. They seemed petrified, because she was an old customer who couldn't be pleased easily.

'Show me only pinks,' she spoke huskily. One salesman tumbled in, holding a huge tower of ghagras, straining under their weight as he placed them on the counter. One by one, he rolled out the designs and my breath quickened when I noticed some pretty ones flash by. But Q kept flicking them away, asking them to bring more. My mother was obviously going to take Q's advice and not mine, so I kept my mouth shut and watched the lovely designs unfurl before us.

I noticed another salesman coming with two more ghagras in his arms from the corner of my eyes. I stiffened when I saw the one on the top. It was an oyster pink delicate confection that was absolutely gorgeous, with the right amount of bling. It glittered and winked and beckoned me, and I gave in, touching the silky material lightly. I could envision myself stunning all the guests at Y's wedding when I wore it. I could probably blow dry my hair as my friend X keeps suggesting and leave it open or tie it at the nape with a ribbon. Or I could. . .

Wait a second. No one had said they were buying this for *me*. As the salesman spread it out with a flourish, I picked up a corner and read the price and almost stopped breathing. It was ₹75,000. Ammi too had seen the price and she paled, hoping that Q wouldn't select it. She'd apparently been hoping for something around the range of ₹15 to ₹20,000.

Q looked at the oyster pink ghagra critically. She inspected it more thoroughly than the others, lifting a handful of the silk and letting it go through her fingers sensually.

'Keep this aside. I want it for myself,' she spoke briskly. The salesman nodded his head quickly, relieved to have brought her something that finally met with her approval.

'And we'll take the other one as well,' she said and got up. Ammi looked at her, merely surprised, but I couldn't bring myself to get up immediately. What? *The other one?* I shot a look at her again to see if she was serious, and she was.

The bride's ghagra was also pink, but I can't quite describe the colour without going into palpitations. The oyster pink ghagra was like the queen while the other one was like the queen's poor relation dressed in all her fake finery. It was a violent shade of pink, the kind that erupts when a halwai accidentally drops more pink colour into the sea of coconut barfi he's making. Which is where the name mithai pink was probably born.

13

Three years ago, Shahid realized he was in love with Saba. He was twenty-one and she was only sixteen, not more than a girl just out of school. The onset of his feelings wasn't sudden, but identifying them as love, and separating it from brotherly love, had happened just then. The realization had jolted him thoroughly.

Of course, he *could* get married to her. They were just second cousins, and if you went back that path on the family tree, they were probably not even related directly. But his mother and hers were good friends and she'd ended up calling him 'bhai' in the same way as she addressed Zohaib.

When they were young, he'd been happy to have her around filling the space in his life for a sibling. He'd always tried to protect her from the other cousins who could get pretty rough when adults weren't around, making sure she did not get hit too hard. But the life changing moment came when discussions about Rabia's marriage started.

Her parents wanted to get her married, but she wanted to pursue a course in fashion designing and they'd agreed reluctantly. At a family gathering, his mother had joked that if Rabia had been younger than Shahid, she'd have become her bahu already. Rabia had straightened her back and flung her long hair back, saying that she wouldn't have married him even then and looked at him as though he were a flea-bitten dog.

It had been a starkly embarrassing moment for everyone. His mother had laughed nervously and, trying to diffuse the tension, jokingly suggested that maybe Shahid should marry Saba.

Shahid's head had shot up and his eyes had sought out Saba who hadn't heard the conversation at all. She was sitting across the hall talking to another girl, and when she saw him staring at her, she'd stuck out her tongue at him. He'd laughed at that and all of a sudden it was as though something sharp had splintered his guts and his face closed up. The realization that marrying Saba would be the best thing to happen to him was painful in its stark clarity, because it seemed as though all his brain cells were shouting out together to him—*You love Saba.*

He had excused himself from the gathering and gone for a walk to assimilate his thoughts. He couldn't marry her! Or, could he? The thought came almost immediately. But he was only twenty-one and still studying! And she was too young. There was so much to do before he could ask his mother to speak to Saba's parents on his behalf. He had to get his MBA degree and he had to set up his business to become worthy of her.

At first he'd tried avoiding her, but it soon became unbearable, and so he made excuses to visit their house, even prepared to be cordial to Rabia.

Over the last three years he'd seen her grow into a young woman and his heart ached so much with his love that it took an immense amount of control not to blurt it out. She'd be horrified. He needed to make a place in her life and make her realize that he could be more than a cousin to her. But that was easier said than done.

Even now, whenever she called him 'bhai', he felt his heart constrict a bit. Would it work out? Would she be willing to see him in a different light? He had no idea. Even then, he had set up his business in the hopes of impressing her father and making himself eligible for her.

A few days ago when he'd seen her with her friend outside her college, he almost drove away before she called out to him.

He was seeing too much of her and it was getting more difficult for him to control his reactions to her. But he'd stopped anyway and offered to drop them home. He'd been a little amused when her friend started flirting with him. Saba was completely occupied with her mobile phone and she seemed to be texting someone constantly. That was why he'd suggested coffee, so he could spend some more time with her. But her friend Riya, or Priya something, had taken it upon herself to entertain them that evening with all that had happened in college.

He had dropped them off later, only noticing that Saba was unusually silent. He'd always behaved with decorum around her, never letting his feelings for her show. But her silence was unnerving and it upset him a bit when she went inside the house without even turning to wave at him in her usual exuberant manner.

Well, she was almost twenty now and if he could wait a little longer, he'd be able to tell his mother that he wanted to marry her. He'd often debated about when he should tell his mother, because although he wanted her on his side, he didn't want her to go rushing off to Saba's mother, thrilled with the news. He wanted Saba to be in love with him *before* he approached her mother. He needed her to want him as much as he wanted her. He wanted to become the most important person in her life. And for that he would have to wait.

14

Countdown to 6 March

POSTED BY THE OTHER T, 01-03-12

At home, everything seemed to be happening at once. The rush for clothes and jewellery for the bride had barely subsided when we had to buy clothes for ourselves and I had kept putting off mine until the very last moment. I'd looked for a time when Q wouldn't be around so that I'd be free to wear what I wanted, but she had decided to camp at our house until the engagement. It seemed like she was avoiding her husband, so he too had simply decided to stay here at our house!

Apart from Q and her husband, a few of the bawdy aunts had also decided to stay with Ammi to lend her a 'helping hand'. Read that as loud and raucous gossip sessions that lasted till midnight. Actually, it wasn't that bad. I'd been deflected from my studies and recruited to help them in packing the bride's clothes and it had taken a good three hours to pack her ghagra in an elaborate design. But this was accompanied by mirth and laughter going around and I realized that it was all quite a lot of fun.

With just five more days to go for the engagement, I'd been busy, and came face to face with T only today. I hadn't seen him at all since that episode with my friend X and I had stopped thinking about him. Well, almost. Apparently, he'd been hanging around at home, becoming indispensable to Ammi in every way. But he was gone before I got back home from college. It kind of looked like he was avoiding me, when the reverse was true. Somehow, it seemed okay if I didn't want to see him. But him not wanting to see me hurt for some reason.

Today I hadn't gone to college because I was too tired. I'd slept late last night and hadn't been able to get up. So when I walked into the hall rubbing my eyes, sleepily squinting at the clock to see the time, I felt a sudden jolt when I saw him sitting there talking earnestly to Abbu about something. He looked at me and for a moment I thought I saw something flash in his eyes before he smiled at me and said 'salam'.

I launched an attack at him directly. 'Why have you been avoiding me?' I asked him, and Abbu looked at me, surprised.

T, on the other hand, looked uncomfortable and quite at a loss for words. 'I. . .I've been busy,' he said.

'No, you're always here during the day when I'm in college, but you disappear when I come back.'

I cringe to think how childish and recalcitrant I must have sounded. He probably *was* busy. Just because he always was around for me when I was younger didn't mean that that would continue forever. He was entitled to a life of his own, after all.

Someone called out to him and he went, looking relieved. After he left, Abbu gave me hell for talking to T so rudely. 'He's your cousin! Show some respect!' he said.

T had been sent out to get something and as he got into his car, I looked at him from the window, wondering what it was that X had seen and I had been unable to see in him. He looked the same to me.

Anyway, today was the right time to pick up something for myself to wear at the engagement, I thought. I went to Ammi but she shooed me off. Literally.

'Shoo! Go! Go! Don't disturb me! Take money from your father and go buy something,' she said, as she rummaged through her closet. I scowled and went to Abbu. I had no idea how much a good dress would cost and I didn't know how much money to take from him.

Abbu was surprised that I hadn't got my clothes ready yet. To my dismay he called out to Q, asking her to take me to a shop and get a dress. No, no, no!

Q didn't hear him thankfully, so I managed to convince him that I could get it myself.

'But are you sure?' he looked doubtful. 'Somehow, the clothes you buy always seem so drab.'

I *had* to roll my eyes there. He had noticed that my clothes were drab, but hadn't seen *why* that was the case. Men!

'Yes, Abbu. I'll buy something bright and pretty. Just give me the money!' I was desperate now and looked around almost fearfully, but Q hadn't emerged yet.

Abbu gave me ten thousand rupees and I was taken aback. I almost pushed it back into his hands saying I didn't want to buy such an expensive dress, but he shook his head. 'Get something good. You're representing this family and I won't have you wearing dowdy clothes at your brother's engagement.'

Yeah well, whatever. I took the money, grabbed my burkha from my room and was wondering where I could possibly go and buy a nice outfit. With the money I had in my hands, I could buy it anywhere, but I was confused. I wished X hadn't gone to college or I would have taken her along with me, but then she'd have been shocked at the kind of dress I would eventually buy. X is the kind of girl who would wear a cotton-silk salwar to a wedding and think she's chic. If I wore something chic, chances are I'd be disowned.

I stepped out of the house and saw that T was just parking his car inside our gate and he stepped out, his eyes on me. 'Hey!'

I nodded but walked on. I was a bit embarrassed about my

childish outburst a while back. It was only T after all, one of my best friends, but. . .

'Hey wait up!' he called. I turned around, my face sulky.

'What's up? Where are you off to?'

'I. . .I haven't yet bought a dress for myself for the engagement so. . .'

'And you're going alone?' he frowned.

'That's not the problem. I just want someone for a second opinion. But everyone is busy and I don't want to go with Q,' I shuddered.

'Come, I'll take you,' he offered, and I narrowed my eyes. Maybe he hadn't been avoiding me and maybe he had just been busy as he had said. But he wasn't meeting my eyes. Maybe he was having girlfriend problems or something like that. I shrugged and got into the car and waited for him to drop off the package he'd been asked to get.

We went to Commercial Street and amazingly found parking on the main road itself. After a bit of browsing around different shops, I was getting confused. I couldn't make up my mind about what I wanted. Finally we went to Mysore Udyog.

I don't know why, but the salesman thought we were a couple. 'Your husband will love this colour on you madam,' he said as he opened an unstitched, deep orange salwar kameez.

'My husband!' I repeated, shocked. 'Do I look married to you?' I asked the man and from the corner of my eyes I saw that T was laughing soundlessly, his shoulders shaking. The salesman hurried away offering to get more designs.

'You're upset that he thought you were married, and not because he thought I was your husband?' T asked when I settled deeper into the chair.

'Huh?' I turned to face him and, I'm shocked to admit, we had a moment. You know. Those moments that make you go all 'aww' in romance novels and movies when the hero stares at the heroine and they're unable to break their gaze? Exactly. I was, no, *am* still shocked. I don't know what happened but he continued looking at me with such intensity that I finally had to look away.

I was flustered and couldn't concentrate on the clothes that the salesman was showing us. T leaned forward and picked up a deep green outfit with gold zari work on it. I demurred because my mind was racing and my stomach was working itself into knots.

Finally, I settled on a chocolate coloured crepe silk outfit that winked alluringly with delicate sequins and gold zari work. I told myself repeatedly that nothing had happened and nothing had changed as I paid for it. We both walked to the car and T asked me if I wanted to eat something. I *was* a bit hungry but I shook my head. In the car, probably for the first time ever, we sat without speaking to each other and I tried to tell myself that everything was normal. Nothing had changed. But as I glanced at his profile as he drove confidently, I knew that wasn't so. It was like looking at a jigsaw puzzle that had been rearranged subtly into a new design and you couldn't quite pinpoint what was different. The more worrying aspect was that I was getting quite entranced by the new design.

15

Someone take me away please

POSTED BY THE OTHER T, 03-03-12

The air in my house hangs heavily, pulled down by the weight of all that sugar syrup that's evaporated and made everything so sickly sweet.

My idea of what a halwai looked like was fed by popular culture or, rather, Hindi films. So I was expecting a rotund and cheerful 'lalaji' type man who would be dressed in a dhoti and leave his upper body bare (I was wondering about how hygienic that was. Wouldn't his sweat start dripping off into the. . .Ugh, okay, never mind.)

But when I opened the door to the man who would be making laddoos for the engagement, I thought he was a salesman and I almost shut the door in his face telling him that we didn't need another water purifier, when he said something about laddoos. I called out to Abbu and in minutes the man got down to work.

From the garage outside, I heard sounds of scraping and banging and I went to the window in my room to inspect. Abbu had arranged for the halwai to work there which included getting him a stove, a huge kadhai and lots and lots of ghee.

I watched for some time as he fried the boondi, briskly moving the little round orange balls in the hot ghee, scooping them up with a slotted, long handled spatula and draining them into a huge vessel. When I went back to the window after a while, he was still doing the same thing, except that there was now a young chap of maybe seventeen with him, who was chopping cashews with almost manic speed. I observed them for a while, watching the mound of boondi grow, wondering why these two with their polyester shirts and trousers looked least like people who would make something sweet. Abbu sat nearby on a chair and watched them.

Inside the house, things were getting quite chaotic. As the boy's side, we not only had to take the clothes for the bride and the laddoos, but also what seemed like hundreds of other goodies, arranged artfully on trays, wrapped in cellophane paper or clingfilm and decorated with ribbons. All this was a lot of work and Ammi had recruited all the relatives who were free to come and help so there was a lot going on at home.

Then there was also the question of what Y would wear for the engagement. The girl's side would also be sending him clothes, but he would be wearing something else (See? He gets away with *his* own choice.) Abbu felt he should wear a sherwani but Q insisted he wear a suit. For all the urgency Y had been showing when they had been searching for a girl, he didn't seem much bothered about things any more. In fact, he had about as much enthusiasm as I'd probably have for a dentist's appointment.

Speaking of which, I remember my sweet tooth. I find it irritating when girls proclaim how much they *hate* eating sweets. I've seen girls shudder and run in the opposite direction when faced with gajar ka halwa. But if it's a tiramisu, they might titter and complain about how many calories it is and elegantly touch the rim of their spoon to the edge of the little swirl of cream on top and whisk it off, and then taste it gingerly and then make all sorts of orgasmic faces.

Okay, where was I again? Right, I was talking about my sweet tooth which is a bit of a monster. So, I'd been eagerly waiting for the day when the laddoos would be made because then I could sample all I like. But for some reason, the smell of the ghee and the sugar syrup was making me feel queasy.

I tamped down the feelings and went outside to taste and test some of the laddoos.

'I was surprised that you hadn't come outside yet,' Abbu remarked. I watched mesmerized as the man and his assistant started making the laddoos, deftly taking the syrup drenched boondi into their hands, rolling it around and making balls that they dropped into a large plate.

It was evening by the time they finished and I'd already eaten three laddoos and was feeling sick. Everything seemed sweet and sticky to me, right down to the air, which seemed laced with sugar and cardamom.

Okay, the laddoos were just an excuse for me to write this post because this blog is about my brother's wedding, blah blah blah. Actually, I'm DYING to talk about T to someone, but I can't speak to anyone. Usually I unload all my problems on T whenever he comes. But he's out of the question, obviously. In recent times, X has also been a pretty good listener, but I find myself reluctant to tell her about T.

I mean, what will she *think* of me? T is my cousin! I call him 'bhai' and everything. Won't she think I'm all weird? Also, she raved about T for all of three days after we met him outside our college and she thinks she has a crush on him, so I can't really out-crush her, can I? And I don't have a crush on T. That's absurd. Maybe I imagined that eye contact. Maybe he'd spaced out and I *mistakenly* thought he was looking at me as though I was the most cherished woman in the world. Yeah, except that I don't know what to think anymore. It's all so confusing.

Also, it looks like T's avoiding me again. No, I didn't bunk college today so I could bump into him, silly. We didn't have many classes and I wanted to help in the house. No really! I'm not Q, who expects to be pampered all day and was at the salon getting spa treatment. But I'm also super annoyed with myself. Each time the gate opens or I hear a car, I look up, wondering if it's him. Somebody please knock some sense into me. Or find me another guy I can have a crush on.

16

Rabia inspected her face in the mirror that covered half the wall in the enclosed room of the salon. She lifted her neck, ran her hands over it and then lowered her neck again. She was wearing her own shift because she refused to wear what the salon provided, and she tapped her fingers impatiently on the bed where she was sitting sideways as she waited for the girl to bring the waxing kit. The girl stumbled inside, smiling at Rabia uncertainly, and because Rabia was pleased with her image in the mirror, she smiled back at her. Instantly, the girl became more radiant as she enthusiastically waxed Rabia's arms and legs.

Rabia hardly felt the twinges of pain as the strips were ripped off repeatedly, revealing her smooth and fair skin. She was thinking of her husband with a good deal of annoyance. He was behaving as though he couldn't live without her for even a day and she was getting tired of his constant attention. It wasn't like he hadn't left her alone and gone on business trips before. But now that he was staying *here* with her, everything was different. Her mother was constantly on edge, trying to make sure he was comfortable.

When Rabia asked him why he was staying with her, he had put his arm around her shoulder, squeezed her firmly and said, 'But it's my only *saale saab's* engagement. I don't want to miss out on the fun.' And true to that, he had stayed up with them late into the nights, gossiping with the aunts, flirting with dumb Saba and making everyone giggly.

She no longer looked forward to Zohaib's engagement and wanted everything to be over so things could just go back to being normal. No one fussed over her anymore because they were so busy packing all those things for that girl.

Rabia pondered over the girl her brother would be marrying. She was very pretty, but of course, no match for her, she thought as she brushed a strand back into the wide band that held her hair in place.

'Ma'am! You have. . .' the girl broke off looking at Rabia in consternation.

'What?' Rabia asked, narrowing her eyes.

'You got some wax into your eyebrow,' the girl said looking terrified.

'What? Where?' Rabia hopped out of the bed and inspected her eyebrow in the mirror in horror. Some of the wax on her arm had got stuck on her eyebrow.

'I'll wash it off,' she said, running towards the wash basin stand in the corner, but it had immediately hardened into a tiny ball. She tried to remove it carefully and it came off eventually, but not without uprooting some of the hair at the corner of her eyebrow.

'It's all your fault!' Rabia shouted at the girl. 'How will I go for my brother's engagement with a quarter of my eyebrow gone?'

The girl looked aghast. She ran outside to get help, leaving Rabia at the mirror inspecting her face. She looked comical and no longer in charge of her beauty.

When she left an hour later, she was seething with anger although her eyebrow had been drawn into place with a pencil. It didn't look the same, but there was little she could do. She'd been thinking of Zohaib's bride when the incident had occurred, so obviously it was *her* fault. Rabia checked off on a mental list about why she hated this girl already: a) she was prettier than she had a right to be and with Zohaib's looks, the two of them would become the most envied couple in the family; b) She cost Rabia her eyebrow.

Rabia reached home to see Shahid's car leaving the gates. This was one more thing about the engagement that she hated. Shahid's constant presence in the house. Even as kids he had seen right through her, at the things about herself that she didn't even acknowledge. So naturally she resented him.

Seated next to Shahid was Zohaib who looked bored and annoyed. Normally she and Zohaib got along well enough, but in recent times he had withdrawn from her completely. Around the time she got married, he had started his job and the two major events in their lives had driven them further apart. Even the times when he dropped her home, he was silent and refused to come inside, but she'd never given it a second thought. Was he all right? Happy with what was happening? Well, he should be, because he'd been so insistent on getting married so soon.

All concerns for Zohaib dried up when she went inside, hoping no one would comment about her missing eyebrow.

17

'I can't believe you haven't decided what you're going to wear!' Shahid said as he drove out of the lane.

'Why are *you* getting so worked up?' Zohaib asked, turning to look outside the window.

'You're getting engaged on Sunday. And it's Thursday already,' Shahid reminded him, echoing the words that Zohaib's father had said a while back.

'So? We just have to go to a store and pick up some clothes. Big deal!' Zohaib replied, fiddling with the music system in the car.

'Okay. Where do you want to go?' Shahid asked, glancing at the bunch of CDs on his dashboard that Zohaib was examining.

'Wherever,' Zohaib shrugged. 'Look at you! Are you twenty-four or forty-two?' Zohaib was turning the CDs in his hands and looking at them critically. 'I cannot believe you listen to ghazals. Dude! Are you for real?'

Shahid actually blushed. 'Uh, I. . .'

'Wait a second. These are all Abbu's favourite singers. Ghulam Ali and Jagjit Singh. He used to drive me nuts listening to these ghazals every time we had to do a road trip somewhere.'

Shahid cursed himself for not having stashed those CDs away. 'Are you trying to impress my father for something?' Zohaib asked him quietly.

'Of course not!' Shahid replied immediately. 'I like them too!'

The truth was that ever since his own father had passed away many years ago, he had turned to Zohaib's father as his own and had been hoping to surprise his uncle by playing the CDs whenever he took him in the car. And also to stack the brownie points in his favour for the time when he'd ask for Saba's hand. But so far it hadn't happened.

Zohaib cocked his head and looked at Shahid as though seeing him for the first time. 'Are you trying to make him invest in your business? You don't need to do all these things, you know? He'll do it if you simply ask him.'

'What nonsense!' Shahid exploded. 'It's nothing like that. Here, take some of these CDs.' He handed Zohaib some more that were lying around and Zohaib stared at him for a few more seconds before taking them.

'So, have you decided what you'll wear?' Shahid asked, hoping to change the topic.

'I'll wear what I usually wear. A shirt and trousers.'

'Fine.'

The two of them were quiet for the rest of the way. Zohaib bought an off-white shirt with dark trousers and Shahid looked at him disapprovingly as they paid and left.

He wanted to shake Zohaib and remind him that it was his engagement but he didn't say anything because his mind had moved automatically to the time he'd taken Saba shopping. It had been delightful listening to her comments about the clothes that she was being shown, her expressions of horror when she recounted the colour that Rabia had selected for the bride and her inability to choose something for herself. But when the salesman had thought that they were a couple, he'd felt a little bubble rising inside him and he forgot to keep his feelings from showing on his face. So when she looked at him, he'd been unable to look away and yet he'd had to clench his hands so he didn't reach out for her. She looked very disconcerted as it was.

It was a repeat performance of the day when he'd picked her up with her friend and she'd remained quiet throughout the journey. The only difference was that she'd been busy texting then and now she wasn't, although she did turn and look at him a few times.

Shahid had no idea what she was thinking and he took the easy route out by avoiding her since then. Today when he'd gone to her house, she'd been standing at the window eating a laddoo and he grinned at how engrossed she seemed to be.

'*Zyada khayegi, moti ho jayegi,*' he repeated the jingle of an old commercial that the two of them used to sing to annoy Rabia whenever they saw her nibbling on an apple or biting delicately into a carrot, when they'd been kids. Of course that used to piss Rabia off and the two of them would crack up in laughter.

Saba turned to him and it seemed that she had forgotten what had passed between them two days ago. Shahid felt a little sad, but still smiled at her indulgently when she completed the jingle defiantly, saying, 'I—don't—care.'

She smiled back at him brilliantly and he walked away to Zohaib's room wondering how he would stop himself from speaking his mind on the day of the engagement when he'd see her wearing that beautiful dress that the two of them had picked out together.

He turned to enter the corridor, but stopped and glanced back over his shoulder. She looked away swiftly because she'd been staring at his back. She was confused by him. Maybe it was a good way to edge into her life, he thought, feeling a tiny pulse of optimism.

Had Shahid known how things would change in the next few days, he would have preferred to hurtle himself into her life immediately. But he hadn't known, of course.

18

Oh. My. God.

POSTED BY THE OTHER T, 06-03-12

Today has been the most awesome day of my life. Yes, my brother was getting engaged and all that, but it was still *my* day.

First of all, Q's husband found out about the ₹75,000 oyster pink ghagra that she had bought. She had split the charge between two of her cards, but the card company had texted him about the huge expense, getting her into trouble. It wasn't like he didn't like spending money on her. He was just pissed that she hadn't bothered to tell him. Moreover, he felt that the ghagra was too grand for an engagement, so he insisted that she wear it for the wedding.

Since Q never listened to anyone, she had decided to wear the ghagra anyway, but on the morning of the engagement we heard her scream. Ammi and I ran to her room and saw her husband sitting on the bed, legs stretched out and grinning.

'You hid it?' she asked him, her voice high and squeaky, and I had to stop myself from smiling.

'Just give it back, please!' she pleaded when he didn't reply. He shook his head.

'Jaan, you know how obstinate I am,' he said. 'I mean, I forced your parents to get you married to me. You think I'll give in for a ghagra?'

'Fine. I won't go for the engagement,' Q said, sitting down on the bed in a huff. Ammi was torn between placating Q and smiling indulgently at her son-in-law for the cute trick he'd played. More like juvenile, but I wasn't complaining.

'Ammi, you go and get dressed. I'll make sure she'll come downstairs,' he assured Ammi who nodded as we walked out. It still felt a bit strange when he called my mother Ammi, because that made him more like my brother than brother-in-law. But I'm SO glad Q got married to him and not some sop who would give in to every wish of her's, although I wondered how he planned to make her wear something else. I could hear her complaining about not having the right accessories as we walked downstairs.

That was the first sign, and I should have known that better stuff was coming my way. The engagement was in the afternoon and after a hurried breakfast we all went to get ready. I took a shower and wore the chocolate brown dress that I had bought with T. Our tailor Khaja had done a splendid job with it because he hadn't been visited by Q this time around. It fit perfectly, clung where it should and fell into graceful folds along the bottom. I brushed my hair and pinned it up using some bling-ey hair accessories that Q's husband had got for her and me on his last visit to Hong Kong. As I ran a raisin coloured lip gloss over my lips, I briefly wondered where T was and whether he was coming home or going to the engagement directly.

I waited in the hall with the other aunts and Ammi, hoping that Q would stop throwing things around and wear something and come.

'If I was her husband, I'd make her wear a towel and go,' an aunt said, her face glowering and we all tittered, except Ammi who looked offended.

T's mother had stayed with us the previous night and she was on the phone talking to him. We were waiting for everyone to assemble and then we'd all have to leave in a flurry of cars.

'He's stuck in traffic,' she said as she ended the call. 'I told him to stay the night here but he wouldn't listen,' she continued, shaking her head.

There was some more idle chit-chat and then Q came down wearing a light green saree, which made her look like a very delectable kiwi mousse. She wasn't wearing any gold jewellery, but stones flashed from everywhere as she descended haughtily. She was followed by her husband who kept grinning and gave me a conspiratorial wink.

It was nearly 12.30 p.m. by the time we left. T had arrived and I braced myself wondering how I would feel when I would see him. But he barely looked at me, because he was very busy. I did get a good eyeful of him, dressed in a black shirt and jeans. He'd also shaved and I almost told him that I preferred the stubbled look but kept quiet, a little unsure about the changed equation between us. He went off to Y's room immediately, from where the two of them emerged a little later and both joined the other cousins and boys who had come home.

Finally, when it seemed that our house couldn't contain all the people anymore, we left, piled up in different cars. I wore my special burkha that Ammi had got for me from Dubai last year and I couldn't help feeling pleased that I looked nice in it. It has these Swarovski crystals lined up on the stole and the sleeves and I instantly felt more glamorous when I wore it. I know, I know. . .the burkha is not meant to add glamour, but rather to detract from it, but it was my brother's engagement after all.

Then we got into the cars and I found myself squeezed beside one of the bawdy aunts who was inspecting my face closely.

'You girls wear too much make-up these days,' she commented, looking at my eyeliner and then at my lipstick.

I raised an eyebrow and rolled my eyes in the rear view mirror thinking it was T, because I was used to sharing these things with him. To my horror, I realized that it wasn't T but an uncle who was driving and he saw me roll my eyes at him in an exasperated manner. He narrowed his bushy eyebrows and almost turned to look at me when I turned away, pretending to see the road.

We reached B's house (B for Bride, get it?) which is in Benson Town, a very posh locality where you are likely to find most of the upper class Muslims of Bengaluru. We parked the cars in lanes and got off outside, and I could overhear an aunt murmur to another, 'They probably wanted us to see how big their house is. That's why they're holding the engagement here. Show offs!'

I shook my head at their pettiness as I made my way towards the door, holding a tray. Since I was an unmarried girl, I wasn't supposed to be seen *or* heard, but Abbu would have none of it. He lambasted an aunt who suggested they leave me at home and go.

The door was open and there were chairs outside in the lawn. (Yes, they had an actual lawn.) There was a huge marquee put up there and someone in their family was probably a big fan of *Hum Aap Ke Hain Kaun*. Or *Monsoon Wedding*. They'd strung marigolds everywhere.

We walked inside and there was a hushed silence before the women started welcoming us, showing us where to go, telling us to remove our burkhas and generally making a huge fuss over us. A pretty teenaged girl smiled at us and held a tray with glasses of watermelon juice. Tiny bits of watermelon floated on the top and the rims of the glasses were coated with powdered sugar. *Please take note.* People like X simply assume that ALL Muslims serve only rose milk or Roohafza to their guests, thanks to Hindi movies and commercials. But see?

We settled down in a room and I wondered if it belonged to B. It was painted white and seemed as though it had leapt straight from the pages of an interior design magazine. Ammi was nervous and Q looked at everything disdainfully. If we'd been kids she might have even erupted, saying, my house is bigger or prettier. Thankfully, she sat down on a chair and crossed her hands over her knees.

That was when he came inside.

Oh. My. God.

He saw all the women seated inside but didn't seem deterred by it at all as he came right near me (near ME), almost brushing his thigh against my knee as he opened a wardrobe and rummaged inside it.

I knew my face had to be flaming red. Like fire engine red. I quickly looked at everyone and saw that after that collective gasp, all the women had averted their faces from him, some hiding their faces with their saree pallus and others turning their entire bodies away from him. Okay, don't misunderstand me. There was nothing wrong with him. The thing is, our women keep communication with strange (as in whom they are not related to or don't know) men at a minimum. Only Q and I hadn't done the whole hiding-our-faces-from-him thing. I don't know about Q, but I couldn't look away from him.

I knew I'd get a proper tongue lashing from Ammi later on, but I couldn't move! He was standing so close to me, it felt as though a whole army of ants was marching up and down my entire body in a pleasant and tingly kind of way.

He finally pulled out a shirt and then inspected it against the trousers he was wearing. And then he spoke to me.

'Do you think this shirt goes with these trousers?' he asked, and I wish my throat hadn't blocked up completely, as I didn't know whether to look at his face or his hands or the shirt or. . .

'Yes it does,' Q answered regally from where she was sitting. It looked as though only the three of us were there in the room amid a sea of colourful sarees and clothes. His face lit up when he saw her and he smiled almost conspiratorially. Then, with a smart salute to the two of us, he stepped outside.

I won't describe the angry confusion that broke out when he left, or the heated whispers about such inappropriate behaviour or about how the girl's side could have humiliated everyone this way, sending a strange man into their midst. One aunt actually stood up, saying that she wanted to boycott the engagement and go back home.

My mother had to soothe everyone's ruffled feathers and when that didn't work, she had to call B's mother and ask for an explanation. The poor woman was shocked too when she heard about it.

'Uzair came *here*?' she asked, her voice turning shrill.

Uzair. I ran the name over my tongue feeling a tingle run down my back. Oh shit! I've used his name instead of initials. But I don't really care now. I mean, I just have to hit the backspace key and delete it, but I can't think of calling him by a mere initial. He's too. . .too larger than life for that.

'That *boy*! Apa, I'm so sorry! I have to keep reminding him about our culture and traditions, but that boy! He's been living abroad for too long and he just doesn't care,' she sniffed.

'Is he your son?' one of the bawdy aunts asked with a speculative glance. I knew the maths running in her head. Drop dead gorgeous son+ huge bungalow+ NRI. I could actually *see* the WOW! swimming in her eyes.

'No!' B's mother looked almost horrified at the suggestion. 'He's my sister-in-law's son. He lives in London and he just came last week for some work and my husband asked him to stay for the engagement.' She made a face as she said that.

'So is he going away?' the bawdy aunt continued and B's mom flashed an angry look at her.

'Actually, no. He's staying here until the wedding. I'm so sorry, I'll make sure he won't come again and disturb you people this way. I'm so embarrassed!' And true to that, she had turned pinker than the salwar she was wearing.

Of course, bawdy aunt was looking beady eyed and maybe she already had plans of her own. For some niece or neighbour's daughter, of course.

You know what? I quite like the idea of living in London.

19

Zohaib checked all the boxes and hit the delete button without a qualm. All the congratulatory emails landed in his virtual trash can and he smiled with grim satisfaction. While he was almost relieved now, there were times when he wished all this was over and he could continue with his life normally. But nothing would be normal again. He was going to have to put up with a new person and she was going to share his life, his room, his bed and even his bathroom, he thought with a twinge of unease.

He remembered Shahid's concern before his engagement, 'Why are you going through this if you're going to be so uninterested?' Zohaib had kept quiet with a great deal of difficulty, because he was on the verge of snapping at Shahid's concern.

Maybe when Shahid got married, he would jump and dance and *show* everyone how happy he was. For him, getting married was the only available option.

He picked up his phone and flicked through the photos until it came to hers. He tapped idly and the photo filled the screen. He brought his thumb and forefinger together on the screen and let go, and the picture zoomed. He had to admit that she was very pretty. Even though she was dressed in a very disturbing pink ghagra, she had a wonderful complexion, almost luminous as though it was lit up from inside.

He shook his head and then ran his forefinger across the screen to see the other pictures. There he was, sitting on the sofa in his in-law's house, looking quite like the lamb being taken to the slaughter as Shahid had implied.

'Dude, why didn't you call us for your wedding?' Sampath slapped Zohaib on the back. Zohaib coughed, cleared his throat and straightened up.

'I didn't get married,' Zohaib explained but Sampath and a few other guys had already grabbed his phone and were scrolling the pictures.

'THAT'S your wife?' someone asked and Zohaib nodded.

'Yes. My fiancé,' he replied wishing they'd give back the phone so he could continue with his work.

'Man, she's hot,' the same guy, whose name was Kunal, commented. 'You lucky dog, you!'

'What's she like?' Sampath asked.

Zohaib shrugged. 'I haven't met her, so I don't really know.'

'What?' Kunal asked, and the others looked at him as though they couldn't believe him.

Zohaib nodded. 'I *haven't* met her. My mother found her for me.'

'You just said that like she was some pretty shell your mom found for you on the beach, dude,' Sampath remarked, scrolling the pictures again.

It wasn't too far off the mark, Zohaib thought, but didn't say anything because they had let out a whoop again.

'Who's *this* babe?' They were checking out Rabia.

'That's my sister' Zohaib said stiffly.

'Why didn't you invite us?' a fat guy called Deepak asked. 'We could have seen these pretty ladies *and* we could have had biryani as well.'

'You should have invited us to your house, at least,' Sampath said, and the others nodded. 'At least we'd have been able to see the pretty ladies.'

Zohaib thought of telling them that no matter where they went—his house or his in-laws'—the 'pretty ladies' were always going to be beyond their reach.

'Hey, I like this one also,' Deepak said as he zoomed a photo.

'That's Saba, my other sister,' Zohaib said, feeling a little protective suddenly. He reached out and took the phone back.

'She's pretty. . .not stunning like your other sister. . .but there's a nice quality to her face,' Kunal said almost sanctimoniously.

'Yes, thank you for noticing that,' Zohaib replied with sarcasm that didn't reach them, however, because they were already comparing the attributes of the three women they had seen. He wished he hadn't handed over his phone to Shahid to take photos. Shahid had apparently given it to someone in the ladies section, asking her to take pictures of everyone, especially the bride.

'Shall we get back to work?' Zohaib reminded them, at which they dispersed, and Zohaib sighed in relief.

'Did you just say you got engaged?' Maya asked as she walked by with a folder in her hands. She reached her table but didn't sit down. Instead, she perched her butt on the edge and looked at him, as though waiting for an explanation.

Zohaib didn't say anything. He briefly observed how Maya's skirt had ridden up a few inches, and her feet swung lazily as she toyed with the string on her folder. She pulled at it and then let it go with a twang. He swivelled around to face his computer to get back to work. There was no way he was letting Maya distract him.

'So, were you even planning on telling us about it?' she asked, jumping off the desk.

'I thought everyone knew,' Zohaib replied. 'I've been deleting congratulatory emails since morning, because they've been clogging my inbox.'

Maya stayed silent. 'What's her name? What's she like?' she asked after a moment as though she couldn't contain herself any longer.

Zohaib drew in a breath. He looked around and saw that everyone was busy. Apparently. But they were probably clued in to their conversation as well. He wanted to tell Maya that he'd never been interested in her from the beginning, that she had been the one who kept trying to draw his attention. But it was too open a space to say that. He didn't want to IM her, OR send her a text or email, because all those things were incriminating later on, as he knew from bitter experience.

Well, thank God he had never taken her up on her offer. Offers. But she looked hurt and he wished there was some way he could assuage it. It really wasn't his fault that she'd had such an obvious crush on him.

'Her name is Ashrafa. I haven't met her yet, but my cousin took pictures of her yesterday,' he said finally, hoping she wouldn't ask to see the pictures. He turned away from Maya, but he glanced at her briefly as he spoke. Her face was blank and she too was sitting before her monitor. Whew! Apparently she didn't want to see.

How does one sweat in an air-conditioned office, Zohaib thought as he dabbed at his forehead and nose with a handkerchief. But it wasn't guilt, he thought. It was relief.

20

What's happening?

Posted by The Other T, 07-03-12

What a relief it was to find that I was hugely attracted to Uzair. At least now I could put behind all that stuff with T as temporary insanity. Now, whenever I see T, I think of Uzair and I can immediately identify how different both feelings are. With T, I really couldn't pin it down. It was too tremulous and almost scary. With Uzair, however, I know, because I've been there already but not to this extent probably.

You know how, when you have a crush on someone, you dream about opening the door to see them standing there or answering the phone to hear their voice. As filmi as that sounds, that kind of happened today.

It was Monday and almost all the aunts had left after the engagement. Q was supposed to return to her house in the evening, although she looked reluctant. But it was a relief to have the house as it was before everyone had invaded it.

I was just idling away thinking of how pretty B had looked even though the ghagra we took for her was ghastly. There was an alluring quality to her face and, at a quick glance, I saw that her make-up basics were correct and *I* could take lessons from her if it came to that. Y was definitely not marrying some country bumpkin who was going to put rouge on her cheeks in two round circles.

When we got back home, the talk was divided between how

beautiful she was and what an idiot that boy who had barged into the ladies room had been. You know how these aunts are, na? They love to embellish facts, and if I hadn't been there myself, I wouldn't have known whether to believe them or not. One aunt almost implied that he'd *changed* his clothes in front of them! Oh, come on, woman! Don't you actually wish he had? After we came back, Y went off to his room, unwilling to participate in the festive atmosphere and T had disappeared too, which was a relief in a way because I could think about Uzair freely.

I hadn't gone to college because I was tired and after lunch, Abbu had also gone to his shop and Q's husband was in his office. Q had decided to take a nap because *she* was so tired. Right.

When the doorbell rang, I made a face but went to open the door. There he was. His smile widened when he saw me and I think I forgot how to breathe. What was he doing here? What was I wearing? I couldn't possibly look down and see and I couldn't remember. Not fair!

'Hey gorgeous!' he said and I *knew* I'd blushed because my face felt hot. He called me gorgeous, my mind screamed repeatedly.

I stood still at the door, uncertain whether to let him inside or not. He straightened up after giving me another heart-stopping smile (I know, I know—bad cliché. but it did feel like that) and spoke again.

'I've been asked to drop off these things to your house today. And to apologise to the ladies about barging in without any warning yesterday.'

That was when I noticed that behind him three men were unloading plastic covered trays of mithais and dry fruits and fruits and myriad other things. He leaned closer to me and I stepped back involuntarily.

'But you know what? I'm going to skip the apology,' he said and winked at me!

No one had ever spoken to me like this. The boys I had interacted with were really a very tiny lot. Mostly cousins and guys from tuition classes and then. . .see. . .that's it. I hardly came across any boys in my life, so to find myself in front of this amazingly good looking boy. . .uh. . .man, who was actually flirting with me, made me feel as though I'd suddenly lost half of my stomach somewhere.

'Are you okay?' he asked and stepped aside to let the men come inside with the trays.

'What's all this?' I asked, my voice sounding rusty and unused.

'So you *do* have a voice,' he spoke, and then stepped closer, 'I have no idea what all these things are but I *think* they're some kind of exchange mechanism. Apparently you guys brought some stuff over yesterday and. . .'

'Who is it?' Ammi's voice came from behind me and he stopped speaking.

'I didn't get your name,' he said and bent his head low, but Ammi had come up to the door by then.

She gasped when she saw that I was actually speaking to him.

'Go to your room,' Ammi admonished me and stood in front of the door like a barricade. He raised his eyebrows when I stepped back and shook his head slightly, raising a corner of his mouth into a smirk. A smile actually.

I went to my room, my heart thudding loudly and erratically. I quickly walked to the window hoping to see him from there. Yes! There was a car parked in the drive and a small tempo from which the men were unloading more stuff. Uzair was standing near his car, but he wasn't looking towards the window.

God! Look this way you idiot, I flashed mentally at him. Nopes. No telepathy whatsoever, because he'd taken out his mobile and was busy with it. I don't know why I felt such desperation at the thought that I'd never see him again and this was the only chance I had to speak to him. I almost thought of calling out to him, but then Ammi would hear me and I didn't want that.

I stared at his tall form, drinking in his features as he looked up from the mobile and saw that the men were done unloading the stuff. Have I described him before? I haven't? Okay, I'll do my best, but you should know that I'm a bit biased towards him already, given that I have this massive crush on him. So he's around six feet tall. Umm. . .T's around five feet ten, and Uzair is definitely taller than him. Okay, why did I bring in T ?

Yeah, so he's tall but not lanky. He's got broad shoulders, and today he was wearing this T-shirt that stretched right across his chest in a very sexy way. And his hair! Not too long but casual and. . .again, very different from T's almost harsh crew cut. And he has a tiny little cleft in his chin which made me. . .Well, I will stop now or the keyboard will get wet with all the drool.

He straightened up, turned towards the window and smiled when he saw me. I wondered if he'd walk up and speak to me. After all, my room was on the ground floor. Would he give me his number? Or, would he ask for mine?

I stood there in anticipation, but he smiled again as though enjoying a private secret and then shook his head and got inside his car and drove off! He just drove off! He didn't even wave at me. Okay, in his defence, Ammi was probably standing at the door emitting rays of disapproval at him so he may have thought it best not to do anything that would enrage her further.

The moment he left, I sank into my bed with a feeling of desperation that made me feel so bleak that I couldn't quite understand it. What could I do? How could I get in touch with him? Maybe I could ask T for help?

21

There was silence in the auditorium as darkness descended and then the spotlights came on the stage, highlighting the actors who stood frozen in a montage. There was a thunderous applause and a number of wolf whistles rang in the air as the actors took a bow and walked away from the stage. Riya and Saba clapped hard. Their palms smarted, but that didn't stop them from applauding the rousing performance that the students of their college had given.

There was a brief interval before the last play of the day was going to be staged. Riya nudged Saba to get up and together they left the auditorium unobtrusively, snaking their way between sprawled legs until they reached outside.

'Whew!' Riya let out her breath in a whoosh. 'That was something else!'

Saba smiled. 'I know! They did such a good job of it!'

Riya sat down on one of the stone steps nearby and stretched. Everywhere around them there was the buzz that inevitably sprang up in the air whenever there was an inter-college festival. This time around, they were attending a drama festival that was being held in Christ College, and their college had just finished their play.

'I had no idea Michelle could look so hot,' Riya remarked when Saba leaned back and shut her eyes. She opened her eyes wondering what Riya was talking about.

'Huh?'

'Michelle! She looked so hot as that girl's husband. I mean, so what if we don't have guys in our college. Michelle was totally awesome.'

'Yeah, I know. She was very convincing,' Saba remarked.

'I think I have a crush on her,' Riya giggled and Saba rolled her eyes.

'You seriously need to get a boyfriend,' Saba said. 'Look at you, having crushes on random people!'

Riya made a face at her. 'I mean, I've seen her around in college. But I had no idea she could be so fantastic on stage!'

Saba nodded. Her college had just put up a play that she had scripted and she'd felt a warm glow come over inside her when she saw it. At first, she felt a bit weird. Those were *her* characters there on stage and they were mouthing *her* lines. And they weren't exactly doing it the way she had envisioned. But soon her discomfort vanished and she got engrossed in the play just as everyone else had.

'I wish we could go back home,' Saba yawned. She hadn't been sleeping properly since her brother's engagement and she just wanted to lie down and curl up.

'Yeah, but we have to wait for the results to be announced,' Riya reminded her. 'I have a feeling our play will win.'

Saba shrugged. 'The Joseph's team also did a good job,' she said.

'You know, the script that you wrote was really amazing,' Riya remarked. 'I hope you're planning to continue with your writing after college gets over.'

Saba remained silent. She had joined a scriptwriting workshop in college and, at the end of it, they all had to submit their scripts. The best one would be chosen by the drama team for the inter-college festival and that was how hers had been selected.

'I don't know,' she said after sometime.

'What do you mean?' Riya turned to look at her puzzled.

'I mean, I'm not really sure I want to write scripts. It's not my cup of tea.'

'Oh please! There is actually something you're good at, but you. . .'

'No, no. . .it's not like that. The thing is, I don't have any ambition,' Saba spoke softly.

'What do you mean?'

'I mean, I enjoy writing and I'll continue doing it. But I'm okay if nothing ever comes of it.'

'How can you say that?' Riya exploded. 'Look at me. I don't have a single talent and I have no idea what I'm going to do with my life. You, on the other hand, are fantastic at something and you're just throwing it away.'

'I'm not throwing it away,' Saba argued. 'I'm just cool about it. I mean, I don't have a strong drive to write a novel or get published or become famous.'

'But why not? Do you want to just get married and stay at home? Like your sister?' Riya asked her furiously.

Saba thought of Rabia for a moment, watching American shows like *Desperate Housewives*, thinking she was different from all the other women who watched Ekta Kapoor's hotchpotch. She didn't have any housework to do and all she did was watch TV or log on to Facebook. Did she want to end up like that?

'No. I mean, I *will* do something. I just don't want to push things further,' Saba answered finally, wondering why Riya was getting so worked up.

'I don't understand you. You're talented. But you just want to let it wither away. You're going to get married as soon as you finish college, have three kids, become fat and then watch Hindi soaps with your mother-in-law and then. . .'

'Stop! Stop!' Saba burst out laughing. 'Okay, I promise I won't watch Hindi soaps!'

'Saba! That's not what I meant,' Riya looked exasperated. 'You have to nurture your talent. You're gifted. You can write so well. Why do you want to give it up?'

Saba sighed. 'I never said I'm giving it up. I can always write without getting anyone else in trouble, so. . .'

'What do you mean?' Riya interrupted her.

'See, Rabia wanted to do fashion designing after college. And my parents wanted to get her married. But she had her way and then. . .my parents had to face a lot of flak from all quarters for giving in to her.'

'So? You're going to make things easy for your parents?' Riya asked incredulously. 'I've never heard such a lame thing in my life!'

'No, what I meant was that Rabia attended the fashion designing classes for a year and then she got married. My parents were convinced that if they hadn't let her continue there, she would have married someone in our community.'

'Huh?' Riya looked confused. 'Your sister's husband saw her at a wedding and not at her fashion designing classes. What has one thing got to do with the other? And he's a Muslim, right?'

'Yes. But he's a Dakhni boy. And in my community, that's as good as getting her married to someone from a different religion.'

'I'll never understand you guys and your communities,' Riya said with a huff. She turned to Saba. 'So what does this have to do with you?'

'I don't know. I just feel that my parents won't take it too well if I tell them I want to do something more after graduation.'

'But. . .but. . .you should!' Riya said, getting up. 'I'm going inside now. If I sit here talking any longer, I'll probably end up un-friend-ing you.'

Saba watched her leave, feeling slightly indignant. Well, it was *her* life. But her thoughts went to Rabia. Her sister, with all her plans to become a fashion designer had not been able to manage it. And it wasn't like she'd had babies or her husband wasn't supportive. It was because Rabia didn't have the drive to pursue her dream. Which brought her back to what her dream was. She didn't know. She knew she was good at writing and she topped her class almost always, given that all they studied was her favourite subject—English literature.

Well, she was still in her fourth semester and there was plenty of time to decide what she wanted to do with her writing. She dusted her back as she got up and went inside. Riya hadn't gone back to their seats. She was standing at the entrance waiting for her, but her eyes were on the stage.

'This one looks really good,' she whispered and together they made their way back to their seats. Saba watched the play with little interest. Some time later, the actors on stage bowed and left to a very loud applause. She wanted her play to win for the sake of the college drama club. They'd worked so hard at it, and now it looked like this last college had apparently done better than them.

The judges needed time to discuss the results and once again the lights went on. Riya spotted a couple who had been making out in the corner, spring apart. She hid a smile as she saw the girl arrange her mussed hair, looking around nervously.

'While we wait for the results, you might as well tell me all about this new guy you met at your brother's engagement.'

Saba looked at Riya, wondering if she was still angry with her. But apparently Riya had forgotten, so she started to describe the events when Riya interrupted her.

'I can't believe you didn't invite me,' she complained.

Saba looked at her embarrassed. The truth was since it was being held in the bride's house, her father had felt unsure about how many guests they could invite. Even Zohaib hadn't invited any of his friends for his own engagement.

'Okay, okay! Don't go red trying to explain anything now. Just tell me more about this guy. What is he like? Is he hotter than your brother? Or that cousin of yours?'

Saba stared at Riya feeling exasperated. How did she expect her to compare Uzair with her brother and Shahid?

'Think Robert Pattinson and Arjun Rampal,' she replied after some time. Riya's eyes went round and then her shoulders slumped.

'That's a yucky combination,' she said.

Saba stuck her tongue out at her. 'He's gorgeous,' she whispered, shutting her eyes and remembering how she had felt when she'd opened the door to see him lounging at her doorstep.

'Yeah, whatever. What's the point? You don't have his number or vice versa.'

'I'm thinking of asking Shahid to help me out,' Saba revealed.

'Ooh! You ARE serious then, huh?' Riya asked, nudging her playfully.

'I don't know yet. But I'd like to pursue it and see what happens,' Saba replied and broke into a smile. 'You know, he said *I* was gorgeous.'

'Sounds like a flirt to me,' Riya said, narrowing her eyes.

'Yeah. . .' Saba stopped talking when someone came up on stage to announce the results.

'Okay, promise me one thing,' Riya said to her suddenly as the noise in the auditorium started to quieten down.

'What?' Saba whispered, surprised.

'If our college wins *any* prize today, you're going to think about your writing career more seriously.'

Saba rolled her eyes. 'Yeah, yeah, okay. But for now, I'm happy with the blog,' she spoke without thinking.

'What blog?' Riya asked, turning to face her, just as the microphone on stage started emitting screeching sounds. Someone tapped it nervously and then started speaking into it.

'Shh, not now,' Saba said, hoping Riya would forget all about it later.

22

The rocking motion of the train had lulled him to sleep and Shahid jerked awake when his phone vibrated in his pocket. He straightened up, rubbed his eyes with his thumb and forefinger and pulled out his phone, squinting at it.

It was a message from Saba. *'Call me when ur free?'*

Shahid blinked and then rubbed his eyes again. He typed back—*'Anything important?'*

He pressed 'send' wondering what had made her text him so early in the morning. He was on his way to Chennai on a business trip and he almost wished he hadn't avoided her so much these past few days. The more he saw of her, the harder it was getting for him to control his emotions and he was afraid he might do something too soon to scare her off.

During Zohaib's engagement, he'd made it a point not to linger in the house and he'd glanced at her briefly before making his escape. Her image in the chocolate brown salwar kameez was imprinted on his mind though, and he smiled as he remembered how pretty and sweet she had looked wearing it. He looked at his phone again and wondered why she hadn't texted back. It was Saturday and she didn't have college. Maybe she'd dozed off to sleep, he thought, imagining her sleeping in her bed and he rubbed the back of his neck, a little irritably. Grow up soon, Saba, he urged mentally.

His phone beeped again and he looked at it immediately. *'Kind of, yes. I really need 2 talk 2 u.'*

He scratched his chin briefly, wishing he'd taken the time to shave and then he typed back—'*On my way 2 Chennai. Can I call when I come bk?*'

His phone buzzed once again. '*Oh!* ☹'

On impulse, he dialled her number directly. Maybe the sad smiley had done it, but he wanted to hear her voice and she was giving him a great excuse for it.

She picked up on the first ring and sounded surprised.

'Hey!'

'Hey! What's up?'

'I'll talk to you when you get back,' she sounded hesitant.

'Nah! I'm getting bored as it is. Tell me,' he looked out of the train at the mountains that whipped by, cracking his knuckles on the side of his neck.

'It's. . .I. . .I don't know how to say it,' she said and Shahid forgot about everything around him. He edged himself closer to the window even though it was shut.

'Tell me,' he spoke softly, his heart beating madly with some absurd hope that maybe she'd understood how he felt about her.

'I don't know how to say it,' she said again. 'I think I'll wait for you to come back. Maybe we can meet up somewhere and I'll tell you.'

Although that sounded very tempting, Shahid's curiosity had gone up along with his hope. He had to hear what she had to say *now*.

'Listen. You can tell me whatever it is,' he spoke in a low voice.

She sighed. 'Okay. The thing is. . .you remember that guy whom everyone was talking about at Zohaib bhai's engagement?'

Shahid's brow furrowed. He *had* heard about some guy who had barged into the women's room but hadn't paid much attention to it.

'What about him?'

'I. . .I don't know how to say this,' she said, and Shahid felt a sharp pang. 'I. . .I know you think of me as your little sister and everything, but I need your help. As a friend.'

Shahid realized he was breathing hard. He didn't know if he could speak, but he tried nevertheless and swallowed. 'What help?'

'I. . .I need your help in getting Uzair's number,' she spoke softly.

'Why?' Shahid couldn't stop himself from asking in a sharp voice.

'Actually, he had come home the other day. . .'

'When?' he interrupted her, feeling anger rush inside his veins.

'The day after bhai's engagement. So, I opened the door and there he was,' she said shyly.

'Go on,' Shahid spoke tightly.

'And. . .and. . .I think I like him. Very much. But there's no way for me to contact him, without getting into trouble.' She sounded hesitant and a little afraid. Before he could tell her exactly what he thought of her hare-brained idea, she continued, 'Please? Please bhai? I really, really need your help. He's going back to London in June and I. . .I don't know what to do, so. . .'

Shahid swallowed again. From the time she'd joined college, he'd been a bit afraid that she'd fall in love with some random guy she'd meet at some fest. This was worse than that. Why hadn't he staked his claim on her before this guy had come along? What was he going to do?

'Do you think this is such a good idea?' he asked in a level voice, trying to control his anger.

'I don't know anything anymore,' she sounded despondent.

'You just saw him at the engagement and you think you're in love with him?' Shahid asked, unable to keep the sarcasm from his voice.

'I. . .I never said anything about love,' Saba replied, surprised at his tone.

'Why are you asking me for help?' he asked, wiping the sweat that had beaded on his forehead. His stomach was clenching and unclenching and he had the urge to smash his phone.

'Who else can I go to? And you know how my parents feel about all this since Rabia got married, right?'

'And they'll never find out that you made the first move?' he asked,wishing he could control himself and not blurt out something hurtful.

'I. . .I don't know why you're getting so angry,' Saba said, sounding a bit angry herself.

Shahid breathed deeply, trying to get his emotions under control, but it was proving to be very difficult. The man sitting next to him looked at him concerned. Maybe he thought Shahid was having a heart attack.

'Look. I'll meet you and we'll talk about this, okay?' Shahid asked her, wishing he could stop the train right that moment and turn it back so he could return to Bengaluru and throttle Saba's neck or, rather, shake her so hard that she realized how foolish she was being.

'I. . .I don't know why you're getting so upset at this,' she repeated as though she wanted him to bless her and *not* have puppies. Or whatever it was that he was having now.

He bit the inside of his cheek and then spoke. 'I'm coming to your house tomorrow and we'll talk about this. About whether or not I'm going to help you. . .' Just thinking of mediating between Saba and what's-his-name made him want to pull his hair out.

'But whatever, what ever happens, you have to promise me one thing,' he added recklessly.

'What?' she asked, a bit surprised and confused.

'You are NEVER going to call me 'bhai' again,' he enunciated each word clearly.

'Huh? Why? But you ARE my brother, right?' she asked, sounding shocked and surprised.

'*Never*. I was *never* your brother,' he said vehemently and, with that, he ended the call and shut his eyes, wondering how everything could have gone so wrong. The first thing he wanted to do was kick that guy on his backside. Kick him so hard that he'd land right back in London.

He almost wished he hadn't added that bit about not being her brother at the end, but he'd been right. Let her get confused. Let her wonder what he meant.

23

Saba stared at the phone in her hand as though it would talk back to her. She shook her head, her sleep completely gone. WHAT the heck was that all about? She sat up, looking at her mobile and wondered if Shahid would call back to explain what he had meant.

She decided to talk to Riya about Shahid's outburst instead of blogging about it, because at the moment, she needed someone to talk back to her. She didn't want to rant at empty cyberspace.

She fell back on the bed, deciding to call Riya after some time, but the more she buried her head in her pillow, the more she remembered Shahid's intense voice. She couldn't figure out the reason behind his anger or his taunting tone which was so totally unlike him. And he wasn't even letting her attribute the over-protectiveness to brotherly feelings. A new thought began worrying her. What if he told her father about this conversation?

She knew he wouldn't squeal on her and do something so drastic. Punching her pillow back into shape, she closed her eyes and tried to think of Uzair with his dancing eyes and irreverent charm. Thinking of him, she dozed off with a smile on her face. When she woke up a little later, she yawned and then picked up her phone to see if there were any messages.

None. With a sigh she dialled Riya's number, wondering why she had expected Shahid to send a message to her.

'Mmm,' Riya's sleepy voice came on the other end.

'Wake up, sleepyhead. It's 10 a.m.' Saba laughed.

'Mmm,' Riya seemed incapable of saying anything more than that, but Saba couldn't wait. She launched off into an explanation about what had happened and when she was done, she asked Riya, 'Did you listen to anything I said?'

'Mmm,' Riya replied and Saba groaned. But then Riya finally spoke.

'Just go over everything again. A little more slowly this time,' she said and Saba sighed and repeated the whole story to her.

Riya was fully awake now.

'Whoa!' she said finally.

'I know! What's wrong with him? Why's he behaving like some bear bit his backside?' Saba asked, walking over to her window.

'Dude. . .I think your cousin has a thing for you,' Riya spoke. Saba had been looking at a street vendor stop near their gate and she didn't quite catch her words.

'Huh?'

'Yeah. I think that's what this is all about,' Riya spoke excitedly.

'What? What's this all about?' Saba asked puzzled.

'Didn't you just hear me?' Riya asked, making a 'tch' sound.

'I. . .uh. . .' Saba faltered.

'I said. . .' Riya started and then continued, 'Oh, what the fuck! I said I think your cousin is in love with you.'

Saba's phone slipped from her hand and she quickly caught it in the other palm.

'What?' she exploded, placing it back at her ear.

'Don't make me repeat this again,' Riya warned her. 'I said. . .'

'No, no! I got that! I mean. . .that's so absurd!' Saba spoke quickly. She whirled away from the window to sit down on her bed.

'You can't be right,' Saba said a minute later, her heart thundering loudly.

'Look, I'm not an expert, but going by his reaction and especially his last statement, it sounds a lot like he's got stronger feelings for you.'

Saba shook her head in disbelief. Deep inside, she knew that there could be some truth in what Riya was saying. But she didn't want to acknowledge it. She didn't want to accept that the 'moment' they'd shared before Zohaib's engagement in the shop had been more than her imagination.

'I don't know what to do,' she whispered, falling back on the bed.

'Wow! Look at you! Having to choose between two hot guys,' Riya joked and Saba felt a flash of irritation towards her.

'Shut up! This isn't funny,' she muttered, pulling at a tendril of her hair that had fallen across her face.

'I haven't seen Uzair, so you can keep him. But give me your cousin!' Riya sounded almost petulant.

'Riya, this is not a joke. What if you're right? And he said he'll come and talk to me. What if he tells me his feelings then? What will I do?' Saba rushed on, sitting up in her bed again.

'Look, just relax. Let him come and talk to you first. But it's a good thing that you've got the upper hand now since you know what's driving his protective feelings for you.'

'What nonsense. We have no idea if what you just said is true,' Saba protested, although a part of her had started wondering already.

'Yeah, right. Whatever. Just chill and relax. Nothing has happened yet, so wait for him to make the first move,' Riya instructed. Saba grimaced at how pretentious Riya sounded and couldn't stop herself from asking her, 'What makes you the expert on relationships?'

'Uh, the fact that I've already had boyfriends in the past?' Riya asked her sardonically.

'But this is different,' Saba muttered, wishing she'd never told Riya how cloistered her life had been.

They talked for some more time and then after ending the call, Saba sat down in front of a mirror staring at her own reflection.

Would it come to that? A point where she'd have to choose between Uzair and Shahid? She blushed when she thought how weird her thoughts were getting. Firstly, she didn't know whether Shahid actually had any feelings for her. And secondly she didn't know what was going to happen with Uzair. When she'd asked Shahid for his help, it was merely to get to know Uzair and *then* think about something else. With those looks and charm, he probably had a *dozen* girlfriends back in London, she thought sourly.

24

March madness

Posted by The Other T, 15-03-12

After the engagement, Q moved back to her own house and Ammi constantly felt bereft. She started getting worried over small things and she would need to talk to Q to feel better and she would call Q who merely needed an excuse to land back at the house.

The talk now was of jewellery. As the boy's side we had to take jewellery with us for the bride, which we'd make her wear during the nikah. The jewellery usually included a gold chain, sometimes with black beads (our own version of the mangalsutra) and *then* the choice expanded to include what you could afford. Some people chose bangles, others brought necklaces and still others got longer ones that rested near your belly. Some, of course, took all of the above.

Right.

For some reason, my mother had decided to be one of those who took *all* the jewellery I have just described. Abbu sat her down one day with a calculator and the current gold prices, which shocked me into silence.

'We can't afford eight lakhs just on the bride's jewellery,' he explained to her and I hovered nearby wondering what was going to happen. I sidled towards the end of the dining table and lowered myself into a chair to listen to them.

'But. . .but. . .'Ammi looked distraught.

'But what?' Abbu asked almost gently.

'Q told me how much jewellery people wear these days and. . .'

'Yes, yes,' Abbu interrupted her, irritated. 'Q is in a different community now, so it's all right for her to talk,' he glowered.

Ammi made a face at the criticism. 'It's not her fault, you know that,' she defended Q.

Abbu shrugged. 'Look, let's not talk about that. I have many more expenses to cover in this wedding, right from the wedding hall for the Valima to the clothes you're taking for the bride.'

'Shouldn't we do that. . .that thing to Y's room?' Ammi asked, looking a bit lost.

'What?'

'That thing. . .they change how the room looks and they make it like one of those. . .those houses in a magazine?'

Abbu looked at her mystified. 'What are you talking about?' he asked her, scratching his head.

'Abbu, she means renovation,' I suggested, and he glanced at me, realizing I was sitting there.

Ammi's face changed as she grasped the word. 'Yes, that's what I meant,' she pointed out to him.

Abbu pondered over the suggestion, wondering if he really needed to think about this extra expense. They also had to paint the house before the wedding and so much had to be done.

'I'll think about it,' he said, getting up when Ammi stopped him.

'Okay. Suppose I said we didn't have to take the big necklace?' she asked.

'Not good enough. You either choose a smaller necklace or bangles.'

Ammi's face fell.

That was the discussion about the jewellery. And then there was the day they were talking about how many sets of clothes they were going to buy for the bride. Ammi insisted that we take twenty, while Abbu thought ten was good enough.

'Why are you skimping so much on your only son's wedding?' Ammi asked him almost outraged at his suggestion.

'Because, everything costs money. And I have to provide you with that money,' he said simply. I cringed when I thought of how calmly he had handed me ten thousand bucks to buy the dress for the engagement. It had cost only five thousand though, and when I had given it back to Abbu, he actually told me to keep it!

'Look. Everyone will ask how many dresses we took, and ten is not such a nice number,' she tried to reason.

'Well, go for eleven then. Knowing you and your daughter, each will cost a bomb. So it should be enough,' he finished.

'But. . .'

'Look! We have to get clothes for Q also. Even though Q is married, we have to stitch an outfit for her, and if I know your daughter well, she'll choose something that will bankrupt me. Then, there are clothes for T as well. Your *other* daughter,' he reminded her pointedly.

'She doesn't need grand clothes. She's not married,' Ammi replied and Abbu shut his mouth grimly at that. I was in the kitchen making tea when this argument was going on.

'Well, what about clothes for Y? He's the groom,' Abbu asked, and Ammi fell silent.

'We can afford, no? Why you're getting so worked up?' she muttered.

The arguments went back and forth and I'm just wondering that, if this is the beginning, where will it all end? I mean, we hadn't even started the wedding preparations and Ammi and Abbu were fighting over all the details. I could just about envision how crazy it was all going to get when the wedding date got nearer.

∽

Okay. Something weird has definitely happened in my life. I've always had a very boring kind of existence and suddenly it's like the Maker decided to pull up the picture of my life and dribble colourful paint on it everywhere.

So what happened was that I called up my cousin T and asked him to help me in contacting you-know-who. You know who, right? I'm not going to mention his name here again.

And my cousin T nearly bit my head off. And he gave me some other bullshit about how he wasn't my brother, which *really* confused me. Despite my misgivings with her, I called up X and she suggested that T was in love with me! Can you imagine?

So I got all worked up when T texted that he was coming home the following day to talk to me. I mean, what if X was right? How would I deal with it?

T came home after lunch and I wondered where we would talk. My room? It kind of felt strange to go there alone with him, knowing that he probably had feelings for me. He resolved the problem by suggesting we go to the terrace. Almost glad that I didn't have to sit with him in my room alone, I followed him upstairs, only vaguely noticing what nice shoulders he had. (No really! The thought registered in my head all on its own.)

We had a few chairs on the terrace for days when we wanted to sit there and enjoy the evening breeze. I sat down on one of them and watched him pace the terrace.

He finally plonked down on a chair opposite me. I held my breath wondering what he would say and for the life of me, I couldn't bring myself to meet his eyes.

'I got his number for you,' he said, and my head shot up. What?

'I also found out about his personal life. No girlfriends back in London. He's single.'

I didn't know what to say. I mean, I thought that he was going to tell me about his *own* feelings for me now. But, instead, he'd already found out about you-know-who, so soon!

'Wow! You were fast,' I muttered, still unable to meet his eyes. I was thrilled that he'd got the number and found out that you-know-who was single. But. . .there was a part of me that was wondering what had happened to him on the phone the previous day. Would he offer any explanation?

When he didn't say anything, I looked up, meeting his eyes for the first time. They held a bright spark, which I uncomfortably recognized as anger.

'Why are you behaving like this?' I asked, and he glanced away, shrugging.

'It's hard to accept that people grow up so soon,' he said.

I couldn't argue with that. He handed me a slip of paper with a phone number on it and my head felt light. I smiled tremulously as I took the paper from him.

'Thanks, bh. . .' I stopped myself and looked down at the paper. He had told me never to call him 'bhai' again. I felt strangely bereft, because it felt like some strong connection between us had been severed.

He got up from the chair and walked towards the parapet and looked down, his hands in his pocket. Was it safe to assume then that X was an idiot and had got everything wrong? If T had feelings for me, now was the time to have declared them instead of getting me another guy's phone number.

He whipped around and walked back towards me and I felt a frisson run down my back. It wasn't fear, but I didn't know what it was either. My back prickled when he offered his hand and I took it, noting how warm and dry it was as I got up from the chair. But he didn't let go of my hand. He grasped it tightly, and I blinked. Was he going to say something *now*?

I noticed that he'd shaved recently and I took in his face, his familiar loved features that stared back at me from a stranger's eyes. He pressed my hand tightly again and then released it, but his eyes never left mine, as though he was desperately asking me to understand something.

X thinks I should have asked him outright if he was in love with me. Can you imagine? What would I have done if he had laughed at me? I knew I couldn't get the words out anyway, without sounding foolish.

'Just be careful,' he whispered and then walked away. I watched him leave, feeling despair deepen inside me. Everything had changed, especially the easy camaraderie we'd shared. I stared at the piece of paper in my hand, at the numbers written in his bold handwriting, but I couldn't bring myself to smile.

25

'I never thought I'd be one of those girls.'

'Huh?'

'Especially in this day and age,' Saba continued.

'Okay, what are you talking about?' Riya asked, shading her eyes with her palm.

'I'm going to join that queue there,' Saba pointed to the five or six girls who were waiting in line to make a call at the PCO in their college.

Riya sat up and brushed the grass from her skirt. 'Well, I think it's silly. Just text him from your phone.'

Saba didn't answer as she saw the queue inch forward as other girls joined.

'Why are those girls not calling their boyfriends from their mobile phones?' she mused.

'Who knows?' Riya muttered as she stretched and pulled out a ragged looking copy of *The Tempest*. She flipped the pages and got engrossed in some of the lines, tuning out Saba instantly.

'Sending a text to him from my mobile or calling him could be dangerous,' Saba said.

'Tch! You act as though your family was the mafia,' Riya muttered and Saba laughed.

'So, are you going to call him or not?' Riya asked, although her head was still buried in the book.

'What do you think?' Saba turned to Riya, who finally looked up.

'*Would I might but ever see that man,*' Riya quoted dramatically from the text, and Saba started laughing.

'Call him,' Riya said briskly. 'No harm in that.'

'Wish me luck,' Saba said and got up.

'Come back soon! Lunch hour gets over in ten minutes,' Riya reminded her. Saba stopped.

'What will I tell him? Like how I got his number and all that?'

Riya shrugged. 'Make up some story. Tell him. . .tell him your mother asked you to call him, because he didn't apologize enough.' She laughed at that while Saba rolled her eyes. She was still finding it funny that the women in Saba's family had been offended by this guy walking in on them.

Saba walked away towards the PCO, but came back a few minutes later. Riya shut her book, looking at her interested.

'What happened?'

'I spoke to him,' Saba replied, her face flushed.

'And?'

'I was too confused to say anything properly. So I told him the truth.'

'What?' Riya's eyes were round. 'What truth?'

'I told him that we had met at my brother's engagement and later at my house.'

'Oh. . .okay,' Riya looked relieved.

'Then he wanted to know how I got his number,' Saba went on, looking down.

'What did you say?' Riya asked sharply.

'I told him I got it somehow.'

'Then? What else did you guys talk about? Did he ask you why you called?'

Saba nodded, not saying anything.

'What did you say?' Riya asked.

'I asked him if he'd like to meet me for coffee,' Saba muttered, looking at her feet. She glanced at Riya who looked shocked, her mouth open.

'You. Asked. A. Guy. Out?' she asked her, each word sounding like a bullet. Saba felt her face grow hot as she blushed.

'Not like that. I just asked him casually. Like, let's meet up for coffee sometime,' Saba defended herself and Riya shook her head.

'Whoa! Sweet girls like you never do these things,' Riya commented, and Saba looked at her irritated.

'What is it about me that makes you want to patronize me all the time?' she snapped at Riya.

'Ooh! Take it easy!' Riya said, putting her book in front of her chest, as though to protect herself.

'See, you're doing it again. I mean, why can't I ask some guy out?' Saba asked, glowering at her.

Riya shook her head, but Saba could see that she was getting annoyed too. 'Okay. Have you ever had a boyfriend? Has any boy ever held your hand? Have you ever been kissed? Did you make out with a boy in a. . .' Saba raised her hand to stop the tirade.

'Okay, okay, I've done none of these things,' she admitted, although in her mind she kept thinking of Shahid holding her hand the last time she'd seen him. It wasn't the same thing, right?

'See. That's what I meant. You've had a protected upbringing. So for you to ask a guy out. . .just doesn't sit well.'

'I'm sorry if I no longer appear to be a paragon of virtue in your eyes,' Saba said sarcastically, rearranging the books in her bag.

'Okay, don't get pissed off now,' Riya responded. 'What did he say? Is he meeting you?'

Saba was silent for a moment and then hitching the strap of her bag on her shoulder, she nodded.

'I'm meeting him at Barista,' Saba said.

'When? Today? The one here in Koramangala?' Riya almost screeched and Saba grimaced.

'Not today. He's busy. But he said we could meet up tomorrow.'

'Okay. Then I have to come and see this Adonis guy who's got you breaking all your own rules,' Riya said as the bell rang.

'Obviously, you have to come. But what rules?'

'You know, the ones you've made for yourself. *I shall not meet a boy outside college*, etc., etc.,' Riya smirked.

Saba slapped her arm and they both walked into class, Riya rubbing her arm and making exaggerated noises. They had a test on *The Tempest* the following hour and for the first time ever, Riya scored higher than Saba.

26

What went wrong?

Posted by The Other T, 18-03-12

If you're thinking that this blog is losing its focus as I'm hardly using it to bitch about my brother's wedding, you're quite right. But things have suddenly slowed down over the last few days on that front and my own personal life has picked up pace like crazy.

So I called you-know-who and we decided to meet for coffee! Yes! Can you imagine? I don't know how I got the nerve to ask him but I didn't have an option because you never know what these NRI types might do. What if he decided he didn't want to stick around till the wedding?

When I returned home I toyed with the idea of calling T and telling him what had happened. I sent him a text instead, thanking him for getting me the number. I knew he wouldn't reply but still I waited. When he didn't reply after an hour, I knew he wouldn't. Thinking about him made me feel despondent so I put him away from my mind firmly and decided to focus on the meeting with you-know-who.

So, the next day after college, X and I rushed to the restroom to freshen up for this non-date. I refused to call it a date while X just rolled her eyes and observed me as I scrubbed my face with a face wash and applied a thin line of kajal. 'Lip gloss,' she reminded and suggested that I leave my hair open.

I removed the scrunchie that held my hair in place and brushed it out but I tied it back at my nape and she frowned.

'It's your best asset!' she insisted but I shook my head. Leaving my hair open wasn't a good idea. It was too long and attracted way too much attention.

X was going to come with me and once she met him, she'd make an excuse and leave. I was all jumpy and nervous as we walked to the Barista near college. I was comforted by her presence but also worried that she would flirt with him like she had with T. Still, her opinion mattered to me and we both walked inside the dimly lit coffee shop.

Inside, I could make out a few occupied tables but he wasn't there yet. So we sat down and waited for him to come and ordered cappuccinos. At home, I'd told Ammi that I had special classes and would be late. She was preoccupied as usual and probably didn't even hear me and I quelled the tiny little voice in my head that was troubling me for having lied to her.

Two cappuccinos and a trifle pudding later, he still hadn't turned up.

'Does he have your number?' X asked, putting her head down on the table wearily.

'No.'

She lifted her head and shook it slowly.

'Come on! The guy has no way to get in touch with you. Text him now. Ask him where he is! And if you're scared to use your own number, use mine,' she said, offering her mobile.

I shook my head and decided to text him from my own phone. He replied almost immediately.

'Sorry! Running late!'

'Later than this?' X fumed and she got up.

'Where are you going?' I asked her nervously. She dropped a hundred rupee note on the table.

'I'm going. That's my share of the bill. I can't wait anymore,' she huffed.

'Wait! Don't go yet!' I panicked.

'I'm sleepy and tired and. . .'

'But you just had coffee. . .' I averred.

She sighed loudly and sank back. 'Okay. But I'm here only for fifteen minutes.'

Come soon! I muttered a litany in my head. I wasn't sure I wanted to meet him alone without X acting as a buffer.

I was shredding a napkin to bits looking at the entrance all the while when suddenly, X said, 'I haven't met this guy, but given a choice, I'd go for your cousin any day.'

I looked up impatiently. 'But there *is* no choice,' I said, trying to push away thoughts of T that had been intruding in my head all along. Maybe it was this place, because we had met here the last time with X. But from the moment I had walked inside, I kept thinking of his calm manner and his low voice, his amused face and his smile as his eyes connected with mine over something funny X had said, and I realized that that day had assumed more importance for me than I'd ever thought it would.

'Why not? I'm quite sure he has a thing for you,' X argued.

'Are we back to that again?' I asked her, feeling irritated.

'Yes. And if I recall correctly, the last time we were here, although he kept talking to me, his gaze kept wandering to you. He kept looking at *you*,' X said, crossing her arms.

I looked up at her disbelievingly. That was. . .that was. . .true? So it hadn't been my imagination?

'That's impossible,' I said, 'the two of you were flirting like crazy.'

'And she says I patronize her,' X replied in an aside that didn't seem funny to me at all.

'You mean. . .'

'Yes, I meant. . .' X stopped talking. 'WOW. Is that him?' she exhaled.

I turned to the doorway and there he was. I nodded, feeling the blood come rushing to my face.

'He's. . .' X had run out of adjectives apparently.

'Hi girls!' You-Know-Who smiled and pulled up a chair before us. 'Sorry to have kept you waiting but I got stuck in traffic.'

(*Right now, as I'm writing this, I'm trying hard to recall the details of that conversation, but I'm coming up with nothing. I just can't remember what we talked about. Sorry!*)

I only remember that I smiled a lot and X alternated between worshipful glances at him to giggling like a little girl.

She left after some time and texted me the moment she reached outside.

'W*O*W' was all it said.

I shook my head and then realized I was expected to make conversation with him but I couldn't. He was leaning back in his chair and smiling at me.

'I can't believe I'm sitting here with you,' he said finally and my heart raced.

'Why?' I asked.

'On the engagement day, that whole fiasco happened, right? Me walking into what is actually *my* room? Bloody hell! Everyone yelled at me that day man! All those daft people refused to believe me, that I'd gone in to get a new shirt!'

'Oh!'

'Yeah! I had to deaf them out for a whole lot of time.'

'Deaf them out?' I asked.

'Tune out?' he amended. 'Yeah, so I managed to do that by thinking of the two pretty girls I'd seen that day.' He leaned forward. 'Do you know who that other girl is? The one in the green sari?'

I looked down, literally hearing all sorts of crashing sounds in my head. He was asking about Q.

'Yes.' But before he could get all eager, I spoke quickly. 'She's my sister and she's been married for two years.'

'Oh!' He looked disappointed. His question changed the tenor of our meeting. I'd seen that look in many other eyes before. If he was smitten by Q, then this guy was clearly out of my league.

I collected my bag and got up, and he looked surprised. 'Where are you going?' he asked.

'Home. It's quite late as it is,' I replied tightly.

'But I just got here. Do you have any idea how far I've travelled in this bloody city's bloody traffic?' he asked, his voice rising a bit.

Okay. So you don't like Bengaluru's traffic. No one asked you to come here. Then get the hell out, na?

I didn't speak those words, of course. When I'd called him up, I hadn't known what to expect when we actually met. I suppose I'd forgotten how Q affected my life, even when she wasn't around. This was a mistake, asking him to meet me. I just realized the enormity of what I'd done. What if he told someone in his family that he'd met Y's sister for coffee? That would not just jeopardize Y's wedding (and weddings have been called off for lesser 'crimes'), but seriously lower my own chances in the marriage market. Especially when word got around that *I* had been the one to initiate the meeting. Was this what T had meant that day? Then why had he given the number to me? Why couldn't he have been more insistent and refused? It was all *his* fault.

'What happened?' he asked, looking at the play of emotions on my face.

God, I had to get away from there. I tried to move out and he quickly reached forward and held my hand.

'Wait,' he said.

'No, no! I have to go,' I said, trying to pull my hands out of his, but his grip only tightened further.

'Stop making a scene,' he spoke in a low voice and I stopped struggling. 'You were fine one minute and the next you're going crazy. What happened?'

I sat down on the chair, wondering how I could get out of this mess.

'You know, I'm not going to eat you,' he remarked casually as he called the waiter for the bill. 'What happened to you suddenly?'

I shook my head. Could I pretend that I had a headache or I was getting fever? Could I just forget all this ever happened?

'You know what? I don't even know your name yet,' he said and I looked up, hope surging through me. It was true. He hadn't asked for my name on the phone and I'd just told him that we had met on the day of the engagement. Apparently he'd remembered me because Q and I were the only ladies who hadn't covered their faces in front of him. And when I texted him sometime back, I had forgotten to add my name at the end.

Why do they make this look so easy in the movies? I mean, all this falling in love bullshit? Two people meet and they fall in love in a snap! And here. . .the moment he asked about Q, it was like someone had lifted a heavy curtain from my head. Or, thrown a bucket of cold water over me.

'You were *speaking* just now!' he said, leaning forward. 'What happened to your voice dammit?'

It was almost comical, the situation I was stuck in. Bizarre. Like something out of a seriously whacked up movie.

'Nothing,' I muttered. 'I'm sorry for asking you to meet me here,' I said.

'That's okay,' he dismissed it magnanimously with a wave of his hands. 'But. . .'

'I just realized I have a test tomorrow and I need to study. That's why X left so soon,' I said, getting up again. He didn't stop me.

I was just going to have to hope he wouldn't mention this meeting to anyone.

'So we're cool then?' he asked and I whipped my head back to look at him.

I didn't know what he meant by that so I merely nodded.

'Then I'll call you sometime?' he asked and I froze.

'Everything has changed in this bloody city,' he went on. 'I haven't been here in five years and I come back and nothing is the same!'

I stood there with my lips pursed as he went on and on and on about how much Bengaluru had changed and all for the worse. Was he expecting me to feel sorry for him? I hated people, especially outsiders who whined about the traffic here. Okay, so it was bad. What did they expect us to do? Lay out a carpet of roses just because their highnesses have descended?

'I'm desperate for some decent company! All I have are these aunts and uncles and these cousins who I can't get along with, you know?'

'What about your friends?' I asked.

'They all seem to be busy. I'm thinking of going back to UK and coming for the wedding. Imagine sitting here for another three months!' he shuddered.

'That's a great idea!' I said, wondering if it was the same me who was going all melancholic thinking of him going back to London.

'But my uncle isn't letting me go,' he made a sad face which was appealing in a very boyish way. But I was able to view him objectively, especially as he went on, 'Apparently, I'm the bride's *brother* and I need to stick around and help,' he mimicked.

The bride had another younger sister, but no brothers. I knew how much my mother too counted on T to help during

Y's wedding. What was it about brothers that we sisters lacked? Organizational skills? Manpower?

'Anyway, so I'm stuck here till the wedding. Let's meet again sometime? I'd do anything to get away from the house, you know?'

I didn't know what to say. I nodded and left wondering at the way my dreams had collapsed and yet, I wasn't as devastated as I thought I'd be.

27

When Rabia was five, her grandmother used to tell her stories about fairies and jinns and spin hundreds of fantasies around them. Rabia loved listening to stories about golden haired princesses and their handsome princes who would defeat the jinn and how they all lived happily ever after.

Later on, she was shocked to discover that her family believed in the existence of jinns. 'But they're just fairytales!' she protested to her mother who shook her head in an all-knowing way.

'Of course not. They really exist. They haunt old houses and some people can even see them! In fact, some jinns can even impersonate human beings!' her mother had whispered in a conspiratorial way.

Rabia, who was then twelve, scoffed at her mother. 'What nonsense,' she said, but a part of her was thrilled. If jinns existed, then why not the handsome princes? But they would come only if there was a princess in the reckoning. So naturally Rabia went all out to become as princess-like as she could. As she grew older, she forgot about the stories, but the princess demeanour was something that didn't leave her.

When she'd gone to her friend Sheetal's wedding three years ago, she had no idea her life would change, just as it happened in books and movies. At twenty-three, she was the most stunning girl in their family. She'd left home looking respectable enough (hair tied up and dupatta covering her shoulders), but once Zohaib had dropped her at the five star hotel where the wedding was being held, she'd gone inside the ladies room and emerged with her waist long hair left open. She'd had her hair straightened so it hung down her back like a thick, straight curtain and she loved the way it swished when she walked. She wore a dusty rose crepe silk tunic that ended just above her knees, paired with a flared shalwar of the same colour. The dress was one of her more subtle ones, lightly embroidered and very chic, as compared to the full on bling that she usually wore at weddings among her own community.

Her make-up had also gone up significantly and she carelessly slung her dupatta around her neck. The overall effect was of a girl-woman, and with her smooth complexion, fabulous cheekbones and sultry lips, there was no way those girls in the backless ghagra cholis were going to deflect any attention from her, she thought. There was no one from her family to see and berate her, so she smiled and danced during the sangeet, wondering why the weddings in her family were so dull and dreary.

Much later, after the ceremonies had got over, she sat down on a chair, pleasantly tired, sipping on a minty mocktail. She'd received compliments from so many people that it was like a buzz. Someone came and sat down next to her and she stiffened when she realized it was the same man who had been staring at her from the time she'd come out of the ladies room.

He was very good looking, but she'd avoided him because his stare was too intense and disturbing.

'Rabia, right?' he asked, crossing one leg over the other and settling deeply into the chair. Rabia felt perturbed by his presence but she nodded looking down at the remnants of her drink.

'When we're married, I want you to leave your hair open only in the night, so only *I* can see how beautiful it is,' he remarked leaning forward.

At his words, Rabia felt a thud in her chest, a kind of heat that blossomed outwards, almost painful in its intensity.

'Are you insane?' she asked him, shocked at his intimate tone and his words. What really threw her off balance was the way her body was reacting to him. She looked around at the people in the wedding and no one seemed to have noticed that anything was amiss.

'Absolutely. I want to marry you, Rabia,' he spoke in a low voice and he covered her slim, fair hands with his. Rabia looked up at him and her throat felt dry. She couldn't speak so she merely shook her head.

'You can't say no. You know you're mine already,' he whispered and Rabia closed her eyes, not willing to believe how much his voice was turning her on. It seemed as though her body had become a liquid embodiment of desire. He got up and yanked her hand gently and she followed him, unable to think clearly. The sangeet had got over and people were eating, so no one noticed the two of them disappear towards the garden.

They walked for some time quietly until he stopped, turned her around and pulled her close. She gasped as he bent his head to kiss her, lightly at first, but when she put her arms around his neck, he pulled her flush against his body and deepened the kiss. She didn't know what was happening, except that she couldn't stop herself. When they broke apart, they were both breathing heavily.

'My name is Rafiq,' he said, and Rabia covered her lips with her trembling hands, unable to believe she had acted this way, without even knowing the *name* of the man. She turned around to leave but he stopped her with a hand on her arm.

'I meant it when I said that I want to marry you,' he said.

'But you don't even know me!' she protested and his grip tightened in response.

'I know enough,' he said gruffly and turned her around to drop another light kiss on her lips before letting go.

Getting married to Rafiq had been an uphill task. She had become the talk of the family in the worst way possible. Everyone seemed to have different versions of how Rafiq had seen her at a wedding and fallen madly in love with her. What's more, she didn't like all the drama that was being enacted at her home because of her. But she just sat back and watched Rafiq win her parents over, no matter how reluctant they were.

During the time when everything at home seemed to be going haywire because of Rafiq, Rabia would often shut her eyes and think of how he was like those handsome princes she'd heard about in her grandmother's stories. She remembered the feel of his lips on hers and the touch of his hands on her waist and she knew that all her life had been hurtling towards this moment when she would get married to him. She wasn't *in love* with him, but that didn't matter. He was crazy about her, and that was enough. And what's more, she was having a fairy tale wedding even if it greyed her mother's hair prematurely, and even if her father lost whatever little he had left on his head.

Rabia stared at the strip of plastic in her hands, unwilling to believe her eyes. She turned it around a couple of times and got up from the toilet seat slowly.

She was pregnant.

The two pink lines had undoubtedly been the cause of cheer for many women, but also the reason for despair amongst numerous others. Rabia, however, felt numb. She couldn't possibly be pregnant. She was on the pill. How could she have got pregnant despite that?

She surveyed her face in the mirror and it looked the samc to her. She pulled her nightgown against the top half of her body so her figure stood out. No bulge. Nothing. But it was ten days since she'd got her period and she had taken the test idly, as she always did whenever her period was even a little late. She had assumed that maybe the stress of Zohaib's engagement had delayed her period. But. . .

She wasn't expecting this! She couldn't talk about it to Rafiq yet. She leaned against the cool tiles of the bathroom, her brain working rapidly. Okay. Okay. Okay. This was all right. Lots of women got pregnant, she tried to convince herself, but panic had edged inside slowly. She'd seen women bloat up and then waddle like ducks. She'd seen stretch marks and then. . .the babies! God!

She sat down on the toilet seat again, clutching her head. She was not ready to become a mother yet. She didn't want to go through all that pain and she wasn't ready to house a human being in her body for nine months. Nine freaky months, she thought, anger surging against Rafiq.

Rafiq was the root of all her problems. How was it that when he wanted something, it happened almost instantly? She'd never understood the power he had over her, and the way things fell in place around him almost magically. He'd wanted to marry her, and it had happened. He'd wanted a deal to be completed last month in Singapore, and it had happened. She could name all the things that went his way but. . . How was it possible?

She got up again and paced the white tiled bathroom nervously. A knock sounded on the door and Rabia jumped.

'Do you want me to come in and get you?' Rafiq called out laughing, and Rabia shot a look at the door, quelling an urge to throw up.

She opened it to see him standing outside, his face gleaming as he pulled her to him. She went to him reluctantly, wondering whether she should tell him yet. Maybe there was a way to make this work for her.

'You're pregnant, right?' he asked, nuzzling her neck and she froze.

'What?'

'I saw you take the pregnancy kit with you inside,' he said, pressing his open lips against the side of her neck, his hands drawing firm and insistent circles on her back.

'I. . .'

'I knew it!' he said triumphantly, hugging her hard. 'You've made me so happy today.'

As his face came closer to hers to kiss her, Rabia backed away in fright. But behind her there was the bathroom door and she had nowhere else to go.

'I love you so much, baby,' he said, but Rabia couldn't move or speak. She'd just had a thought that terrified her completely. His face loomed above hers again and Rabia fainted.

28

'He's an asshole.'

'He is *so* not.'

'You know what? Just forget it.'

'Yeah right!'

'Why are we even fighting?' Saba threw her book at Riya who dodged just in time.

'You are the most indecisive and fickle-minded girl I have ever seen,' she remarked as she caressed the book that Saba had thrown at her and shut it.

'Of course not,' Saba replied, but she looked up anyway. Riya had invited herself home that day after college and Saba was glad none of the bawdy aunts were around to judge Riya based on her clothing, particularly as Riya was wearing a pair of frayed jeans and a ragged looking T-shirt. You never knew which aunt might ask Riya how she could afford college when her parents were so obviously poor.

'No, you really are,' Riya insisted, getting up from Saba's bed. 'You had a *serious* crush on this guy and now there's nothing?'

'I spoke to him and there's no connection. What can I do? He *annoys* me!' Saba said, flinging her hands in the air.

Riya rubbed her forehead and shook her head. 'At least give him another chance? How can you decide so soon that you don't like him?'

Saba was silent for a moment, wondering how she could explain the whole situation to Riya, particularly since she herself hadn't understood it. Her irritation at his obvious interest in Rabia had combined with the fear of discovery, making her want to run from there and never meet him again.

'It was just too. . .'

'Dangerous?' Riya ended for her wryly.

'You don't know the half of it. After all the hungama with my sister, my parents want a simple arranged marriage for both me and my brother,' Saba started.

'Who even talked of marriage?' Riya asked, raising an eyebrow.

'But. . .'

'Oh come on! You see a guy and you happen to like him. . .and what? You have to get married to him? Please! Grow up!' Riya laughed.

Saba looked uncomfortable. Her upbringing had not involved boyfriends. There were only potential suitors.

'Jeez! You were thinking of *marrying* this guy?' Riya asked, her eyes all round in her face and she burst out laughing again.

'Of course not!' Saba protested, although a vivid blush on her face had given her away. Riya held her stomach and laughed uncontrollably.

'Why are you laughing so much?' she asked, irritated.

'So are you going to marry your cousin then?' Riya retorted, breaking into giggles again.

'Shut up!' Saba muttered looking away.

'Why? What's wrong with *him* now?' Riya asked.

'Nothing. I'm not interested,' Saba said as she tidied her desk.

'Why? What happened?' Riya persisted. 'It's not like you're planning to do anything with your life anyway. Might as well marry your handsome cousin and have his kids.'

Saba gasped. 'What a mean thing to say, Riya!'

'But it's true, right? You don't want to do anything. You said so yourself.'

'That doesn't have anything to do with this,' Saba replied, her voice taut with anger.

'It has everything to do with this. You're going to finish college, get married and have babies. That's it,' Riya mocked.

Saba shut her eyes. Put like that, it sounded pretty lame.

'I'll do something,' she said, but her mind was racing.

'Yeah, right. The moment you finish college your parents will get you married. Right?' Riya asked, picking at some fluff from the bedspread.

Saba sat down at her desk heavily. 'What's wrong in getting married and having kids?' Riya looked at her and shook her head.

'Stop being so judgmental,' Saba continued. 'I like things the way they are and I'll be perfectly fine if I have to get married after college gets over.'

'But don't you have the desire to do something?' Riya asked, her brows furrowing in confusion.

'It's probably lying dormant somewhere. We still have time to figure out what we want to do, right?' Saba replied, wishing they'd talk of something else.

Riya seemed to have got the message almost telepathically, but she went back to the earlier topic.

'So, have you met your cousin lately?'

Saba shook her head. Shahid had completely disappeared. He never dropped by these days, didn't reply to her texts and never answered her calls. She'd once called from the fixed line at home, but he hadn't answered that either. She was almost tempted to call him from another mobile number, to see if he would answer that. But she was scared, because if he did answer, it would confirm that he was truly avoiding her.

Riya saw the play of emotions on Saba's face and offered her phone. 'Try calling from my phone.'

Saba shook her head. She'd been thinking of going to Shahid's house and confronting him. She didn't want to talk to him on the phone.

'Maybe he's pissed off with you,' Riya suggested and Saba made a face at her.

'That's very helpful of you. Of course he's pissed off with me,' she said.

They both fell silent, each apparently thinking of Shahid. Riya, for some reason, couldn't seem to let go of the topic and Saba didn't want to talk of him anymore, because it hurt.

'Give me his number. I'll call him,' Riya said and Saba shook her head, horrified.

'Let's forget this. I'll go to his house and talk to him over there,' she said. She really needed Riya to stop going on about Shahid.

'Hey, do you want to see the clothes we got for the bride?' she asked suddenly.

'Of course,' Riya replied. They both got up and went to Ammi's room where she had kept all the things they had bought for the bride in a separate cupboard. Riya was amazed at how heavy and ornate everything seemed.

'Did *you* go shopping with your mother for these?' she asked as Saba shook out a moss green silk outfit that was covered in bedazzling sequins.

'No. Q did,' Saba replied and bit her tongue.

'Q?' Riya asked, looking up although her hands were gliding over the silk slowly.

Saba didn't know when the transition from the blog to real life had taken place, but Riya would not leave her until she extracted all the information from her. Maybe she could show her the shoes they had got for the bride?

29

Bad things happen in threes?

Posted by The Other T, 28-03-12

Bad things really happen in threes.

Abbu had gone to meet B's father to discuss a few details regarding the wedding hall a couple of days ago.

I was quite scared when Abbu went there. What if that idiot (you-know-who) blabbed about meeting me? He didn't know my name but he did know that I was the bridegroom's sister. Wait a second. He didn't know that too. I felt relieved when I realized that, although I was still nervous until Abbu came back.

My mouth dried up when I saw that Abbu looked livid when he returned. I knew something had gone wrong. Abbu sat down on the sofa, breathing heavily. I made tea for him and Ammi sat down next to him and they spoke for a little while. I took the tea to him and he barely glanced at me as he took the cup from the tray.

I could just make out snippets of the conversation.

'. . .Not all boys turn out like that,' Ammi was pacifying him.

'. . .Absolutely no sense of what to say and when to say. . .' Abbu muttered.

'. . .Maybe he's just a bit simple in the head?' Ammi suggested.

'. . .Nonsense. . .'

Okay, what the heck were they talking about? I found out only later that you-know-who had apparently made another faux pas. I couldn't find out much about what exactly he'd done without looking too interested in him, but I just heard Ammi telling T's mother on the phone about how glad they were that they hadn't sent Y abroad.

'These kids just forget their culture and don't have any sense of how to talk to elders and blah blah blah,' she went on. I tuned out because I was wondering if T was around and if I could make Ammi get him on the phone without arousing her suspicion. But Ammi was emotionally involved in the conversation already.

'Can you imagine? He *kept* asking about Q!' Ammi exclaimed and I blanched. Hadn't he understood when I said that Q was *married*?

'I know! Y's father was very angry at his impertinence. Apparently this boy was asking him if Q was happy with her husband! Just look at his guts!'

Uh, no thanks, I thought, I didn't want to look at his face, or his guts for that matter, as I escaped to my room. What had I been thinking, setting up a meeting with *this* guy? Just the thought of having asked T for his help made me feel so foolish, I wanted to dig a big hole in the ground and bury myself there forever.

I had texted T to tell him what a disaster my meeting with you-know-who had been but I was really irritated when he didn't respond to even that message. Shouldn't he be worried about me?

Nevertheless, you-know-who came across as a complete fool and he'd made Abbu very mad. Technically, this wasn't one of the trio of bad things, but it was an eye opener. Abbu was still furious that he was showing so much interest in his married daughter. Of course, I couldn't imagine what Abbu's reaction would be if he found out that his other daughter had met him for coffee.<shudder>

(From this moment onwards, I'm renaming you-know-who as the Idiot. When the Maker was bestowing intelligence, the Idiot probably skipped his turn thinking that he had the looks, and that ought to be enough.)

The second bad thing to happen was Q. See, Q is a bad thing to happen to anyone, especially a younger sister, on a normal day. But now, Q had moved into our house permanently. I couldn't figure out what she wanted. Her husband adored her and was crazy about her. So much so that *I* blushed at the way he'd look at her, even after two years of marriage.

But Q? She obviously didn't care for him in the same way. She enjoyed the attention, but love wasn't a part of it. When I was walking past her room the other day, I heard her crying and was tempted to go inside to see what would reduce *her* to tears, but I stopped when I heard Ammi's voice.

'I've booked an appointment with the gynaecologist tomorrow,' Ammi said.

'Okay. Whatever. I know I'm already pregnant. So why bother,' Q replied in a dull voice.

Q was pregnant?!

I was so thrilled that I forgot one of Q's fundamental rules that she'd laid down for me. I was never to enter her room unless she invited me. I barged inside her room to see her sitting up on the bed and Ammi sitting next to her. Both of them looked at me, surprised.

'You're pregnant?' I gasped. I was shocked when she burst out crying and Ammi looked at me irritated.

I slunk out after that, my euphoria at becoming an aunt fizzing out. Why was she so upset? Didn't she want kids? Okay, that was a stupid question. Of course she didn't want kids.

Normally, having Q in the house was pretty painful. But a pregnant Q was worse. She expected us to wait on her, bring her juice, bring her milk, bring her biscuits, bring her magazines, bring her chocolates, bring her chikki, bring her chana bhatura, bring her chips, bring her just about everything she wanted. Even stuff that she wouldn't touch on a non-pregnant day. I couldn't understand why she was stuffing herself so much when all she did was throw up a little later. And whenever her husband came, she refused to be alone with him. She expected me or Ammi to be in the room whenever he was there, and it was quite embarrassing.

Her husband always sat by her side, holding her hand (like she was an invalid!) and he spoke to her softly. Most of the times, Q looked at the ceiling when he was talking, or out of the window. . .anything to avoid looking at his face. I don't know why, but my heart went out to him each time I saw him look at her, his eyes blazing with pain at her rejection. I once caught his glance when she was looking outside as he spoke and I *cannot* describe how bad I felt for him.

And finally, the third bad thing to happen.

Y wanted to call off the wedding.

30

Zohaib rotated the pads of his thumbs around his eyes slowly, hoping that the massaging action would dissolve the tension that seemed to have seeped there and settled for good. He leaned back in his chair, looked up at the ceiling and then snapped back instantly into work mode. Worrying never really made a difference to the problem, but the uneasiness was weighing like lead in his stomach.

He'd dropped the bomb on his parents a couple of days ago. He hated putting his parents through so much anguish, but there was little that he could do. Everything was a mess in his life and there didn't seem to be any way of resolving all his problems without hurting someone in the process.

His eyes lingered over the email that had changed his life in the past few days and made every nightmare come true.

He'd been busy as usual, working hard at a project when the email had dropped into his inbox. At first he hadn't paid any attention. Then he went to get a cup of coffee and checked his mail. And there it was.

The coffee in his hands grew cold as he clicked on the email and read it. A part of him had wanted to drag the email directly to the trash folder but he didn't want to take any chances and he had read it again and again until it seemed as though his head would explode.

Actually, he had been expecting something like this to happen over the past few months. Even then, expecting it didn't make it easier to regulate his breathing and stem the churning in his stomach. Sometime in November last year, the first email had come. It was from Meenakshi, his ex-girlfriend who had moved to Mumbai earlier last year. She claimed she was still in love with him and moving to Mumbai had been the worst thing she'd had to undergo.

Love. He shuddered when he thought of her. She was the clingiest, whiniest and most annoying girl he'd ever known. Why he had been with her in the first place was beyond his own understanding now. Even so, they'd been together for just a few months, but when he'd broken up with her, she refused to accept it.

That was it. She refused to believe it was over. She just smiled and said that she knew he'd come back to her. By the time she got transferred to Mumbai, his working life had become hell. She was there wherever he turned and she'd taken to sabotaging his projects and his reputation. When she left, he had breathed easily for a little while, enjoying the attention from the ladies again, but he was too daunted to burn his hands again and therefore stayed away. Maya had been tempting him from the time she had joined but he'd decided not to fall for that again. He'd firmly stayed away from her and all the other girls who pouted their glossy lips whenever he passed by.

In November, he got a slight shock when he heard from Meenakshi. She was trying her best to get transferred to Bengaluru again and apparently she was sure that nothing would keep them apart once she got back.

Either she was actually stupid and couldn't understand that he'd broken up with her, or she was deliberately trying to make him nervous. That was when he thought that it would be a good idea to get married before Meenakshi decided to come back. Maybe the fact that he was *married* would actually get through her thick skull?

Of course, things hadn't happened so smoothly on that front. His sister and mother had taken very long to find a girl for him. Then he saw the picture of his bride and he'd felt a little alarmed at how pretty and sophisticated she looked. But she seemed like the only silver lining in the mess that was soon becoming his life. Maybe he could get out of this whole thing with something good to show for it. He'd taken to seeing her photo every morning before leaving for work, just to accustom himself to the idea and now it had become a habit. That was, until Wednesday.

The email that had him paralysed on his chair was once again from Meenakshi. Yes, she was coming back from Mumbai, but the best part of the news? She was going to be his project manager! Meenakshi was going to come back the following month and he was getting married in two months.

That was when he decided that he couldn't take any more of this. He couldn't face getting married when Meenakshi was around and there was no saying what she would do to sabotage that as well. In retrospect, he realized that rushing into marriage was not going to help anyone. It wasn't fair to the girl either that he would be bringing the baggage of his past to their marriage.

So he'd confronted his parents and told them that he didn't want to get married. Abbu was furious and Ammi was shocked. Both of them tried reasoning with him but he'd made his decision. Maybe he'd marry later, years later, but first he had to deal with Meenakshi without using his bride's pallu as a shield. But he couldn't explain all that to them, so he'd simply said that he didn't want to get married.

At home, the situation was fraught with anxiety. Rabia was living with them and it seemed like she didn't want to go back to her husband. His parents were already very worried about her, especially as she was pregnant. But now there was cold war at home. Zohaib's parents weren't talking to him at all.

This morning, his mother had come to his room and told him in a stilted voice that they wanted him to think about it again. There was no way they could live down this scandal and he had to think of others as well. Such as Saba. Who would marry *her*? He hadn't replied to that.

He'd thought about the alternatives. Could he quit his job? Bloody unlikely. Not in this economy. Should he tell everything to the bride's parents? Speak to her father and tell her he didn't want to marry? That would be a bigger scandal, he supposed. There had to be a solution to this. Maybe it was time he spoke to someone and came clean about the whole mess. He mentally ticked off names in his mind, friends whom he hadn't met in a long time and friends who wouldn't understand his predicament. And then he stopped at Shahid.

31

Dew drops had crystallized on the blades of grass and they crunched beneath his feet as Shahid jogged diagonally across the park, planning to head back home. He had left his iPod behind because, for a change, he wanted to listen to his thoughts and try to make some sense of them.

It was more than a month since he'd seen Saba and he'd resolutely avoided her calls and deleted her messages before reading them. He had no plan in sight. He could see his love for her being overshadowed by that glamorous London guy and he was frustrated that he couldn't do anything about it. He wished he was the manipulative type who would have warned off that London guy or pretended to Saba that he had been unable to get his number. He wished he'd told her about how he felt. He wished he hadn't behaved like a coward and stayed away from her.

As he jogged towards the exit turnstile, he wiped his brow and stopped, his heart beating loudly in his ears, his blood rushing to his fingertips, his chest heaving because of the sudden inactivity. Saba was sitting on one of the park benches looking at him. Had he conjured her out of his thoughts or was she really here, in Koramangala 6th Block at 7.15 a.m.?

She smiled uncertainly and it seemed like the block of ice he'd become was just melting around the edges and that too at a very fast rate. What was she doing here? Was she in some sort of trouble? Yeah, obviously. Why else would she come to him, he thought bitterly. Had Uzair done something?

Pulse rate quickening, Shahid walked up to her, still breathing heavily. He towered above her but she continued sitting on the bench, staring back at him.

'Sit,' she said, patting the bench beside her and he sank into it without much thought. He edged away from her because he couldn't think clearly sitting so close to her.

'Are you in some trouble?' he asked her without any preliminaries. He turned his head to look at her, wishing he'd brought his towel along so he could wipe the sweat that was running down in a column at the back of his neck.

'Trouble?' she repeated after him. 'Why would I be in trouble?'

He shrugged, all the while mentally adding up the reasons why she could be here. Was it to *thank* him again for getting her together with that guy?

'What have I done to make you so angry?' she asked softly. Shahid continued looking at her but didn't say anything.

'You don't come home these days. You don't answer my calls or my texts. You don't want to be a part of my life any more, is it?' she asked, looking down at her lap.

In the early morning light, Shahid observed how the fine hair on the back of her neck glistened. He noted how her hair was coming out of her braid on one side and a patch of skin on her back gleamed richly above the maroon kurta she was wearing. He didn't want to talk to her. He wanted to absorb the very essence of her and not move from there. Like ever.

'Say something!' she urged, looking up at him, but he only stared back into her eyes. He noticed that the kajal rimming her eyes made them look more luminous. And she was wearing a peach lip gloss that was making it very hard for him not to stare at her lips.

He sighed deeply. 'What do you want me to say?' he asked. 'I have a business to run.'

She lowered her gaze and mumbled, 'So you weren't ignoring me then?'

'What do you think?' he asked finally and she looked back at him again.

'I think,' she reached into her bag and pulled out a water bottle and handed it to him. He took it from her gratefully, opened the cap and drank from it finishing almost all the water. He capped it and then shook his head a bit, as though to dislodge the different thoughts that were running inside.

'I think,' she continued, 'that you got angry with me when I asked for Uzair's number.' Before he could say anything, she put up her hand and went on. 'Don't tell me it isn't true.'

Okay, so she'd cornered him. 'So if you know the reason, why are you sitting here?' he asked and made to get up, when she covered his hand with hers.

'But why should that make you angry? And you're saying it's not even brotherly concern.'

He settled back into the bench, noting absently how soft her hands were. 'So how's he? Is he everything you dreamed he would be?'

Saba was silent and she withdrew her hands. 'I. . .I can't believe you didn't even read my texts,' she murmured and got up.

'What?' Shahid asked, feeling a little uncomfortable.

'Nothing. This was a waste of my time. I'm going to college,' she said more firmly and moved towards the turnstile. He watched her walk away and then ran after her and stopped her with a hand on her shoulder.

'Did he misbehave with you?'

'As if you cared!' she exploded, turning around and shaking his hand off her shoulders. 'I don't know why I took the trouble to come and see you. Obviously, you're not bothered.'

One moment she was almost timid and sweet and the next she was a spitfire, Shahid thought, wondering if that was one of the reasons why he loved her so much. She looked furious and he had visions of Uzair touching Saba, instantly making him feel sick.

'What did he do?' he asked in a low voice, his hands on her shoulders again.

'If you'd read my messages, you would have known,' Saba bit out the words, trying to twist herself away from his grasp.

'Let me go. You're making a scene,' she said curtly.

'Okay, I didn't read your texts,' he admitted. 'It just hurt too much.'

'What hurt too much?' she asked, stopping her struggle.

'You need to answer me first,' he reminded her.

'I met him for coffee with my friend Riya and he turned out to be a whiny idiot whom I couldn't stand for more than ten minutes. Plus, he was more interested in *Rabia*. I said as much to you in my SMS,' she said.

Relief flooded Shahid's body and it was so intense that he pulled Saba to him and hugged her tightly, not bothered about who saw them. He winced when he remembered how sweaty he'd been and he moved away from her gingerly. She looked surprised and shy and Shahid decided that he wasn't going to take his chances by waiting any longer.

'I'm sorry for ignoring you all these days, but it hasn't been easy,' he said, without letting go of her arm.

'But why?' she asked, finally meeting his gaze.

'We need to talk,' he said, leading her back to the bench where they had been sitting. An elderly couple walked past them vigorously and shot him a dirty look. He waved at them but turned his attention back to Saba.

'This wasn't how I intended to say this,' he said, taking her hands in his. She looked at his face intently and Shahid wondered if she'd guessed.

'Say what?' she asked, her voice husky, as though speaking from a dry throat.

'I'm sweating. I need to shower. And there are a hundred ways I'd planned to do this, but I can't wait anymore.' He was suddenly scared. What if she just laughed at him and said he was being outrageous?

Rubbing her warm hands in his, he drew circles on her palms with his roughened thumb and then took a deep breath to speak.

'I'm in love with you, Saba.' There, he'd said it. Now, all he had to figure out was whether the look of shock on her face was a good thing or a bad thing.

32

Saba's phone rang and interrupted the silence. Startled, she hunted for it in her bag and pulled it out.

'Who is it?' Shahid asked.

'Ammi,' Saba said and pressed the green button, turning away from him slightly so she didn't have to look at him. She didn't want to see his disturbingly attractive shoulders or his broad chest and neither did she want to see how sexy he looked, even with the sweat dripping off his face, while she spoke to her mom. Gosh, this was Shahid she was thinking about! Shahid, who had just told her that he was in love with her!

'I'm in college,' she lied as her mother asked her where she had disappeared.

'Yes, I have a project in college and I had to come early. What time will I be back?' she wished she hadn't turned to face Shahid as she answered this question.

He was staring at her intently, shook his head and raised an eyebrow. 'Late,' he mouthed.

'I'll b-be late,' she stammered and then ended the call, dropping her phone inside her bag. She was almost glad the phone had rung, shattering that tense moment, but now she had to face him.

'Can you wait here for a while?' he asked, leaning forward suddenly and getting up.

'Why? Where are you going?' she asked, surprised.

'I can't talk to you any more like this,' he said, pointing to his T-shirt that had stuck to his body. Tearing her eyes away from his chest, Saba looked at his face.

'Give me five minutes. Ten at the most. I'll shower and be back before you even know it. Don't go to college,' he added as he jogged out of the park and broke into a run.

Saba stared after him and then pulled out her phone again to text Riya. It felt as though her heart was jumping crazily inside her.

'Awake yet?'

Her phone buzzed when Riya replied.

'I am now 😐'

Smiling, she called Riya and told her everything. She was rewarded by a shriek that made her keep the phone at some distance from her ear.

'Are you bunking college? Are you going off somewhere with him?' Riya asked, her sleep completely gone and excitement tinging her voice.

'Of course not!' Saba replied, her sense of propriety kicking in.

'Arrey you idiot! Go somewhere with him. Have fun,' Riya chided her.

'But. . .'

'The guy JUST told you he's in love with you. And you're going to come to college and listen to Shakespeare and Donne?' Riya sounded outraged.

'But. . .it seems so awkward. What should I tell him?' Saba asked feeling distressed. She was glad Shahid had gone away momentarily. Or she would have done something stupid, like lean forward and feel his muscles.

'Tell him how you feel about him,' Riya said, as though it was completely obvious.

'What feelings? I don't have any feelings for him,' Saba replied, although in her mind, she added the word 'yet'.

'Well, all that is for later. Spend some time with him. Get to know him,' Riya urged her. 'I will personally kick you out of college if you come here.'

'He's back,' Saba spoke and ended the call even though Riya was still talking at the other end.

'Hey!' he said and came to sit down next to her. It was almost eight now and getting quite warm.

'Why am I going to be late?' she asked the first thing that came to mind.

'Because you're coming with me,' he said, resting his hands near her nape. Her back prickled as his hand lightly toyed with a strand of her hair. Saba forced herself to think clearly.

Okay, so this was Shahid. Her cousin. And he claimed he was in love with her. So did that give him the right to start acting towards her in a proprietary manner? She moved away from his hands.

'What are you doing?' she asked, her breath catching in her throat. She wanted to be annoyed with him but was finding it difficult because it seemed like she'd *just* now noticed what a slow and sexy smile he had.

'You never told me how you knew I'd be here,' he said, ignoring her question. His hand was still in the air and he let it drop lightly on the bench.

'You showed me this place some time back,' Saba replied, casually observing that with the jeans and deep blue T-shirt he was wearing, he didn't look like a businessman at all.

'And you remembered?' he asked, looking a bit incredulous but pleased.

'What's going on, bh. . .?' Saba stopped herself in time. 'I can't bring myself to call you Shahid yet,' she said, lifting her hands and dropping them in her lap.

'You're going to have to,' he affirmed as he moved closer. 'Shall we go somewhere else? This bench is getting really warm.'

'No, you have to explain all this to me,' Saba stopped him. And where else *could* they go? It was too early in the morning to go to a restaurant.

'Okay, at least let's sit somewhere in the shade,' he said and moved towards another bench that was located under the sprawling branches of a tree.

Saba followed him reluctantly.

'So, what do you want to know?' he asked as he sat down. Saba sat down at the edge.

'None of this makes sense. You say that you are. . .in love. . .with me,' Saba paused. She turned her head a fraction to look at Shahid and he nodded, his face serious.

'But. . .you gave me Uzair's number,' she pointed out. 'Why didn't you say anything then?'

Shahid was silent for a moment. 'I don't know. I thought that maybe you were infatuated and the more you stop someone, the more drawn they get towards that person. I wanted it to play itself out but I was also very angry and frustrated,' he spoke softly.

Saba shook her head. She rubbed her temples with her fingers.

'What if I'd fallen in love with him? You'd have just sat back and watched?' she asked.

Shahid twisted his mouth and nodded. 'I'd just want you to be happy.'

Saba was overcome with a number of emotions but she couldn't distinguish one from the other.

'So. . .when did you. . .' she started hesitantly and stopped when Shahid covered her hands with his.

'I've been in love with you for years,' he said, turning her palms over in his hands.

'Years?' Saba asked, shocked. 'But you've always treated me like your kid sister, pulling my braids and teasing me,' she reminded him, although her stomach was churning now.

Shahid was quiet but continued rubbing his thumbs over her palms. 'What?' she prompted him and he shook his head.

'You don't want to know,' he sighed and looked away pulling out his hand.

'Now I *have* to know,' Saba said settling back into the bench and turning to look at him.

'Well, I had to behave like an elder cousin would, right? I've had to wait so long for you to grow up and then you ask my help to get another guy's number,' he reminded her, raising his eyebrows in a way that comforted Saba because it looked like the old Shahid, the one she'd known all her life. But his words embarrassed her.

'Do you have to bring that up every minute?' she asked, looking away.

'I've been tormented all these days wondering what was happening,' he admitted and Saba turned back to glare at him.

'Why wouldn't you read my messages?'

'After that first message when you *thanked* me for getting his number, I didn't want to read about how your love story was progressing,' he shrugged.

'Couldn't you have told me about your feelings that day on the terrace and saved us all this trouble?'

Shahid looked a bit perplexed himself as he pushed his hair back from his forehead in a gesture that was familiar to Saba. But she couldn't bring herself to relax around him any longer. She could no longer escape into the comfort zone that had always been there between them.

'Okay, why are we arguing?' he asked.

'I don't know. I still can't understand any of this,' Saba said, looking at Shahid from a completely new perspective, wondering if he'd been this hot all along or was she seeing him clearly only now. She was finally getting what Riya had been harping about all these days.

Shahid made a sound of annoyance. 'What's there to understand? I'm in love with you and I want to marry you,' he said.

Saba leaned back on the bench. 'Give me some time to get used to this idea,' she said in a shaky voice. She opened her eyes to see him looking at her as though he was absorbing her face in his mind.

'Okay,' he agreed but continued staring at her.

'I think I'll go to college anyway,' Saba said, feeling a little nervous about the emotions that were roiling inside, but he laid a hand on her lap and stopped her.

'No, wait.'

'Okay,' Saba gulped. His hand remained in her lap and she felt slightly light headed. She forgot why she'd been angry with him in the first place.

'You were asking how I used to pull your braids and generally tease you,' he stated and she nodded.

'Do you want to know what I really wanted to do each time I saw you?' he asked.

Time stretched between them as Saba wondered at the implication of his words. She shook her head finally and, through a voice that hardly sounded like her own, using words she never thought she'd say, she spoke, 'I'd like you to show me, instead.'

33

OMG totally!

Posted by The Other T, 05-04-12

My blog is now finally public. Apparently, I'd fiddled with the privacy settings when I started it and made it a private blog. That's why I haven't received a single comment from even random lurkers (so I'd been ranting at empty cyberspace all along). X pointed it out to me and yes, she knows about the blog. She *made* me tell her.

So, where was I the last time I was here? About Y calling off his wedding, right? Yes, I'll get back to him but OH MY GOD, I HAVE TO SAY THIS NOW.

T and I are a couple.

Yes, that's right. If you're wondering what happened between my last post and now, I'm afraid I'll have to keep you wondering. I know, but it's personal. Okay, I'll make an exception just this once and give you a short version.

I confronted T and asked him why he was avoiding me and then he admitted that he was in love with me. There's definitely something between us, though I don't yet understand my feelings, so I've just gone ahead with the flow. Also, it's like he's become super attractive overnight. I mean, he just looks at me in this particular way and my knees go shaky and my stomach drops as though someone pitched it from a height.

Although I'm blushing a bit while writing this, I have to say it. T kissed me in the park. He just leaned forward, took my face in his hands and kissed me in front of a bunch of old people on their morning walk. Then we had to go to his car because the old people looked like they were either going to faint or call the police and we kissed there too. A few times. That's it. Nothing else happened. Really.

I bunked college and spent the whole day with him and we sat around in a couple of coffee shops, and just talked and talked. But every fifteen minutes or so there was a lull in the conversation and I'd find him staring at me in a way that made me blush. And have I ever mentioned that he has the most dazzling smile I have ever seen on a guy? I'm probably biased I guess.

Then we met up with X for lunch, who couldn't stop telling me 'I told you so'. She was very pleased, as though she'd been the one to get us together, and I was amazed at how well the three of us seemed to click. So much so that T and X ganged up against me and teased me mercilessly for having a crush on the Idiot and then T made up for it on the way back home. Sorry. No details this time.

T has never looked this happy and I cannot believe I am the one to put that look on his face. I wish I knew if this was love. I've never experienced anything like this before, so there's no reference point. But I'm so happy, it's like I'm in this shiny rainbow-coloured bubble which I'm afraid will pop anytime. Some of my trepidation has to do with Y and Q.

Yes, Y and Q. Those two are having the strangest set of problems and there's nothing my parents can do to take their worries away.

Y has refused to get married and he's not telling us why.

Q, on the other hand, has changed drastically. I went with her and Ammi to the gynaec and only then noticed that she'd put on a lot of weight. Her face looked chubby and her skin had spots. She was also losing some hair, going by the strands I saw on her hijab.

Ammi held her hand because it looked like she needed comfort and I actually felt bad for her.

Her husband came to the hospital directly from his office and he sought us out, looking worried. Q tensed when he sat down near her, as if she'd frozen up inside, and it was painful to watch them. He was no longer playful and she couldn't muster up her haughtiness.

The doctor seemed friendly and approachable and she took Q behind the curtain for an examination while we all waited and then, suddenly, we heard the strangest sound coming from there. Thupp! Thupp! Thupp! It went on rapidly and I heard Q's scared voice. 'Why is it so fast?'

'A baby's heartbeats are always fast, dear,' Dr Shanthi assured her. Q's husband, who was seated in front of the doctor's empty table, swallowed audibly. 'Is that my child's heartbeat?' he asked, his voice husky.

'Yes, yes!' the doctor said, smiling as she came around the curtain, snapping off her latex gloves. 'That's your baby.'

Colour suffused his face and he looked at Ammi who smiled back at him uncertainly and then at me and I grinned, seeing how happy he was.

'Can we do an ultrasound to check if the baby's fine?' Q asked as she walked out from behind the curtains.

'But everything *is* fine!' the doctor said. Q insisted she wanted an ultrasound.

So we waited outside the ultrasound room for our turn and then Ammi and Q went inside because only one person was allowed inside with the patient. And Q didn't want her husband with her. She actually said that out loud.

The two of us stood outside the door and then sat on the plastic chairs. The silence between us was grim and finally he spoke.

'Will someone tell me what's happening to my wife?' he looked down at the ground as he spoke, clutching his head in his hands.

'I. . .'

'I shouldn't have forced her to have a baby,' he spoke as though to himself. 'I had no idea she would become. . .'

'I'm sure. . .'

'I can't tell you what she means to me,' he said, speaking quickly as though the words would dry up. 'She's everything to me. And she's treating me like a monster.' He covered his face with his hands and I gulped.

I looked away, wishing I didn't have to witness this passionate display of emotions, because it was really disturbing. Was it the hormones that were making Q act this way? She'd never behaved like she was lovelorn around him but she hadn't acted this way either. T texted me and I read his message a hundred times like a litany, hoping to erase this dull ache in my chest.

'Love you. Miss you.' That's all it said but I read it until the words blurred.

I wanted to help Q and her husband, but I had no idea what was wrong in the first place.

'Maybe you could take her to a psychiatrist? For counselling?' I suggested but he shook his head.

'She won't spend even five minutes with me,' he said, sighing heavily. 'Isn't there anyone in your family she would listen to?' he asked.

'She was very fond of my grandmother,' I remembered but shook my head. 'But she passed away a few years ago.' His shoulders slumped.

'I don't mind her staying at her mother's house for the entire duration of her pregnancy, but what after that, what will she do? What will *I* do if she doesn't come back?'

It's very difficult to see your heroes crumbling before you. Q's husband was pretty much my hero because he'd taken her away from our house *and* kept her in line.

'I. . .I'll try and talk to her,' I promised, before I realized what I was saying. Q would dismember me and throw the pieces to the crows before listening to what I had to say. But I had to try, for his sake at least.

Q and Ammi came outside and, without looking at her husband, Q walked slowly (she walked as though she was already eight months pregnant) towards the exit.

'Is everything fine, Ammi?' her husband stood up and asked my mother who looked stricken for some reason.

'Y-yes! It's f-fine,' she struggled with her words and then beckoned me.

'Come. Come, let's go,' she said and we walked outside the hospital. I turned to look at him and smiled as if to reassure him, but Ammi pulled me away and we went back home.

34

Over mutton biryani and chicken kebabs at The Empire in Church Street, Zohaib and Shahid got talking. It was now the end of April and Zohaib's parents were in a state of complete panic, because just the day before, Zohaib had threatened to go and speak to the girl's family if they didn't call off the wedding.

'How can we?' his mother asked. 'They've already started giving out invitation cards and they were a bit concerned that we haven't started ours yet.'

Invitation cards! That was it! His father rarely spoke to him now and he'd looked at Zohaib coldly as he stomped off. Zohaib had gone straight to his room and called Shahid, asking him to meet him the following day as he had to talk about something important.

'So, tell me what's bothering you?' Shahid asked as he rubbed his fingers together in the hot water that the waiter had brought in a bowl, with a wedge of lemon floating on top.

Zohaib scratched his jaw absently, and then sighed and settled back into the chair. Most of the lunch patrons had left and the servers had been eying them to see when they would leave too.

He looked at his place mat as he spoke, observing the squiggly lines and swirls in the design, just so he wouldn't have to see Shahid's face. When he finished speaking, he flicked the place mat away and finally looked up. Shahid looked impassive.

'So, by refusing to marry, who exactly are you helping?' Shahid asked, his brows bunched together.

Zohaib looked uncomfortable. 'What do you expect me to

do? I can't get married now with Meenakshi looming over my head like this.'

'Keep this up and you'll never get married,' Shahid snorted.

'Stop being such a wise ass,' Zohaib muttered. 'Tell me what I should do.'

Shahid stared at Zohaib's face for a moment, startled to realize the similarity between him and Saba. They both had the same nose and the same upper lip. Bending forward to talk to him, Shahid said, 'Okay, what exactly is your problem with getting married? I don't quite understand the issue here,' Shahid said, beckoning the waiter for the bill.

Zohaib sighed. 'You don't know Meenakshi. She'll sabotage my wedding. She'll come over there and create some kind of trouble. Or she'll even find the bride's family and go speak to them and make a big mess. I'm just saving everyone all that embarrassment and shock.'

Shahid was silent for a moment. 'You could quit your job,' he suggested.

'And do what? I don't have a brain suited for business like you, dude. And why should *I* quit my job?'

'Exactly how serious was your relationship with this girl? Are you planning to pick it up when she's back? Were you in love with her?' Shahid asked, frowning. It was disconcerting to see this side of Zohaib.

'No way! I don't want to see her ever again,' Zohaib stated vehemently and then looked down. 'She was my girlfriend for a few months, but love? No. It was definitely not love.'

Shahid wasn't judgmental, so he kept quiet but how could he possibly help Zohaib?

The waiter placed the bill before them and there was a minor argument over who would pay it. Shahid finally wrested the bill from Zohaib and dropped the money in the tray. His mind was racing as he sought out ways in which things could work out for Zohaib. Also, he really cared about Saba's parents and didn't want to see them hurt this way.

'My parents are talking about the scandal this will cause and who will marry Saba and. . .' Zohaib continued, a pained look flashing across his face. 'What did I know? I just wish things were different.'

'Have you thought about how your bride will feel when she finds out?' Shahid asked.

'Exactly. That's why I don't want to put her through this,' Zohaib muttered.

'Why don't you try and talk to her about this?' Shahid asked, and Zohaib looked at him unbelievably.

'What is wrong with you?' he asked him and Shahid sighed. But he couldn't let go of the idea.

'Why should it be difficult? I can get you her phone number if you like!' Shahid said, trying not to remember how odd it was that he'd procured Uzair's number for Saba just some time back.

Zohaib rubbed his forehead anxiously. 'I. . .I. . .what will I tell her? I'm calling off the wedding because my ex-girlfriend is going to be back in town?'

'No, but you can come clean about everything. You can try and establish trust between the two of you,' Shahid said, toying with the place mat on his side.

'And then? You think she'll want to get married to me? What if she goes and tells her father? I can't take that chance of this story getting back to my parents,' Zohaib said, shaking his head.

Shahid felt exasperated. Zohaib wanted help, but wasn't willing to listen to options.

'How about you get married to her and then tell her everything?' Shahid hated the sneakiness implied by the idea. It wasn't fair to Zohaib's bride at all.

'Dude, that's all easier said than done. She's a stranger to me. What if she's more psycho than Meenakshi?'

Shahid dropped his hands heavily on the table. 'You want help, but you're not willing to act upon my ideas. What can I do? I don't like the last option but, seriously, if you get married, things will be easier for everyone. Of course, you'll have to work harder at convincing her that you're committed to her. See, don't tell her the details, but inform her about Meenakshi, so that if she ever contacts your wife, it won't come as a rude surprise.'

Zohaib snorted. 'You're talking with the assumption that I'll get married without any problems. That's not going to happen, you know.'

'Ask your project manager if there are any projects overseas. Anything. Just take that and leave now, so you won't be here when Meenakshi comes,' Shahid said, annoyed with Zohaib for not being in charge of his life. Shahid was aware that this step was tantamount to running away, but what else could he suggest?

'What?' Zohaib asked, startled, but the idea appealed to him as Shahid thought it would.

'Why not? I'm sure there will be something you can get. Go for it.'

Zohaib sighed as he got up. 'That's the problem with you businessmen. You think everything is in your control. It's not easy to get an overseas assignment and what about the wedding?'

'Oh, you have to be back in time for it!' Shahid was worried now. What if Zohaib decided not to come back?

Both of them got up and left the restaurant. It was close to Zohaib's office so Shahid had agreed to come down and meet him. Together, they walked towards Shahid's car.

'Thanks for the advice, Shahid. I just needed to talk to someone who wouldn't judge me. I'll see what I can do,' Zohaib patted Shahid on the back as though he was the one who needed consoling.

Shahid unlocked his car and got inside. 'Think about it. It's better than calling off the wedding, right?' he said as he started the car.

Zohaib nodded. He was almost convinced. He was leaning inside the window when he spotted something on the dashboard.

'Isn't that Saba's scarf?' he asked, surprised. Shahid turned to look at the yellow silk scarf, dotted with crystals along the edge, and felt a rush of anxiety go through him. Just yesterday, Saba's golden face had been framed in his hands as he leaned forward and touched his lips to hers. Her widened eyes as he pressed kisses on her neck and pulled out the scarf impatiently flashed before him and he turned around to Zohaib.

'She must have left it here by mistake,' Shahid spoke slowly, hoping his voice was normal and his face did not betray anything.

'Really?' Zohaib asked. He remembered the scarf because *he* had got it for her on a trip abroad sometime back.

'Really,' Shahid affirmed.

35

In April, the sky was so blue, you had to squint to look at it, and even then tears would pool at the edges of your eyes and you had to look down. But it was just another unpredictable month in Bengaluru. Saba and Riya were among the many who groaned when the skies opened up and rain fell in huge torrents without any warning.

'Shit! Hurry up!' Riya yelled and covered her head with a book as the two of them ran into the nearest building.

Saba pulled at her clinging kameez and brushed the drops from her hair. They watched the rain lash the ground and all the girls scurrying for cover. Rain *had* to come and ruin their lunch break. The bell rang faintly in the distance, its sound not more than a squeak above the downpour.

'Archana won't give us attendance if we go even five minutes late,' Saba muttered.

'And you really need your attendance, don't you?' Riya smirked. Saba's faced flushed at the reminder of how many days she had recently bunked college to meet Shahid.

Saba rubbed the bridge of her nose and sighed. 'I don't know, Riya. Everything has changed suddenly. I mean. . .two months back I was just another girl, dreaming about a good life and worrying about my exams. But so much is happening at home and Shahid. . .' she broke off.

'Go on,' Riya said, making way for a teacher to walk past them. The teacher looked at the downpour and debated whether or not to venture out and, finally, covering her head with the attendance register, and the other hand holding up the pleats of her saree, she made a dash for it.

Saba continued, looking uncertain. 'The more time I spend with him, the more convinced I am that he is the one for me.'

'I mean, how did he manage to hide such strong feelings for me all these years? I would never have been able to do it. It's so difficult for me to pretend he's just a cousin when he comes home,' Saba said, looking out at the rain that was showing no signs of relenting.

'Wait a sec. Is that a. . .' Riya pointed to the tiny mark on Saba's collarbone as she leaned forward.

'Shoot!' Saba muttered and pulled up her dupatta, blushing even more if that was possible. She was glad that the building was dark because of the rain, but Riya wasn't going to let it go so easily.

'Is that a hickey?' she asked Saba, still in shock. Saba nodded and refused to look at Riya who started guffawing.

'Man! I'm jealous. I want a boyfriend too! And exactly what do you two get up to when he drops you home?'

Saba shook her head. 'We just kiss. A lot. There's not much you can do in a car!' she said, her face flaming.

Riya narrowed her eyes. 'Really? There's quite a lot that you can do in a car if you really want to,' Riya said.

'Actually, we're waiting till we get married,' Saba said.

Riya stared at her and then giggled non-stop for about five minutes. Saba didn't know whether to be angry at her or to join her.

'How come no one finds it odd that he's dropping you home every day?' she asked when the giggling had stopped.

'He doesn't come inside and I get off the car a little away from the house.'

'Ah! Young love!' Riya said, pulling down the corners of her mouth in a sad grimace.

Saba grinned at that but then, as though she had an after thought, she started speaking again. 'Things are so crazy at home that Shahid is the only thing that's keeping me sane.'

'Why? What happened?'

'Zohaib bhai thankfully decided not to call off his wedding. But he's gone off on a project to France. My parents are really worried that he won't be back in time for his own wedding!' Saba said.

'I also promised Rafiq bhaijan that I'd speak to Rabia but. . .' Saba paused. The rain had stopped just as suddenly as it had begun.

'Tell me on the way,' Riya said and both of them stepped out, gingerly avoiding the puddles.

'Nothing more to tell! I haven't got the guts to speak to her. And Shahid thinks that Rabia is just being silly and moody, but I think it's something else.'

'Your life is like a soap opera,' Riya snickered.

'Shut up! You don't know the half of it.'

'Whatever! And you're the pretty heroine sporting love bites and all. And that sexy hero of yours. . .' Riya made Shahrukh Khan's trademark gesture, flinging her arms out.

Saba burst out laughing as the two of them walked up the stairs to the class. Luckily for them, Ms Archana hadn't arrived yet.

36

'That is the most ridiculous thing I've ever heard!'

Saba paused outside Rabia's door, holding a tray. Ammi had sent her to Rabia's room with milk, some sandwiches and fried pakoras. Saba eyed all the food with envy, thinking that it must be really cool to get pregnant if you were actually *allowed* to get fat.

At Rabia's door, however, she heard her father talking to Rabia.

'Do you even *know* what you're saying?' her father thundered again.

Saba couldn't hear Rabia's voice and it made Saba uncomfortable to stand outside overhearing them. She balanced the tray on one hand and lifted the other to knock, when her hand paused in the air.

'So what if things always go his way? He's just a lucky man!'

More murmurs from Rabia's side.

'How do you think Saba was born? She was an accident! Your mother was also on the pill. That didn't mean that. . .'

Saba felt herself grow still as she heard the words. The rest of her father's sentence was drowned out by the rushing sound in her ears. Her father made it sound as though they'd been happy with their two perfect kids when she'd decided to come along. Of course, that wasn't true. Her parents loved her, but Saba often felt that she'd got the leftovers when it came to parental love. Everything else had been lavished on Zohaib and Rabia.

Before her father spoke again, she knocked on the door firmly and opened it without waiting. She walked inside and her father's face flushed when he realized that she had heard him.

She placed the tray on the bedside table and looked at Rabia, who was staring at the wall opposite her bed sullenly. Abbu stopped her as she was about to leave. 'Saba, I need to talk to both of you,' he said.

'Yes?' she asked. She was still feeling hurt though.

'Sit down,' Abbu said, pointing to a stool near the dressing table.

Saba sat down, wondering what was in store. Her father paced the room and the silence was punctuated when Rabia munched on a pakora.

'Rabia has an interesting theory and I want you to listen to her and tell her how foolish she sounds,' he spoke suddenly. Saba didn't speak. She waited for him to continue.

'She feels that either her husband is possessed by a jinn or is a jinn himself.'

Saba flashed a look at her sister who refused to meet her eyes. What? That was ridiculous!

'Apparently, she feels that the very first time they met he put some kind of spell on her and *made* her marry him. And now she says that it's uncanny how everything works out his way and how everyone else caves in to his demands. And the fact that she got pregnant when she didn't want to.'

'But. . .but that doesn't have to mean a thing,' Saba protested.

'Exactly. Now will someone please tell this girl that she's being silly?' he asked both of them.

Rabia folded her arms across her chest and looked out of the window.

'*You* wanted to marry him, remember?' he snapped at her.

'But I told you, now I know the reason why,' Rabia said, looking at Abbu.

Saba observed how her eyes looked sunken and her face looked drawn. She *really* believed it. This was so absurd!

'Does Ammi know?' Saba asked and Abbu nodded.

'She's almost convinced her mother too. That's how I got to know why Rabia is staying here,' he said.

'Why do you feel this way, Rabia?' Saba asked her, swallowing, hoping that Rabia wouldn't decimate her with a withering glance. She was surprised when Rabia pursed her lips and looked at her directly.

'He can't be human,' Rabia said, shaking her head.

'But. . .'

'Do you know that the first time he saw me, he told me he wanted to marry me? That I *belonged* to him?'

'So?' Saba ventured bravely, 'He's a romantic at heart. He fell in love with you the moment he saw you.'

Rabia waved her hands at her, looking irritated. 'No, that's not what I meant. He's had this weird control over me which I can't explain. I didn't want a baby and here I am, pregnant even though I was on the pill.'

Saba listened to her with growing unease. It was the first time in memory that Rabia had spoken to her without insulting her. She also felt a little embarrassed about listening to this with Abbu around. But because this situation was strange, normal limits of propriety were missing.

'Maybe there's an explanation for all of this,' Saba spoke slowly. 'But I'm sure that he's as human as you or me.'

'Prove it,' Rabia said, looking out of the window again.

'P-prove it?' Saba repeated, looking at Abbu for assistance. He looked impassive.

Rabia flashed an angry look at her. 'Look at you. You're nothing but a mere tadpole. You don't know what real life is like. You have no idea about men and women *or* love.'

Abbu got up and left, shaking his head, and Saba was glad to see him leave. This conversation was getting very intense and personal. Rabia, however, continued unperturbed.

'What do you know about falling in love and how men behave when they want something badly from you? You're just bothered about your books and your studies and then when you finish college, Abbu and Ammi will find a nice boy for you and get you married. You have a clean slate. You get a clean start. Look at *me*! I don't want to see my face in the mirror. This thing that's growing inside me is changing me *as* we speak. I hate the world. I hate everyone. But above all, I hate Rafiq for coming into my life!' Rabia was impassioned and her voice quivered and tears fell from her eyes rapidly.

Saba felt a strange set of sensations inside as she heard Rabia. There was annoyance mingled with pity and she was amazed that Rabia was actually jealous of her. How would she react if she ever got to know about her and Shahid? Saba didn't want to find out anytime soon.

She was also concerned about how seriously Rabia was taking this whole thing.

'Rafiq bhaijan is the nicest man I've ever come across,' Saba said and instantly knew it was the wrong thing to have said. Rabia's eyes grew round.

'Didn't I just tell you that you don't know a thing? What do you know how it feels when a man touches you? Or kisses you before even telling his name? And when his very touch makes you feel as though you were melting inside?'

Saba flushed uncomfortably. She shook her head to clear the images of Shahid and her that had immediately formed when

Rabia was talking and she realized her voice was husky when she spoke.

'Fine. I'll prove that he's not a jinn,' Saba couldn't believe she was saying this to Rabia. Jinn! Whoever heard of such a thing?

Rabia snorted. 'Go right ahead.'

'If I prove it, you have to go back to him,' Saba added.

'Why? You have a problem with me staying here?' Rabia asked, her eyes narrowed as she selected a sandwich from the plate.

'No. But I know he loves you and *needs* you.'

Rabia scowled. 'Yeah, right.'

'No, you said I don't know anything about men and women, but I do know that whether he is human or not, he loves you. With all your faults and everything. No one else can love you as much as he can.' Saba got up and walked out even though she heard Rabia calling out to her angrily.

37

Wedding update?

POSTED BY THE OTHER T, 09-05-12

My brother Y has gone to France on a project and although he calls regularly, my parents are really worried that he might simply stay away and bunk the wedding. Even so, they are carrying on with the preparations because there's nothing else that they can do.

With Q out of action (for various reasons that I will explain later), Ammi has reluctantly turned to me to help her with the shopping. I feel torn between helping her, studying for my semester exams which are next month (eeps!) and spending time with T. Still, we went yesterday and bought the last few sets of clothes for the bride (except the wedding ghagra) and are now busy getting the clothes stitched.

Ammi finished the jewellery shopping some days back. Abbu came back with her, looking physically ill. He mumbled about how expensive gold had become and it was ridiculous the amount of money they were spending on their son's wedding when they had a daughter to marry off too.

Ammi and Abbu got into fights regularly over the same issue—money. Ammi wanted to spend around fifty thousand at least for the bridal ghagra and Abbu was adamantly against it. The three of us went shopping for the ghagra in a section of the city that was renowned for them and ended up wasting around three hours—first deciding the colour, the kind of work they wanted on it and then how much they were going to spend on it. I managed to survive thanks to T, who was constantly texting me.

I asked him if he could join us because it would be a legitimate way to spend time with him, but he said he couldn't. My parents would think it odd if he *happened* to be passing by this place which was way out of his work area. True.

So we finally bought a rich maroon ghagra embellished with gold zari and dark green embroidery. It was lush and a little ostentatious, but Ammi was consulting Q on the phone (seriously!) and they finally settled on it. It overshot the budget that Abbu had in mind by a huge amount.

Also, the wedding cards have come and Ammi's again recruited me for writing the names on the covers and God, there are so many! Also, there's a particular format to be used when writing and Ammi wanted me to write in big, cursive writing which I've outgrown since second grade. I botched up that job quite badly and Ammi was really annoyed with me. 'What's the point of all your education if you can't write names on an invitation card?' she asked me. Right. That was why I was going to college.

Once I finished that, Abbu and Ammi started the rounds of invitations. Thank God, she can't ask me to accompany her for that, because I'm the unmarried daughter. I was glad to see them both go each day but they'd come back in the evenings dead tired. They also had to go out of Bengaluru for a weekend to invite relatives in other cities as well.

When I explained all this to X, she was like, why can't they just post the cards? Yeah. Why go to all this trouble? But apparently that was not how it worked.

Q's also still here, refusing to go back to her husband, and now when he comes to visit her she doesn't even let him come inside the room.

Actually, I learnt only recently what Q's problem was. . .and I can't discuss it here. It's too personal and, moreover, no one will believe me. In fact, I haven't even shared it with T or X, two of the people I'm closest to. I think even they will laugh at me. Q wants me to prove that she's wrong and I haven't been able to do anything about that yet.

At first I wondered if I could ask her husband directly, but what if he actually exploded into the air angrily like a wisp of smoke?

So, I haven't made any headway on that front, but I really need to do something. I've seen how haggard he's become and the way his face lights up when he hears her voice outside the door of her room. He looks at me with such naked despair in his eyes because she doesn't let him come inside, that it makes me want to tear my hair out. Maybe I should tear out Q's hair and *make* her see that the man she married loves her beyond description.

On an unrelated note, my exams start exactly a week before Y's wedding. How am I going to get any studying done? My house is going to look like a carnival and there are going to be relatives everywhere. I need to figure out something, some way in which I can manage to study, but with Q down, Ammi's going to need me more.

Also, it's my birthday tomorrow. I don't know why, but I'm rather nervous and excited. T is behaving all nonchalant and everything, but he keeps giving me these secret looks and smiles and nodding to himself. It's getting very disconcerting. He also started this countdown on my mobile, sending me SMS messages that say 'thirty-six hours to go', or 'twenty-two hours left' and this anticipation is making me dizzy with excitement. What is he planning?

38

At around eight that night, Saba yawned and stretched before the computer. It was getting warm and she opened one of the windows. Her parents were due to leave the following weekend for Chennai and they would visit all the other towns along the way too. She might be able to finish her studying around then, but if only her mother didn't install one of the aunts at their house so that she and Rabia weren't alone.

She was just about to shut down the computer when she saw that someone new had commented on her blog. So far, the only comments she'd received were from Riya who posted irritating smileys on each post. She opened her email and smiled when she read it.

Seema

May 09, 2012

Are you sure you're living this life and not dreaming it up? It sounds too incredulous to me. Btw, I'm half in love with your T already. Can't wait to see what he's up to. And do share with us what's wrong with Q. We'd like to know and we can keep a secret! Oh and happy birthday!

Saba felt a thrill go through her as she hit the 'approve' button. For the first time in three months, someone had actually read her work and posted a comment.

A little later, however, she felt the enthusiasm drain away when she remembered that she still had to take care of Q's problem. How on earth could she prove that her husband was human and not a jinn? Even the thought seemed ridiculous.

She recalled a conversation between the aunts some years back when the aunts were talking about how a girl had been possessed by a jinn and they had to call an exorcist to get rid of it. It had all seemed like mumbo jumbo back then. She couldn't even ask anyone about this without rousing their suspicion.

Idly, she googled for it and was surprised to see the number of websites that came up. But just as she was going to open one of the sites, her mother called her. She bookmarked one of them and went to her mother.

'Rabia's dinner,' her mother said, handing her a tray, and Saba grimaced. Rabia's room was upstairs and she didn't want to climb up and down so many times because of her pregnancy. But it was obviously okay for others to run around. She wished her parents had given her a room upstairs, but then, she was the afterthought, right? She had to make do with the converted guest room downstairs and when guests did come, they naturally stayed in her room, while she had to find some other place to sleep.

She knocked on Rabia's door, went inside and saw that she was reading a magazine. Rabia had now put on at least five kilos and her face looked puffy. It was hard to reconcile this image of hers with the sophisticated and chiselled face that had often glared at her disdainfully.

Rabia sighed just as Saba was leaving and she turned around reluctantly.

'I don't know what's going to happen to me,' Rabia spoke. For a change, she sounded like she wanted company. 'I hate this thing that's growing inside me, making me hungry all the time, making me want to pee all the time. I wish I'd never got married!' she said fervently, her voice sounding raspy.

Saba wished she could cover the ears of the baby that Rabia kept referring to as 'this thing'.

'It's your baby. Don't say such things,' she said, sounding clichéd.

'Yeah, right! What if it's like him?'

Saba thought back a moment to her handsome and successful brother-in-law, tall with curly hair and charming dimples, and spoke, 'I'd say your baby has some excellent genes.'

'Shut up! You don't know anything yet,' Rabia snapped. Saba shrugged.

'I'm looking for a way to prove you wrong and I know I can do it,' she countered.

Rabia looked confused. 'How? How can you be so sure of anything?' she asked brokenly, looking out of the window into the darkness.

Saba shook her head. 'I'm not sure of anything. All I know is that he loves you more than you deserve it.'

'You're always behaving like he's some martyr!' Rabia spoke, her voice rising. 'Have you seen what his baby has done to my face and my body? At just three months?'

Saba was quiet. Rabia wouldn't have put on so much weight if she'd exercised and eaten healthy food. But who was going to tell her that?

'Look, all I know is that his love for you counts for something. And it's *your* baby too,' she said, walking away. From where had she got the courage to speak her mind in front of Rabia? From Shahid, obviously, who made her feel loved and cherished so that all insults bounced off.

When she was younger, she'd been convinced that she'd done something to upset or irritate her parents, because they never really seemed to notice her. Her confidence was often torn to shreds with Rabia's razor tongue and any feelings she had towards her family were deadened by Zohaib's indifference.

But over the years, she'd managed to come out of that shell and when she looked back now, she realized that it had been Shahid all along who had helped her at every step. She had turned to him whenever Rabia had been particularly caustic and she leaned on his shoulder whenever she needed to cry. And this was before he had even said that he loved her. Did she love him? She thought of him all the time. Every minute she wondered what he was doing and whether he was thinking of her. She made sure to share all the interesting things that had happened to her in college with him when they met. She replayed their conversations in her mind and she dreamed of his kisses. It sounded a lot like love. But like Rabia had asked, how could she be sure?

The doorbell rang and she went to open the door, wondering who it could be. Shahid was holding a helmet in his hands and he raised his eyebrows at her and smiled. She moved aside to let him in, aware that her father was sitting in the living room just five steps away, but she tried to convey with her eyes just how high her heart had soared when she'd seen him.

'Shahid! What are you doing here?' her father boomed when he saw him. Shahid walked into the living room, shaking his head and removing his jacket.

'There's some problem with my car so I've given it for servicing,' he explained as he sat down, without looking at Saba. Saba was aware of his pretence, of behaving as though she was no more important than a female relative, and she lingered near the living room before heading to the kitchen. Her father was insisting that Shahid stay for dinner.

'Shahid's come, Ammi,' she said, before realizing that she hadn't added 'bhai' at the end. Her mother turned to her from the stove, narrowing her eyes.

'Shahid?' she asked, and she turned back to flip the roti.

'Y-yes. Abbu's asking him to stay for dinner.' She escaped into the living room and found her father and Shahid deep in discussion about some trading issue and neither of them looked at her even though she lingered in the periphery.

Later, Shahid sat down with them at the dining table, protesting that he would go back home and eat but Abbu refused to listen. Throughout dinner, Saba stared at Shahid covertly, wondering what he had in mind.

'I had to drop off some stuff for a client this side of town,' he explained ambiguously when her mother enquired. 'Thought I'd drop by for a while.'

'Good! Good! You know, with Zohaib gone, it's so lonely here,' Ammi said.

'How's he?' Shahid asked casually and Ammi shook her head.

'Even now he's not telling us exactly when his flight is scheduled. The wedding is on 20 June and he has to get back in time. Why did he have to take this overseas assignment now?' she frowned.

Shahid looked impassive and Saba felt a little tingle of shock when she felt his toe touch hers. But that had been an accident because he didn't do anything after that and Saba was actually disappointed.

After dinner he sat down with Abbu for another hour and by then Saba was thoroughly irritated with him. She would just go to bed, she decided.

'Abbu, I'm going to sleep,' she said, looking at the clock pointedly. It was eleven-thirty. Shahid yawned and blinked furiously, shaking his head as if to clear something.

'Saba, could you make me a cup of tea before you go to sleep?' he asked, and Saba's head shot up. It was the first sentence he'd spoken to her since he'd come home.

'Tea?' she repeated, surprised.

She'd really planned on going to sleep and now she had to go to the kitchen again. Just as she was turning to go to the kitchen in a huff, Shahid yawned again and kept shaking his head.

'I didn't sleep last night, uncle. Busy with a few accounts,' he explained. He stretched and spoke again, 'Also, I haven't used this bike since college, but I've been on it since morning and I'm just so tired. I can't wait to go home and sleep.'

Her father said something and Saba went towards the kitchen.

'I know! I'm so sleepy, I doubt I'll be able to ride back home. That's why I asked for the tea.'

'Stay here tonight then,' her father said and Saba stopped in her tracks and turned around. What?!

'Zohaib's room is empty. Stay here tonight and go back in the morning,' Abbu said and Shahid refused. But by then Ammi had also joined the conversation. She too insisted that he stay the night in their house.

'Come on, Shahid! You can stay here tonight,' Ammi cajoled him. Shahid looked doubtful and then rubbing his eyes, he shook his head.

'I should have gone home straightaway instead of coming here. Ammi will be worried,' he said.

'I'm calling your mother and telling her that you're staying here tonight,' she said and got up to go towards the phone.

Shahid nodded, looking resigned.

'Okay! I'll stay the night,' he said and called out to Saba who hadn't entered the kitchen, still unable to believe the turn of events.

'Saba! No tea! I'll just go and sleep. Don't want to put you to any trouble on my account!' he said to Saba who looked at him nonplussed.

He had to pass by the kitchen to go upstairs to Zohaib's room and as he walked past her, he winked at her swiftly and Saba felt her breath catch in her throat.

Her mother switched off the light in the living room and her parents went to sleep. Their room was downstairs too, just not on the same side as Saba's room.

Saba stood inside her room, her heart beating at a mad tempo. What was he *doing* here? Without thinking consciously of what she was doing, she changed into her nightgown and brushed out her long hair and tied it at her nape. She scrubbed her face clean and emerged from the bathroom, dabbing her face with a towel. She sat down at the computer, where she saw that her blog had received five more comments, but she couldn't bring herself to even look at them. Her insides were as jumpy as a tadpole on steroids.

She shut down the computer and wondered if Shahid was really going to do something as daring as coming into her room in the night. She didn't have to wonder for too long. He opened the door and let himself inside, and locked the door behind him.

39

Shahid stared at her for a while and then made a move towards her, but she pre-empted him and together they slammed into each other kissing hungrily. When they broke apart for breath, Saba put her arms around his neck.

'What's going on?' she asked, even as she snuggled closer to him.

'Not yet,' he whispered and together they fell back on the bed and Saba felt a moment's panic because of the intimacy the bed offered. But he seemed content with kissing her, although his hands skimmed her arms and shoulders slowly.

'Okay. It's twelve now. Happy birthday,' he said, lifting his face from hers. Saba smiled lazily and pulled him down for another kiss which seemed to go on forever, until Shahid moved away and sat up on the bed. He ran his hands through his hair and was breathing heavily. Saba sat up slowly, an uncertain smile on her face. He ran a finger down her cheek and then shook his head.

'What?' she asked. She almost expected her parents to bang on her bedroom door to ask why her heart was beating so loudly.

He stood up and pulling out something from his pocket, he sat down on the bed beside her.

'Marry me,' he said, handing her the box.

'Now?' Saba joked as she took it in her shaky hands.

'Today. Tomorrow,' he said, rubbing his forehead absently.

Laughing, she opened the tiny box and saw that there was a ring.

'You don't like it?' he asked seeing her expression. Saba shook her head.

'No no! I. . .'

'You hate it!' he said, taking the box from her hands but Saba stood up.

'I never said that. It's just. . .it's just not my type. I mean, I'm really not the kind of girl to wear such a big ring on my finger. And what will I tell my parents and how will I explain where I got it and. . .' Saba realized she was blabbing. The ring was not hideous but, like she said, just not her type.

Shahid looked hurt. Saba wished she'd gone into raptures to please him but she couldn't fake such an important emotion.

'I was planning to speak to your parents about us after Zohaib's wedding,' he stated.

'I s-still have two more semesters in college,' she said.

'I know. But we could get married and you could finish your studies *after* that. My house is closer to your college, remember?'

Saba looked back at him shocked. 'When were you planning to tell me that you wanted to get married so soon?' she asked him.

'Tonight. I don't want to wait any longer, Saba. This. . .this is torture for me,' he said reaching out to take her hand.

'I turned twenty just ten minutes ago. I don't want to get married this year. Or maybe even next.'

'What do you mean?' he asked.

'I want to explore my writing options and see what I really want to do,' Saba said, pursing her lips. The thought had crystallized in her head after her college had won the drama competition earlier that year.

'So why can't you do that after we're married?' he asked, absently lifting her palm and rubbing it on his stubbly jaw.

'Ow!' Saba pulled her hand back. 'Everything changes when you get married! People get pregnant, their priorities change and nothing is the same!' Saba said, feeling a little bold as she knelt on the bed and ran her hands through his hair. 'Please?'

He moved away from her and stood up. 'Do you know what this means?'

'I. . .no. . .I don't know,' Saba said, dropping her hands and sitting down, feeling despair loom inside her. Was he going to walk out of their relationship?

He sighed heavily. 'It means that we're going to have to stay apart and meet each other as distant relatives like before. I can't touch you without wanting to do a lot more than what I should. And if we're going to wait, then I better remove temptation from my way, right?'

Saba was silent. 'Are you. . .are you breaking up with me?' she asked, her voice sounding hollow.

'Of course not! I love you and always will and if you're determined to wait for so long, then I have to manage somehow, right?' Shahid said, already backing away from her.

'But. . .'

'From now on, we're going to go back to what we were before I told you that I loved you. When we meet, we're going to be polite to each other and I. . .I won't be dropping you to college or home.'

'Stop!' Saba cried out. 'It sounds so horrible when you say all this!'

'Shh! Keep your voice down,' Shahid said. 'If you want us to get married on your terms, then you have to let me do the waiting on my terms. This isn't how I'd planned your birthday but. . .' he moved towards the door.

Saba ran and flung her arms around him. 'You're not going to be my boyfriend anymore?'

They stared at each other for the length of a heartbeat before he dipped his head to kiss her gently. 'Don't worry so much. I'm right here. I will always be,' he whispered into her mouth.

'But you're angry and. . .'

He shook his head. 'I'm not angry. Just trying to be practical. We can't keep doing this, Saba. We'll get caught one day and it can become ugly. I just wanted to avoid that so. . .I wanted to speak to your parents.'

Saba wiped the tears that rolled down her cheek as he unlocked the door. She couldn't let him go yet. She turned him around and his back was to the door as she kissed him desperately. She kissed his jaw line and then put her arms around his neck, hugging him tightly. The moment he'd said that he was willing to wait for her, she knew that she too loved him. But she wanted this reprieve almost as badly as she wanted him.

'Why do we have to become strangers?' she asked and Shahid sighed. 'I can't even call you? Or text you?'

He shook his head. 'I'm trying to make this easier for both of us,' he explained, extricating himself from her but she only pressed herself closer to him.

'You have to stop doing that,' he groaned.

'Why?'

'Because it makes me want to. . .' he swallowed and then shook his head. 'It makes me want to rip off your clothes right now and make love to you.' Saba's eyes grew round and she stepped back hesitantly.

'That is why we have to stay away from each other. The only thing is. . .' he stopped.

'What?' Saba asked, her eyes downcast. This emotional roller coaster was no fun.

'You know how much I love you, but. . .what if you. . .fall in love with someone else?' he forced the words out.

Saba's eyes were shining as she shook her head.

'How can I fall in love with someone else when I love you so much?' she asked him, each word painfully blocking her throat. His head whipped around to look at her and when he saw that she meant it, he pulled her to him and with a last agonizing kiss, he left her room.

Saba stood there for a full ten minutes after he left, unwilling to believe what had just happened. She turned to her computer table and saw that the box was still there. She opened it and slipped the ring on her finger.

40

Shahid had already left when Saba woke up that morning. Throughout the night she kept picking up her mobile every two minutes to call him so she could hear his voice again. But she didn't.

No one said there would be physical pain like this, she thought as she got ready for college that day. It was her birthday, but she didn't care. She wasn't in the mood to dress up and look pretty. She didn't want to go to college, but the semester was ending and she didn't want to miss classes.

Shahid had bought a light blue chikan kurta for her last week that she'd planned to wear today. A part of her secretly hoped that maybe this was a test of sorts because he just wanted her to tell him that she loved him. But she knew that he wasn't the type to play such games. He was honest and sincere and even now, he was thinking of her first.

She wanted him as her boyfriend, someone to hold her hand and kiss her and cuddle her and do all the lovely things that couples do, but marriage changed the equation immediately. Marriage meant responsibility and while she was willing to embrace that, she didn't want it so soon. Not while all her classmates were talking about doing their Masters or getting fancy jobs as technical writers or copywriters or going on to writing books or whatever.

In college, Riya took one look at her face and the 'Happy Birthday' scream died in her throat.

'Babe, what's wrong?' she asked, and dragged her to the

canteen where they spent most of the day talking over steel tumblers of coffee.

'I don't know what to say,' she said when Saba had finished talking. Saba looked down, her eyes centred on the ring he'd given her and she blinked at the tears that were about to fall.

'I mean. . .you're also right and he's also right,' she said when Saba didn't say anything. Saba looked up.

'You think I'm right?' she asked hesitantly. On the way to college, she'd kept thinking that maybe she was being mean and selfish and almost began to wonder what it would be like to get married after the semester got over.

'Of course! This was what I meant when I asked you what you wanted from your life. Now you know or, at least, you're willing to find out what it is, and you can't possibly throw it away. He's willing to wait, right?'

'Yes,' Saba sighed.

'You're behaving as though it's the end of the world,' Riya remarked and Saba looked up at her angrily.

'It feels that way,' she said, pointing her finger to her chest. 'It's actually hurting inside! I never thought I'd feel this way about anyone!'

Riya shook her head. 'But eventually you'll be getting married to him, right? That's what you want, no?'

Saba nodded and then she lifted her head. 'He wanted to speak to my parents after Zohaib bhai gets married.'

Riya shrugged. 'Good enough. That way your parents can fix up everything for later.'

'You think so?'

'Yeah, what's the harm?' Riya asked. 'Did you tell him not to?'

Saba shook her head. 'I suppose he can speak to them but it was so confusing last night and we both kind of got carried away in our goodbye kiss.'

Riya rolled her eyes. 'Goodbye kiss, my ass! He hasn't broken up with you, he still loves you, he's planning to wait for you. . .then what's your problem?'

'This whole stranger thing. God knows how long I'll have to wait before I can touch him again and. . .'

'Uh, could you lower your voice a bit?' Riya asked, although she looked like she was going to burst out laughing any moment.

'Huh? Why?' Saba asked, looking around.

'See that group of paavam kutties sitting there?' Riya asked, raising her eyebrow in the direction of a group of three girls who had been eating quietly from their lunch boxes.

Saba nodded.

'You might want to spare them your X-rated stories.'

Saba blushed and slapped Riya's hand. 'Shut up!' but she spoke in a lower voice.

'Look at you! A couple of months back you were just like them!' she said and Saba frowned.

'No way!'

'Anyway, he's your *cousin*! You'll see him every now and then. So what if he says you have to behave like strangers? You know you're not, right? And you can always think up interesting ways to be near him *and* not get into trouble.'

'What?' Saba asked, surprised.

'You're going to get into trouble *only* if you find yourself with him in a locked room, or some confined space where you will eventually end up doing you know what.'

Saba opened her mouth to say something but Riya spoke again, 'Look. Go back to being strangers or whatever, but given the kind of situation that's going to be in your house during your brother's wedding, I'm sure he won't be able to avoid you even if he wants to. And this whole hidden romance thing is so cute!'

Saba scrunched up her forehead. 'I suppose you're right. It

just feels odd not to turn to him for everything and talk to him till midnight, which is what we usually do. But I'll ask him to speak to my father once Zohaib bhai gets married.'

'Yes, do that. Feeling any better now?' Riya asked her.

Saba nodded and hugged her impulsively. The group of three girls was quietly packing their lunch boxes and placing them neatly inside their bags and Riya spoke through the side of her mouth. 'They probably think we're lesbians.'

That elicited another burst of laughter from Saba and together the two of them made their way to class.

That night her phone rang and she leapt towards it thinking it was Shahid. It was a number she didn't recognize.

'Hello?' she said cautiously.

'Hey!' the person at the other end sounded breezy and Saba felt a moment's recognition and a pang of dismay.

'Oh, it's you,' she said, keeping her voice down. Why the heck was he calling her at night?

'You never called back,' he sounded as though he was pouting and Saba curbed the urge to giggle.

'Sorry Uzair,' she said, but in her mind she added, 'was busy getting a boyfriend, falling in love, etc.'

He sighed loudly. 'I can't wait to get back to the UK. I hate this city, man. Can you believe how hot it's become?'

Saba listened to him as he went on about the traffic and the heat and finally told him that she had to study. He wanted to know if they could meet and luckily she had the excuse of her exams. Finally he hung up and Saba shook her head wondering how she could have had a crush on him.

Her phone rang again and she felt the now familiar line up of emotions when she saw it was Shahid. Her heart tightened in her chest, her face heated up and she smiled, realizing that he wouldn't be able to keep away from her as he'd thought.

'Hey!' she sounded upbeat and happy.

'You're sounding quite happy,' he spoke slowly.

'Just because I'm hearing your voice again,' she said, unable to suppress the emotion in her voice.

'I had so many plans for today,' he went on.

'Like what?' she asked.

'I'm saving it for next year or. . .whenever,' he said.

'Okay,' she said, wishing she could see him.

'I had to hear your voice,' he admitted and Saba closed her eyes in relief.

'I miss you so much it hurts physically,' Saba said, standing near her window.

'Don't say such things to me,' he spoke in a low voice and Saba smiled.

'Okay,' she said lightly.

'And could you move a little towards the centre? I can see only one side of you,' he said. Saba's face flushed as she opened the window to see his car parked in a by-lane.

'What are you doing here?' she asked, her voice down to a whisper.

'Just looking at your window, wondering if you'd come and stand there,' he said.

'You foolish, foolish man,' she chided him playfully. 'You're sounding more and more like Devdas. And in another country they might arrest you for stalking me.'

'Well, I was planning to spend this day with you and I have to settle for something less obviously,' he said.

'But how? I mean, what excuse would you have given my parents?' she asked puzzled.

'I'd already thought of something,' he replied. Before she could ask him what he meant, he continued, 'Did anyone in your family wish you for your birthday?'

Saba wondered at the change in his tone and the subject.

'No. No one remembered it was my birthday, but it's okay,' she said hurriedly, defending her family.

'Can you make some excuse to come outside?' he asked and Saba looked at the time. It was eight thirty.

'I don't step outside the house at this time at all,' she murmured. Her parents would find it odd if she wanted to go to the nearby shop to buy something at this time of the night.

'Okay, just come to the front door at least,' he said and Saba flew outside, wondering if he was there. She saw that her father was in his room and her mother was in the kitchen. She opened the door cautiously but no one was there.

She looked down and saw a small pastry box kept on the step. Heart thumping loudly, she picked it up and looked at the gate. It was dark and no one was there, but she heard the sound of a car revving and zooming away. She sighed and went back inside to her room to open the box.

She opened it with a smile and saw a small heart shaped chocolate cake with the lettering, 'I love you' in white icing.

So adorably conventional, she thought, but was thankful he hadn't given her cuddly toys. Why did guys think girls liked that stuff? Since she didn't have a knife, she used her fingers to scoop out a piece and she wished she could have shared it with him. It was a small cake and she hadn't had dinner yet so she was hungry and before she knew it, she had finished eating it all. She closed her eyes as she licked the chocolate frosting from her fingers, imagining she was licking it from his fingers or, better, his mouth, when she opened her eyes and saw Rabia standing there.

'What are you eating?' she asked.

41

R & R

May 12, 2012

Hey, read all the posts on your blog at one go. What happened on your birthday? And I hope you will put up pics of the wedding?

The Other T

May 12, 2012

Thank you R & R, but uh. . .pics would defy the purpose of this blog, right? I mean, I'll really get into trouble then and you wouldn't want that, would you?

Seema

May 12, 2012

So, what did T do finally? And how come you haven't posted anything yet? You can't leave us hanging in suspense like this!

The Other T

May 12, 2012

Before I say anything else, I'd like to know what you mean by 'us'? Are there others too? Why aren't they commenting? About T, it's a long story and I don't really know what to say, but we're staying apart for the time being now.

Seema

May 12, 2012

Nooooo!! Why are you staying apart from him? Is there any problem? A friend pointed out your blog to me when I was surfing the net randomly and I've been reading since then. She's been meaning to comment too, but never got around to it. Still waiting to hear about your sister and her husband.

Kunal

May 20, 2012

Nice! Sounds like you have an interesting life! Your blog is a good diversion when I don't have work and am simply yawning away. You really need to write more!

The Other T

May 20, 2012

Thanks! I'll try to. It's so nice to hear that people are reading my stuff. That will motivate me to write more often as I meant to.

It was good to have readers, Saba thought, even though they were strangers. In fact, it was best that they were strangers. This was her third attempt at starting a blog and it finally seemed to be taking off.

While the blog had started off as a medium for her to rant and complain about her brother's wedding, it had changed its tone over time. She realized she was using it as a sounding board for her own problems and feelings and that wasn't a good idea. It was best to keep the two separate.

She pulled out her Literary Criticism textbook and tried to study for a while but her thoughts went back to the day of her birthday. Rabia had looked very suspicious when she saw Saba eating cake, but of course she hadn't remembered that it was her birthday.

'How mean of you to eat chocolate cake without giving me some!' she exclaimed and Saba stared back at her, amazed at how much a pregnancy could change someone. Normally, Rabia abhorred chocolate cake.

'How mean of you to not even remember it's my birthday,' she retorted. Rabia raised her eyebrows but didn't say anything. Saba felt a little uncomfortable under her scrutiny and got up to wash her hands in her bathroom. When she came out, she was shocked to see Rabia looking at her phone, staring at the screen intently. Okay. This wasn't done. She couldn't just look at Saba's phone like that. Especially when it had messages from her boyfriend.

She walked up to Rabia and took the phone from her hands without saying a word. Thankfully, Rabia hadn't opened the messages folder. Rabia looked at her surprised and a bit taken aback. Then her eyes centred on the ring on Saba's finger.

'What's that?' she asked. Saba was getting annoyed with her sister. She was being nosy and rude and while that shouldn't have surprised her, she was feeling put out. Maybe it was the chocolate cake that she had just eaten, but she was feeling a little let down by her family for not having remembered her birthday. She didn't care about gifts but yes, an acknowledgment would have been nice.

'Nothing,' she said to Rabia who had bent her head to look closely with the expert and trained eyes of someone who wore diamonds regularly.

'That looks like a diamond to me,' she announced and Saba gulped. Diamond?

'Who will give me diamonds?' Saba said trying to change the topic and turned to switch on her computer. To her intense irritation, Rabia did not leave as she usually did whenever Saba sat down at the computer or opened up her books. She sat down on the bed gingerly and it took all of Saba's willpower to not ask her what she was doing in *her* room. Still, Saba kept her face averted from the bed because she was sure she would blush if she recalled Shahid there the previous night.

'What will I do?' Rabia asked and Saba turned to look at her.

'What do you mean?'

'I mean about this baby and my life. What will I do if I have to stay here?'

Saba looked at her puzzled. Rabia had never looked uncertain about anything in her life before. She had always expected everything to fall in place *for* her.

'Abbu and Ammi are so busy,' she went on. Saba sighed.

'They *are* busy. The wedding is in a month's time now!'

'Everything will change once she gets here,' Rabia spoke, narrowing her eyes.

'What do you mean?'

'Our life as we know it will never be the same. Abbu and Ammi will give her precedence over me. Or you,' she added as an afterthought and Saba shook her head.

'I don't see that happening,' Saba said and Rabia made a noise of irritation in her throat.

'Why do you always talk like you know everything? She's going to be their bahu, their daughter-in-law. And I'll be the married daughter who lives in her parents' house with a baby and a fat body.'

'But. . .'

'Yes, I know you said you can prove that. . .that Rafiq is not a jinn. But even then, I don't know if I want to live with him.'

Saba turned to face her fully. 'What do you mean?' she asked.

'Maybe it's my subconscious that dreamed up all this jinn business, but could it be because I don't want to live with him anymore?' Rabia asked her a question. For the first time in her life, Saba looked at Rabia properly, and not just as an annoying and glamorous elder sister.

'You're saying. . .'

'Yes, what if I don't want to go back to him, just because I don't like him? Shouldn't I be allowed to have a say?'

'For someone who was behaving as though he really was a monster, that's a remarkable way of turning things around,' Saba commented. Inside, she felt a deep thud. Whether or not Rabia thought her husband was a jinn, she had no plans of going back to him.

'You were going to prove it, right? Where's your proof?' Rabia turned the tables on her.

'Yes, but what's the point? You're saying that you want to stay right here,' Saba muttered.

'You really hate me, don't you?' Rabia asked and Saba looked at her again, surprised.

'No. I just. . .I just wish you'd treat me like your sister, that's all,' Saba said.

Rabia sighed. 'I don't know what to do anymore.'

'Give him a chance, Api,' Saba said and Rabia looked up shocked.

'You haven't called me Api since. . .'

'Since I was four years old and you locked me in the cupboard for taking your sketch pens,' Saba completed.

Rabia's face flushed. 'Maybe *I* am the monster,' she spoke.

'That's nonsense!' Saba said. Was it the hormones that were making Rabia so maudlin? Or was she actually changing?

'Look. Give me some more time and I'll prove that he's as human as you or me. Give him another chance. He loves you so much,' Saba said.

'That's what you think,' Rabia snorted.

'Why? Has he given you reason to think otherwise?' Saba asked.

'No, but. . .'

'But what?' Saba was getting irritated.

'I don't love him as much as he loves me!' Rabia admitted, although she looked pained as she said that.

'I'm twenty-six, having a baby and I don't love my husband,' she continued.

'So you're admitting this whole thing was an excuse?' Saba asked.

Rabia shook her head. 'No, I *do* think there's something strange about him, but. . .'

'Okay, here's what we'll do,' Saba said, getting up and sitting next to Rabia.

'I'm going to prove that he's a man, just like any other. And you're going to give him a chance to get back into your life. And having a baby is not such a bad thing. Lots of women have babies and are perfectly fine. About love. . .he loves you even if you don't love him and he'll do anything to keep you happy.'

'You really have grown up, haven't you?' Rabia asked her, looking at Saba as if for the first time.

Saba smiled, thinking how little she knew.

42

Not quite what I expected

Posted by The Other T, 20-05-12

Did you ever expect to bond with someone whom you couldn't stand until a few minutes ago? I felt that way when Q came up to me and spoke her heart out. Now I don't know whether to hate her, pity her or help her.

Anyway, here's the thing. T and I are not going to be together for a while because we feel that's the most prudent thing to do as of now. I still can't believe how we went from being a couple to this. . .this state which is neither here nor there.

T called me on my birthday but he hasn't called after that. It's been ten days since I heard from him and I feel miserable. My parents are going to invite people in other cities tomorrow and I heard that T has convinced my parents that he'll drive them down and his mother is accompanying them. Felt so odd when I heard this news from my father.

Just some time ago, I knew everything that T was doing, right from the moment he woke up to the time he went to sleep. Now, I felt bereft and although I'd always laughed at Hindi film heroines who sighed and lamented when their heroes were gone, I seriously know what it feels like now.

Y called to wish me late at night on my birthday and I was really surprised. He's not an affectionate brother and it often seems like I hardly figure in his head most of the time, as he seems to be wrapped up in his own problems. But I was pleasantly surprised to hear his voice.

He wanted to know how I had spent my day and I almost told him everything. The whole story of how T and I were not together any more, about how Q had actually come to my room and discussed her fears with me, and how I had just polished off a chocolate truffle cake that was leaving me a little queasy already. But I didn't, of course.

I asked him when he was coming back because, deep inside, I was a bit scared that he might decide not to show up. What would my parents do? It would be the disaster of the decade and much as I resented my parents for not giving me enough attention, I still loved them and didn't want them to be hurt or ridiculed.

He deliberated over his words, saying that his project should get over by 10 June and he'll be back soon.

'Are you sure?' I asked, wondering why it felt like he was hiding something.

'Yes, yes!' he assured me. 'But I could get delayed by a few days.'

We talked for some more time and he wanted to know if I preferred chocolates or perfume as a birthday gift. I couldn't quite make up my mind so I told him to get both.He sounded indulgent when he said goodbye and I ended the call thinking that it did help to be the youngest at times.

So that's that.

Saba hit the publish button and sat back, chewing the tip of her pinkie finger without realizing she was doing it. Would people comment straight away? Yeah, like they had no better work to do than lurk on her blog.

Sighing, she got up and stood near the window, wondering what Shahid was doing. This whole thing seemed silly in retrospect. They loved each other so they should be together and there were times when she felt that Shahid was just punishing her for not falling in line with him.

She was bored and she didn't want to study. It seemed that the last two months had been only about that. Studying or spending time with Shahid. She was feeling listless and she wanted to do something. She had just got back from college a while back, but it seemed like she hadn't spoken to Riya for ages, so she called her.

'Hey!'

'Hey yourself!' Riya replied.

'I'm bored,' Saba said.

'Yeah, and now that you don't have a boyfriend you think of me,' Riya joked. Beneath the banter, Saba realized that Riya was right. Although Riya had been thrilled for her, she had probably felt left out all the time that Saba had disappeared with Shahid. She felt a little uncomfortable when she realized how it must have been for Riya when she'd stopped sitting with her for lunch or going out with her to the nearby mall.

'I'm sorry,' Saba said.

'For what?' Riya sounded genuinely surprised.

'I. . .I've been ignoring you all these days and it wasn't nice of me,' she admitted quietly.

'And she sees the light! Hallelujah!' Riya chuckled and Saba laughed. She loved being friends with Riya because of the way she made her laugh and over-dramatized even ordinary things so that they looked out of focus.

'Oh please!'

'So, what do you want to do? Shall we go shopping?' Riya asked and Saba got up, shaking away the listless feeling that had been enveloping her for the last two days.

'Yes! Let's go to Comm Street. It's been ages since I went there,' Saba said, trying not to think of the last time she'd been there. It had been with Shahid when she'd first got an inkling of his feelings for her.

'Okay. As long as you stop moping around and looking like you have a non-communicable disease!'

'*Non*-communicable?' Saba asked as she got up and pulled out her handbag and burkha.

'Yeah! The kind you kids in love have? Like no one else gets how sad they're feeling when they're apart and all that? Like no one else can understand what you're going through?' Riya continued explaining and Saba wished she'd stop. She was feeling terrible already.

'I'll see you there in half an hour,' Saba said, hoping her voice wouldn't give away how much Riya's words had disturbed her. Had she been so full of herself? Acting like only *she* knew what it was to be in love?

Shaking her head, she left her room and went to tell her mother that she was going out shopping with Riya.

'Alone?' her mother asked. Her mother was in her room, stitching the falls onto one of the sarees that they had got for the bride.

'Yes,' Saba said.

'Okay, but try not to go out alone these days. We're thinking of getting you married soon and if people spot you on Commercial Street and all. . .'

Saba sat down with a thud.

'Ammi! I still have a year left in college! Don't talk of marriage now!' she said, looking at her mother almost fearfully.

Her mother shook her head. 'Not me, not me. It's just your father. He's worried with this Rabia thing and how it will affect you if she stays here. He's thinking of getting you married as soon as we get a good proposal for you. Also, all the aunts are asking why we're not getting you married first.' She looked at Saba as she pulled a thread with her teeth and snapped it.

'But. . .I'm a good student! I'm the class topper!' Saba almost screeched. 'You can't get me married off like that!'

Ammi shook her head. 'No one is getting you married tomorrow. Go now. Pah!'

What the heck was the matter with people that once a girl turned eighteen they *had* to start thinking of getting her married? God! This wasn't medieval India.

'Well, tell Abbu that I simply won't get married unless I finish my college,' Saba said. Obviously this wasn't the right time to ask her if she could study further. Saying so, she got up and left the house, feeling an odd mixture of dread about what the days ahead would bring and lightheartedness because she was stepping out of the house.

43

Shahid stepped out of his car and stretched. The day was already warm even though it was just seven in the morning. He turned around to see his mother and Saba's get down from the car, talking continuously about sarees, jewellery and the bride. Saba's father opened the passenger door in the front and he too stepped out.

They'd left Bengaluru early in the morning and had stopped for breakfast at Adyar Bhavan on the highway. Shahid felt a little guilty and shy when he was around Saba's parents now, but he was determined to put it behind him so he could continue to impress them. Since the journey had just started, both he and Saba's father had been quiet but not the two women who had been sitting at the back.

They talked so much that Shahid felt the air vibrate with silence now that he'd stepped away from their immediate circle. But he was happy he'd managed to help out uncle and aunty in one more way and he hoped it would mean a lot for them later.

Saba's mother echoed the same sentiments as they sat down at a circular table inside the crowded restaurant.

'What would we have done without Shahid!' she exclaimed as they started eating.

'Yeah, I'm the designated driver for Zohaib bhai's wedding,' Shahid joked as he poured sambhar over the hot vadas.

'No, no! You're more than that, beta!' Uncle protested. 'You're like my second son!'

Shahid felt a tiny nudge inside, once again that old feeling of guilt, because he'd been seeing their daughter behind their backs.

'No, it's all right,' he said and decided to be quiet.

They continued talking about the wedding preparations and his mind drifted to this morning when he'd gone to pick up uncle and aunty in his car. He hadn't planned on going inside because he didn't want to bump into Saba even accidentally much as he was dying to see her.

Their relationship had lasted for just a month, less than that actually, and yet when he told her that they had to stop seeing each other temporarily, it felt like he'd been with her for years. They'd skipped the getting to know each other phase in a relationship because they already knew each other so well. And in the brief time they were together as a couple, Shahid realized how right he'd been when he knew that Saba was the one for him.

It wasn't just her face that held him in thrall, or her dewy skin that he ached to touch more than he ought to. That was just the attractive package. But even if she'd been wrapped in brown paper, he'd have loved her for the way her mouth curled when she gave what he called her one-sided smirk, her expressive brown eyes, her hearty laughter and the honest way in which she enjoyed everything. She may have been shy with him at first, but he loved it that she didn't mind taking initiative even though what they did was pretty much tame stuff.

So he'd arrived at her house early, hoping she'd be asleep because then it would be easier to continue ignoring her, at least until the wedding. He'd kept the engine running and called uncle on his phone, all the while checking out the windows in her room. Her father said that it would be at least fifteen minutes before they left.

'Come inside. Let's have some tea before going,' he said and hung up.

Reluctantly, Shahid went inside with his mother to see Saba's mother running up and down the stairs like a little girl.

'I can't find my BP medicines. How will I. . .?' She didn't complete the question as she saw them and smiled but before she could say anything further, she ran into the room muttering something about picking out the right slippers.

'She's becoming more scatterbrained as she ages,' his mother commented and Shahid pulled out his phone from his pocket, checking old messages unnecessarily. Saba emerged from her mother's room. Shahid steeled himself to behave normally and not stare at her like a thirsty man in a desert looking at an ice cold glass of water.

'I told you to pack last night, but would you listen?' she called out and stopped when she saw Shahid and his mother. Ignoring Shahid, she smiled at his mother who went inside to help Saba's mother.

'You'd think she would have finished packing last night,' she said to fill the sudden silence that had sprung up when the two of them were alone.

Shahid didn't say anything. He just stared back at her, wishing he'd never made that stupid decision to stay away from her. It was just ten days since he'd seen her and yet it felt longer than that. She was dressed in a pale blue nightie and she flung her dupatta around her shoulders looking a bit self-conscious.

Between them the silence sighed with many unspoken words until she finally spoke quickly, as though she had to say something before the words would evaporate.

'I've missed you so much.'

He nodded briefly and took a step forward, to just run the back of his finger on her soft downy cheek when he heard uncle's voice coming from upstairs. He stepped back immediately and saw the flash of impatience on her face before she went to the kitchen to make tea. Normally, he would have followed her inside and chatted with her as before, but he didn't want to get into close proximity with her especially with her parents around.

He sat down on the sofa waiting for his mother and her parents to get ready. Finally they emerged and Saba brought out a tray with four cups. She sat down on the armrest of the sofa where her mother was sitting, checking the contents of her handbag. Shahid didn't look at her and concentrated on drinking his tea, listening to uncle giving Saba instructions.

'If you're going to college today, wake Rabia up and make sure she's downstairs before you go,' he said. She nodded and took a sip of the tea.

'Tell her to keep the doors locked and open them only when the maid comes and when Aunty comes. I'd prefer if you didn't go today actually,' he continued and Saba looked annoyed.

'I have a viva today. I have to go,' she said. Her father nodded grimly and Shahid looked at the two of them, already missing not being a part of her immediate life.

'At night, make sure you lock the doors and the gate properly and. . .'

'Abbu. I'm twenty. Not two. Now please go and get started!' she said getting up. They all drank the tea quickly and left with brief farewells.

Shahid was the last to leave. He lagged behind the others and when they'd stepped outside the house, he turned around to say 'bye' to her when Saba grabbed his hand and pulled him away from the door and pressed a hard kiss on his lips.

'Drive safely,' she murmured and let go of him, touching the stubble on his jaw with her fingertips.

He smiled at the memory of that brief kiss and realized that his plan was not only foolish, it was impractical. How was he going to avoid her when he'd be in their house all the time next month?

When he tuned into the talk around him, he realized that they had also been talking of Saba. His throat dried when he actually heard what the discussion was about.

'You know Nausheen, I'm only telling this to you and no one else because you're like my very own sister,' Saba's mother went on and Shahid saw that uncle looked uncomfortable.

'But we're very worried for Saba because of Rabia staying in the house. What will we tell people when they ask why our married daughter is living with us? And Zohaib also made a fuss about getting married, *now*. For weeks we were worried about what will happen.'

Shahid's mother looked worried. 'Why didn't you tell me before?' she asked.

Saba's father intervened. 'See, Rabia can stay in my house for the rest of her life if she wants. She's my daughter first. But it also means that I have to get Saba married quickly before talk spreads that Rabia is not living in her own house. I *have* to get her settled fast or what will happen to her?'

Shahid looked from one worried face to the other, feeling panic spread inside his chest because he'd planned for some more time before talking to Saba's parents.

'And she says she doesn't want to get married now,' Saba's mother said ruefully. Shahid cleared his throat.

'I think she's right. Let her finish her studies first,' he said when all three looked at him, wondering what made him step into a discussion that was purely for adults. Adults who could choose at their whim about *his* status as an adult in their presence.

'No, I'm right,' he forced himself to go on. 'Our community needs more educated people, especially women, and Saba is so bright and intelligent. Don't throw it away because you *think* she won't be able to get married easily.'

'Shahid! All you young educated people don't know how the actual world works,' his mother spoke and smiled at him slightly. 'You think it's all so easy and. . .' She stopped when she saw the look on his face.

'Yes, but give her a chance, no? What's the harm in letting her at least finish her studies?' Shahid asked, wondering if Saba would ever know that he'd fought for her.

'We're just afraid. . .that she might get involved with someone, like how it happened with Rabia,' Saba's mother spoke uncertainly as she mixed sugar into her filter coffee.

'Too late,' Shahid muttered softly but, unfortunately, or fortunately, there was a lull in the noise in the restaurant and all three of them heard him.

'What? What do you mean?' uncle asked him, glaring until it looked like his eyes would pop out. 'Has she. . .'

Shahid sighed and took a deep breath.

'I need to ask you something, Uncle,' he said.

All three faces looked at him expectantly.

44

Maintaining the status quo in a relationship is really important. Just like making sure both sides of an equation were balanced. Rabia, who had not been very good at studies, had always been fascinated with balancing equations in Chemistry and had managed to get them right all the time. For some reason, there had been an innate sense in her which knew how to redress the balance.

At present, the equations in her life were so imbalanced that they were in danger of toppling over each other and bringing her down in the process. And it had all started because of this baby.

She wasn't interested in it so she hadn't done what all expectant mothers usually did. She had not bought a book that explained the birth process in graphic detail. Nor had she started looking at cute posters of chubby babies. 'Let them take it out whenever they have to,' she thought. But when the first fluttering started in her belly, she almost wished there had been someone with whom she could share it. To describe how funny it felt. How strange. And almost wonderful.

It was on the morning when her parents left for Chennai. She'd woken up briefly in the morning when she heard car doors slamming and she knew it was probably that bloody idiot Shahid. He must have done it on purpose, just to make sure that she would get up. She had a good mind to get up and yell at him from the window but, of late, she'd felt so ashamed of her appearance that she didn't meet anyone other than her immediate family.

It had been weeks since she'd looked at a mirror and even when she went for a bath, she did it hurriedly, without looking at her stomach, fearing that she might spot ugly red striations as she'd once seen on the stomach of a pregnant woman in the beauty parlour.

She turned to the other side when her father opened the door of her room. He thought she was asleep. He hadn't spoken to her much since that day when he'd brought Saba into the discussion. He skimmed his hands briefly over her head and then she heard some muttering and she felt his breath blow above her head. Even though her eyes were shut, she smiled. When she'd been little, she used to insist that her father read some dua for her, a special blessing and blow it over her head every night. 'But you know them too!' he'd protest and she'd only shake her head and say, 'But I want *you* to pray for me.' And he would, every single night, for his princess.

She decided to turn around and talk to him but he had already headed back downstairs. Just then, she felt her stomach lift a little and drop. Almost as if she were on a roller coaster and, instead of dipping downwards, her stomach had tipped backwards.

Was this. . .the baby moving? Wasn't it too early? Should she go and ask Ammi? By the time she would have managed to get up, they would have left. Still, she made an effort and got up, pushed her feet into her slippers, wishing for her furry ones back in that house and got up. She padded downstairs slowly and was on the landing when she heard the byes being called out. And she saw something that stunned her.

Shahid was leaving when Saba pulled him towards the side and kissed him! What! Rabia blinked, wondering if she was in some weird dream.

She saw how Shahid wrapped his arms around Saba's waist and nodded to something she'd said and he squeezed her gently before letting go. Saba stood staring after him and then finally shut the door, leaned back against it and shut her eyes, her head tilted upwards, her palm resting on her heaving chest.

When she opened her eyes, she saw Rabia standing on the staircase and she lost her composure for a few seconds before smiling at her.

Instead of attacking Saba over what the hell was she doing *kissing* Shahid, she found herself saying, 'I think the baby moved.'

Saba's eyes lit up and she ran up the steps until she came to her and rested her palm on the slight swell of Rabia's stomach.

'Really? Can I feel it?'

The question and the action redeemed her a little in Rabia's eyes, though she shook her head. 'I saw you by the way,' she added.

'Hmm?' Saba pretended she didn't understand as she tucked a strand of her hair behind her ears.

'I saw you kissing Shahid. What's going on?' Rabia asked and Saba's face flushed.

'I. . .'

'What is *wrong* with you?' Rabia asked, thinking that maybe Saba needed to be told about how stupid she was being.

'I. . .'

'How could you?' she asked, walking downstairs gingerly.

'I'm in love with him, Api,' Saba said finally and walked downstairs with her.

'Love? What do you know about love?' Rabia scoffed at her.

Saba made a sound of impatience. 'Of course I know about love! I can feel it inside when I see him. And. . .'

'And?' Rabia asked almost fascinated. Saba had never looked this interested about anything other than her books.

'And I can feel the rush, the heady sense of power when he looks at me as though I'm the only woman for him,' Saba completed, but she shook her head. 'It's more than that. But I can't put it into words even though. . .even though I write so much. Everything I'd say would only sound like a cliché, but what can I do? All these stupid clichés are true!'

Rabia stared back at her, a little surprised and wary but also amazed. What she'd said almost sounded like the way she'd felt about Rafiq in the earlier days.

'Please don't tell Ammi and Abbu about this?' Saba pleaded.

Rabia shut her eyes and opened them, wondering if she'd find herself back in her bed and all this to be a dream after all.

'Please, Api?' Saba repeated and Rabia shook her head amazed.

'Fine. I won't tell them,' Rabia said, disconcerted at all the changes happening around her. Saba left for college an hour later, relaying all of Abbu's instructions to her.

With nothing to watch on TV on a Saturday morning, Rabia thought back to Shahid and Saba. The two of them had always stuck together right from the time they were kids, with Shahid bossing over anyone who tried to come near Saba. They deserve each other, she thought, with a flash of irritation when she remembered the look in Shahid's eyes this morning and the one in Saba's when she spoke of him. It made her feel melancholy.

A while later, she got up and walked to Saba's room. Zohaib had his own laptop which he'd taken when he went and there was only one other computer in the house which was in Saba's room.

She switched on the computer intending to check Facebook and while she was at it, she'd even look at some baby websites to see what she could learn about having a baby.

The computer hummed to life and the monitor started

with a blink and she lingered over the bookmarks, trying to spot Facebook. As she scrolled down towards it, her eyes came across a website and the mouse stopped. Rabia felt herself grow still but the sound of the fan was like a whine. Or maybe it was just the blood pounding in her ears.

Saba had found and bookmarked a website about jinns. Had she found out the truth? Why hadn't she told Rabia about the results? Her stomach dipped again slightly and Rabia looked at it in amazement. Then, taking a deep breath, she clicked on the website and she rested her hand on her stomach lightly for the first time ever, wondering if this was maternal instinct.

The page opened and Rabia blinked at the amount of information there was. It was an FAQ page about jinns. Oh well. The internet had plenty of uses apparently.

Some guy wanted to know how he would know if he'd been possessed by a jinn. Rabia read the answer that had been given to him with interest but soon lost focus and moved to the next question. She read the questions one by one until she came to one that made her pause and gather her thoughts.

Ten minutes later, Rabia closed the window and shut down the computer. She needed to think. According to the website, a human could get married to a jinn. But they could never have a child. And here she was, pregnant. So obviously, Rafiq was. . .human. The thought punctured a hole in the alternate reality that she'd forced herself to live in these past couple of months.

So what Saba had said was perfectly correct. He did love her. He was a charismatic man and that could be the reason why he succeeded in all his endeavours and not because he had some supernatural powers. Rabia felt foolish, exceedingly foolish, and she wondered why Saba hadn't told her about this discovery. Or maybe she'd been too engrossed in her own love story to be bothered, she thought.

The thought that she was no longer the prime focus in the lives of her parents was frightening. They loved her, but when this new girl joined them next month, everything would change. And then there was Shahid who would most likely join their family too. She *had* to go back to her own house, to Rafiq, whether she liked it or not. It was time she started balancing *these* equations in her life.

Slowly and deliberately, she picked up her phone and dialled Rafiq's number, wondering if she was too late. He'd stopped coming home and he hadn't called or texted her in days. At that time she'd been relieved not to have any reminder of him but now she was worried. What if she'd lost that ultimate control she'd had over him? But as the phone rang and he didn't answer, she knew that she'd have to do more than just call to redress this balance.

45

Good news/Weird news

Posted by The Other T, 24-05-12

I have some good news and some very weird news.

My parents came back from Chennai and Abbu called me to the hall to sit with them. I felt a little nervous when Abbu started talking about how Q being in the house could affect my future prospects.

I looked at him annoyed but then proceeded to tell him the good news. Q had gone back to her husband. Just like that. She called him on Saturday morning after my parents left but he didn't come home until evening. I opened the door and saw him standing there, looking expectant but also very sad.

'Q called me,' he explained and I let him in. He didn't go upstairs to her room which he'd used as his own during Y's engagement. He waited for her downstairs and when Q came down, she looked so much better! She'd exfoliated her face so it gleamed and she'd shampooed and conditioned her hair (after ages I'm sure) and she looked almost like the Q we used to know.

Her husband couldn't believe his eyes as she came and sat next to him and told him that she wanted to go back home. I couldn't believe my ears either. Earlier that day she'd seen T and I kissing. Yes, I know! Q saw us! Can you imagine? And what were we doing kissing when we weren't supposed to be together? Long story, which I might or might not tell you later on.

So, was this move precipitated by that? I had no idea. Her husband took her hand and pressed it tightly, looking all the while as though someone had just saved him from life imprisonment. He pressed kisses on her hand and got up, telling her hoarsely that he wanted her to come right away.

Yeah, right. Go back home now, just when we were beginning to bond, and leave me alone with Bawdy Aunty1, I thought irritated. Bawdy Aunty1 was sleeping in *my* room ever since she'd arrived that afternoon.

Q turned to me and sounding quite imperious, much like her old self, she said, 'Help me pack my bag.'

Abbu was shocked when I told him about this new development.

'She didn't even call us before going! Is she all right? She had that whole. . .problem with him, remember?' he asked. Ammi, who had just emerged from the room after freshening up, looked stunned.

'Q went back? With him?' she squeaked.

When Q and I were packing her things, I asked her why the sudden decision to go back. She shook her head and continued folding her clothes.

'Come on, Api! You have to tell me!' I protested.

With a sigh, she went on to explain how she'd come across the website and how the biggest proof that he was human was the baby growing inside her body. (I haven't mentioned it before, but Q was under the notion that her husband was a jinn. Yes.)

And so, she left.

Ammi and Abbu looked at each other as though wondering whether to tell me something or not. Then finally Abbu sighed deeply.

'There's something we want to talk to you about,' he announced.

And then they went on to tell me that T had said he wanted to marry me.

WHAT? Why hadn't he told me anything?

'I know you might find this a bit strange, considering you're cousins and all. But you're not even first cousins and even first cousins get married in our families. So, I wanted to ask you if this is fine.'

How could I tell them without revealing anything? Finally, I nodded and Abbu and Ammi looked so relieved. So they *had* wanted me to marry him, I thought, feeling pleased. I muttered a quick prayer to Allah, thanking him for making everything work out.

Then Ammi started talking about the wedding. At first I assumed it was Y's she was talking about. Then to my horror, I realized that she was talking of *my* wedding with T.

'But I still have to finish my studies!' I protested.

'Yes, yes! T says he'll wait,' Ammi assured me. 'It will be such fun!' Ammi went on. 'I almost can't wait!'

Abbu looked at her and shook his head and smiled. 'I want to talk to Q and see how she's doing,' he said and got up.

Ammi got up to follow him and then she turned around and said something, which is where the weird news bit comes in.

'Oh, and you can't go out in front of T now. He can't meet you or see you until you two get married.'

WHAT?!

But the wedding isn't until. . .a couple of years! Where earlier Riya had reassured me that I would meet him at some family function or when he came to my place, this wasn't what we had expected.

'But. . .' I sputtered.

Ammi turned around and shook her head. 'You're not to come in front of him when he visits the house, okay?'

'Why?' I croaked. First T didn't want to meet me on the sly and now my parents weren't going to let me meet him in our house!

'That's the custom. Do you think Y has gone and spoken to his wife? No. We don't let the boys and girls meet before marriage. You know that, right?' she explained.

I felt my stomach sink. Did this mean that I couldn't spend time with T at all?

Ammi continued, 'I can't tell you how happy I am! We couldn't have asked for a better damaad! He's *such* a good boy. Your Abbu was worried about how Q being here would affect your chances and T quietly said that he'd like to marry you, but only after you finish your studies. Isn't he such a sweet boy?' she asked.

Sweet boy? I wanted to strangle him. Did he know about this? About how we weren't supposed to meet now? Even as cousins?

'I don't know how we'll manage during the wedding, but everyone is going to know about you two now, so we'll find a way to make sure you don't see him.'

I seriously, seriously, wanted to cry.

46

It was the first week of June and Saba's mother realized that now her unmarried daughter was almost engaged. Which meant that she had to wear clothes befitting a girl who was spoken for. Fresh arguments erupted at home and with each day that brought 19 June closer, there was the added worry that Zohaib hadn't returned from France yet.

'I can't imagine why you couldn't have done this before,' she told Saba as they got down from the auto.

Saba kept quiet because she was sure that if she said something, she'd probably yell at her mother. She had *exams* for God's sake! When were these people going to understand that? Just because she wasn't in a professional course, it didn't mean that her exams were irrelevant!

'It's already three days into June now. I don't know if Khaja will stitch your clothes in time,' Ammi muttered as they walked into an air conditioned showroom. Saba remembered the last time they'd been here buying the mithai pink ghagra for the bride and she shuddered. She hoped Nausheen aunty had better taste or Shahid would get an earful from her. Whenever they got married or formally engaged.

Saba banished all thoughts of Shahid as she concentrated on what her mother was saying and realized that she too had been talking of Shahid.

'I don't know what his favourite colour is! What if I buy something for you that he. . .'

'Ammi!' Saba spoke, her voice sounding as though it had

changed texture. 'He's *not* going to be seeing me. So does it really matter what I wear?' Ammi held her gaze for a moment.

'Yes, you're right. But his mother will and there will be photos which I'm sure he'll want to see and. . .'

'Oh God!' Saba rolled her eyes. 'His mother is your friend and cousin and. . .' She stopped at that. She couldn't possibly tell her mother that Shahid wanting to see her photos was *so* archaic. When all he had to do was give her a call asking her to meet him outside her college and she'd go running.

In the end, Saba chose a mustard yellow salwar kameez dress material that had to be stitched. It had gold sequins on the edges of the border and very pretty zari work that added to its elegance. Saba held it against her body and looked at her reflection in the mirror, wondering if Shahid would ever see her in it.

She was glad that things were working out for them. However, there was also a tremor of unease when she thought of marriage. She folded the dress material and looked at Ammi who was talking to Abbu on the phone.

'Yes, I know. Okay. We'll be back in an hour. Hmm,' and she ended the call and looked at Saba.

'You're sure you don't want anything else from here?' she asked and Saba shook her head.

'Don't you think we should call Khaja and see if he'll stitch these clothes in time?' Saba asked, as she ran her hands over the yellow silk.

'You do that. I'll pay and come,' Ammi said and she got up taking the dress with her. Saba pulled out her phone and tamped down her irritation. Why the heck was Shahid ignoring her *now*? He had been incommunicado since they had come back from Chennai and this whole talk of their marriage had sprung up. Couldn't he have called at least once, just to tell her how happy he was? Or anything?

She was searching for Khaja's number on her phone when a voice called out to her.

'Hey! How are you?'

Saba turned around and shut her eyes for a second. God, no! Uzair was standing near a counter and next to him was the bride's mother. And that girl standing next to her was the bride herself!

Both parties were embarrassed for various reasons but they hadn't actually noticed the other's embarrassment. Saba was mortified, because if he spoke about them meeting over coffee, the bride's mother would surely wonder what she had been up to. The bride's mother, however, turned red as she tried to pull back Uzair who had already started walking towards her.

Saba looked around frantically to see where her mother was. She had finished paying the bill and was just receiving the bag and Saba realized that this clash was simply going to happen.

Uzair and her mother reached her almost at the same time.

'You never called me again!' Uzair said smiling, and Saba felt a sickening lurch inside her when her mother spoke.

'Come, let's go.' But her mother stopped when she saw Uzair.

'Call?' she asked, looking from one to the other. 'Who's he?' she asked Saba, eyes narrowing. Then she remembered and her eyes widened.

'You! What are you doing here?' she asked him.

Saba looked at both of them helplessly and watched the bride's mother walking towards them. This situation had just got a hundred times worse now. Saba felt her insides clench as her mother waited for her to answer. Instead, Uzair spoke.

'We met for coffee some days back,' he said warmly.

The bride's mother had hurriedly dispatched the bride outside, to another shop probably, and she came to give her regards to Ammi, who was looking at Saba and then at Uzair.

'Salaam!' she said and smiled, all the while looking a little sheepish as she tried to tug Uzair's arm.

Ammi snapped her head at her and was surprised. She faltered a bit and then smiled back at the woman.

'So, you also shop here?' she asked and Ammi nodded.

'We bought the engagement ghagra from here,' Ammi explained. Saba wondered if it was possible for them to quietly escape, but then Uzair spoke again.

'Great seeing you again! You never told me what your name was, you know. Even on the phone that day?' he smiled, not understanding the havoc he had just unleashed.

'Phone?' Ammi repeated and she looked at the bride's mother.

'Where's the bride?' Saba asked suddenly, hoping to divert the attention from herself. Predictably the bride's mother blushed as though *she* were getting married and Ammi was her mother-in-law.

'Come, come! We should go now!' she said and dragged Uzair away, who looked mutinous. She could be heard muttering something as they both went away and Ammi was left with Saba.

'Could you explain what that was all about?' Ammi asked her coldly.

Saba watched the bride's mother leaving with Uzair, wondering what she would think when he would tell her that *she* had called him and they had met for coffee. She cringed inwardly and then realized that her mother was waiting for her to speak.

'I. . .I. . .' Saba faltered wondering how she could possibly get out of this without getting into any trouble.

'I met him once near college,' she said finally.

'What? Why? How did he know where your college is?' Ammi asked, her voice sharp. Saba knew that this inquisition would never end and it would all boil down to *how* she got his number. What would she say then?

'I don't know. I think he was passing by and saw me,' Saba lied, but her mother didn't look like she believed it.

'And you went and had coffee with him? Alone?' Ammi was now looking outraged.

'I. . .No! Riya was with me,' Saba amended quickly.

'Even then? What were you thinking? He's the bride's cousin! What will they think of us? What will they say when they hear that the bridegroom's sister is so forward and. . .'

Momentarily relieved that the danger was out of the way, Saba felt she could get exasperated without getting into trouble.

'Come on, Ammi! Let's go home,' she said, tugging her arm. 'We still have to find out if Khaja will stitch my clothes or not.'

Ammi allowed herself to be pulled outside although she wanted to pursue the matter.

'What was he saying about a phone call? Did you call him?' Ammi asked. Saba pretended that she didn't hear what Ammi was saying as she walked briskly to the end of Commercial Street where they could get an auto.

'Imagine what Shahid will think if he hears of this!' Ammi said as they got inside an auto and Saba bit the inside of her cheek. Yes, what would he say? That he had helped her get the number?

Saba kept quiet, thinking that maybe she should try texting him again. Surely he wouldn't delete them like before? When they reached home, Ammi was still muttering about the ill-mannered boy and Saba went straight to her room, switched on the fan and sat on the bed heavily. Would he respond to this message? She wondered as she pulled out her phone and typed a swift text message to him, saying, 'Guess who I met today?'

She felt gratified when her phone rang almost immediately.

47

The final countdown

Posted by The Other T, 04-06-12

In around two weeks, Y will be getting married. My exams start next week. I can tell you exactly how much studying I've been doing. Nothing. Zilch. I'll probably fail this year and will join the list of all those girls who get engaged and then flunk their exams because they are too distracted to study.

Y has promised that he will be here in India by 15 June and Ammi and Abbu are very busy getting the house painted. Ammi also insisted on getting Y's room renovated (read, removing his cricket posters which he'd put up when he was a teenager).

Things seem better with Q. She was surprised to hear that T and I were almost engaged and I was quite sure that if she had been the old Q she might probably have blabbed off to Ammi about what she'd seen. But now that she was back with her husband, who was so happy you could probably strike a match off him, she was looking so much better. She also seemed calmer now.

Q and I are not like best friends now or anything. But we can tolerate each other and she doesn't treat me as something that was squashed on the sidewalk recently. She's also got some of her attitude back, and to be truthful I'd missed it. I mean, I missed laughing about it behind her back with T.

T is driving me crazy! He proposes to my parents (sounds weird, no? Like he's marrying them instead of me) ten days after he and I temporarily break up. And then he just disappears. Not a call or text. But I managed to get him slightly jealous yesterday and he called back immediately. What a relief it was to have him talking to me again! It felt like I'd been standing under the relentlessly beating sun and getting my skin parched. And hearing his voice was like a cool shower, washing away all the doubts and worries.

He was quite put out when I told him that I met the Idiot. Yes! That's how I made him jealous, although he says he wasn't jealous at all. Just concerned.

'I can't believe this is happening,' I told him.

'What? Us?' he asked.

'Umm. But this whole thing sucks!' I complained.

'Why?'

'You're not meeting me *outside* the house. My mother won't let me meet you *inside* the house. And you don't call or talk or text. What am I supposed to think?'

'You're supposed to think of how much I love you,' he chuckled and I smiled.

Finally, changing the subject we got talking about Y.

'I hope he'll be back in time,' I relayed my worries to him. 'Couldn't he have gone all these days? Why now? Just before the wedding. And you know, right, that he wanted to call off the wedding? I'm scared he might decide not to come at all!'

There was silence and then Shahid spoke. 'There's something I need to tell you,' he said slowly.

'Hmm?' I asked, idly drawing patterns on the bedspread with my finger.

'It would be better if I explained to you in person, but I doubt we'll get any speaking done if we meet,' he said and I blushed. He was right.

'So, it's about your brother.'

And then he went on to explain to me that Y had had an affair with some girl in his office last year. He broke up with her and she got transferred to another city. But she was back now and she would be his immediate boss when he came back from France. And she wasn't taking the whole break up thing easily.

'Why didn't you tell me earlier?' I asked, shocked.

'He told me this in confidence,' T explained.

'Then why did you say it now?' I asked.

He sighed. 'I thought it would make you understand his motives better. He will come back for the wedding, I'm sure. So don't worry.'

'Don't worry?' I exploded. 'Stop being so patronizing! You gave him the idea to run off to another country and what's going to happen when he returns? She's still his boss, right?'

'Yes. But he'll be married by then, so. . .'

'Oh, that poor girl,' I said.

'Who?' he asked.

'The bride,' I clarified. She had no idea of the drama taking place here.

'Yes. . .but. . .'

'He should come clean with her,' I said, feeling angry at my brother.

'That's what I've told him,' Shahid explained patiently.

'Does this other girl know he's getting married?' I asked.

'No, she doesn't know. And it's better that way, or she might come to the wedding and make a scene!'

'Oh my god!' I exclaimed. I knew it. If everything around us was going so smoothly without any hitches, there was some trouble in the offing. This had just been the calm before the storm.

'What will happen?' I asked him, my stomach working itself into knots.

'Relax! He doesn't want anyone in his office knowing that he's getting married. He'll join work after the wedding. It will all work out.'

'Uh oh!' I said, my neck breaking out into a sweat.

'What?'

'You should have told me this before,' I licked my dry lips.

'What happened? What did you do?' T sounded concerned.

'I. . .I sent an email invite to his colleagues at work,' I said.

'What? Why would you do that? How did you get their addresses?'

I gulped. 'I. . .I thought since he's abroad, he might not have the time to call anyone. So I scanned the card and sent the attachment to his colleagues. I got the emails from an email he'd once forwarded to me.'

There was silence.

'I was just being helpful! I had no idea about. . .say something,' I urged, getting a little worried.

'Nothing. What can I say? What's done is done. You can't undo it,' he said.

'But. . .'

'I'm not blaming you. I should have told you.'

'Yeah. You weren't talking to me, remember?' I said.

'Shows what lack of communication can lead to. I suppose we can just hope that she won't turn up there,' he replied.

'Shouldn't we tell Y?'

'No! No, don't do that or he really won't turn up for the wedding,' T said.

'I've got a coward for a brother,' I stated, feeling angry at Y once more.

'It's easy to judge others but. . .'

'Oh please!' I cut off T. I didn't want anyone to defend Y.

'Okay,' he sighed.

We talked for some more time and I held on to the quality of his voice, wondering when I'd hear him again.

'My exams start on Monday,' I said, trying to prolong the call.

'So why are you talking to me instead of studying?' he asked.

I rolled my eyes. 'X says that I'm a lost cause,' I said.

'Huh?'

'It's so hard to study when all I can think of is you,' I replied, grinning a bit. Okay, mental note. Never say never. I had never thought I'd say this to a *guy*. I'd even laughed at mushy couples and made fun of them relentlessly with X. And here I was. Sometimes I couldn't believe the things that came out from my mouth.

T was quiet again.

'Why do you say such things to me when you want us to get married after two years?' he asked, just as I was wondering if I should end the call.

'I don't even understand the stuff I say these days,' I countered lightly.

'No, think about it. You say you want to do something, studies. . .whatever, and I'm okay with that. You wanted time and you have time. But you say these things which make me. . .'

'When we get married, everything will change, T!' I said, understanding my own motives only then.

'Of course,' he said impatiently.

'No, I mean, we won't be this lovey-dovey couple any more. We'll have to be respectably married and that's okay when we do get married. But until then why can't we just behave like two foolish young people in love?'

He laughed shortly at that.

'Foolish, that's right.'

'And why are you being so stuck up about meeting me?'

'I thought I told you. . .'

'But that won't happen every time!' I protested.

'But. . .'

His constant protests had really begun to grate on my nerves. Why was I protesting when he didn't seem to care at all?

'You know what? Don't bother. I'll meet you *after* we get married, Mr T,' I said and ended the call and dropped my cell phone on the desk with a clatter.

I thought he might call back but he didn't. One more of his ploys to get me to cool down, I thought. At that time it had felt so good, but now it seemed foolish. If he didn't call me, then I couldn't possibly call him back, even to hear his voice. I would lose face and he would take me for granted. Who said that this love business was easy? Could they please come and stand here while I bring out the gun?

48

Two things happened on Sunday. Abbu had invited all the relatives for lunch even before Saba had woken up. The excuse for this sudden get together was that the dry fruit packets had arrived and they needed to be packed with the candies in small boxes which would be given to all the wedding guests next Sunday.

Now, this was a labour intensive job, and Abbu knew that all the youngsters would love doing it, so without even consulting his wife or his daughter, he called up everyone and *then* informed his wife. Of course it was reason enough for another fight, because Ammi figured she had to cook for so many people without any prior notice. Saba could hear them shouting from their room and she came out of her room shaking her head.

'She has exams tomorrow! How will she help?' Ammi shouted.

'But we don't have time at all! The wedding is next Sunday!' Abbu retorted.

'You could have at least told me last night! Why didn't you discuss before calling all your relatives?'

'So it's *my* relatives and *your* relatives, is it?' Abbu's voice had risen a notch higher.

Saba walked in on them glaring at each other and had to intervene.

'Okay, okay! So we'll order food from outside, na?' she suggested and Abbu shot a look at her.

'I can't understand why the two of you have to fight over every small thing!' she chided them. The terse silence was punctuated by the sound of Abbu's mobile ringing and Abbu picked it up from the bedside table and frowned.

'Shh! It's the bride's father!' he said before answering the call.

When he hung up, he looked a little annoyed but grim.

'They're sending over the furniture today,' he announced.

'What?' Ammi squeaked.

'They're sending over the bride's furniture by this afternoon,' Abbu repeated unnecessarily.

'We heard it the first time!' Ammi snapped at him.

'Okay, is that a problem?' Saba intervened.

'Saba, you keep out of this. You have no idea what this means!' Ammi said and Saba made a face. So much for trying to be a mediator!

'It doesn't mean anything,' Abbu said slowly. 'Just that they will send over some people with the furniture, like a bed, cupboard and other things.'

'But his room already has a bed. And a cupboard,' Saba said.

'Exactly. We were thinking that we still had some time to figure out what to do with the existing furniture. But. . .' Ammi responded. 'And now the house will be full of people thanks to your Abbu!' she turned to him.

'Bah! Do whatever you want!' Saba said, flinging her arms and going to her room.

'Saba!' Abbu called out. She turned.

'I've called Shahid also today. So stay in your room, okay? Don't come out. I have to discuss his proposal formally with the other family members.'

Saba's eyes grew round. 'Stay in my room?' she repeated.

'Uh, yes,' Abbu looked embarrassed.

'And when were you planning to tell me about this?' Ammi rounded on him again.

'I told you now,' Abbu countered, but looked defeated.

'No, you don't understand. If Shahid comes over today, he'll want to help with everything and we can't make him do all this work *now,*' Ammi said.

'Why?' Abbu looked mystified. Saba also stood staring at them, shaking her head slowly.

'He's going to be our *damaad*! How can you put him to work like all the other boys?' Ammi screeched.

I can't believe I'm going to be under house arrest or rather, room arrest, thought Saba as she went to her room. She had a good mind to blog about it but some of the recent comments on her blog had begun to disturb her a bit.

Some of the people who had been regularly commenting were showing a little too much interest in the events around her brother's wedding and she was getting a wee bit afraid of having put so much information out there, even though she hadn't given names.

So, she called up Riya and told her about it, and Riya couldn't stop laughing.

'You're family is nuts!' she proclaimed and tittered away. Saba had to concede that it all sounded a bit over the top.

'You're going to be stuck in your room when your boyfriend is in your house,' she continued in the same vein, laughing.

'Tell me about it!' Saba sighed as she yanked the scrunchie from the bottom of her braid and opened out her hair with her fingers.

They spoke for some time and then ended the call. Saba brushed out her hair and tied it up again in a braid and swung it back. She decided that she was going to simply ignore everything that happened outside and concentrate on her first exam.

But it wasn't easy. All the relatives had started arriving and Saba ventured out warily. Abbu couldn't have meant her to stay inside ALL day! She'd have to eat something at least, right?

The hall was filled with people and the bawdy aunts caught hold of her just as she thought of escaping back to her room.

'We heard *all* about you and Shahid!' someone said, pinching her arm above her elbow. Saba didn't know if her face turned redder than her elbow. What did she mean? Apparently they were referring to the proposal and how everyone was shocked that it had come from Shahid directly.

'Maybe he liked her from beginning,' an aunt said, slyly nudging Saba who wished she hadn't come out at all. She pretended to look at the activities with more interest than she had and asked one of the cousins if she could help.

'What? This? You're going to be a bride yourself soon! And your groom is going to come here any moment! Go and hide!' he said.

Saba glared at him. Why was everyone behaving this way? Go and hide? With a huff she went back to her room. She studied for some more time and then heard the sound of a huge vehicle entering the gates. She stood near her window, trying to see what was happening. This was ridiculous. She was a prisoner in her *own* house!

A large truck stood just within the gates and some workers were already unloading things. There was a sofa set, a bed, a dresser, a cupboard, a dining table, chairs and what seemed like hundreds of cartons. Suddenly the wedding seemed more real than it had ever been. These symbols of the bride's imminent presence in their house finally got her worried. *Now* she got what Rabia had been harping about all these days. They were going to have a stranger living with them and both sides had a huge amount of adjusting to do. She was startled when she saw Uzair amongst the group of people who had come from the bride's side to make sure everything was done properly.

She hoped that Ammi wouldn't spot him, but that would be a bit difficult. She still felt horribly foolish when she thought of how she had gone on her own to contact him. And it *really* was Shahid's fault, she thought. Her body gave a tiny little jump as she saw Shahid entering the gates talking on the phone to someone. His mother followed behind him, averting her face from all the strange men outside who were hollering as they carried the heavy furniture into the house.

As though from habit, Shahid glanced at Saba's window and she wondered if he could spot her there. It was a bright day and those inside couldn't be seen clearly unless you peered into the room or switched on the lights, which she hadn't.

She continued standing there drinking in his features, but he had moved away already and. . .uh oh. Uzair had stopped him and was talking to him.

Saba turned away from the window and sat down at her desk, her heart beating madly. She tried to focus on her books, but that was getting exceedingly tough as her room was downstairs and it seemed like the entire Gemini Circus had arrived at her house, elephants and lions, et al.

Just as she was about to shut her book in despair, a young cousin came darting inside her room and sat on the bed breathlessly.

'I just saw the most *divine* looking guy outside!' she panted.

Saba nodded her head and tried hard not to smile.

'God! He's so gorgeous!' she continued. Saba turned back to her book.

'What are you reading? You should be out. . .' Nimra stopped suddenly and slapped her forehead.

'Right, right! Shahid bhai is outside and he shouldn't see you!' she spoke as though to herself and Saba didn't even bother to nod.

'This was so sudden, no? Shahid bhai asking for your hand?' Nimra said as she settled on the bed more comfortably, looking as though she wanted Saba to share her confidences with her. Saba sighed loudly. Nimra had just finished school and, in her holidays before college started, she had finished reading the Twilight Series.

'Doesn't he remind you a bit of Robert Pattinson?' she asked, closing her eyes.

'Who? Shahid?' Saba asked deliberately. Nimra's eyes opened immediately.

'Shahid! *Shahid*?' she repeated as though scandalized that Saba had taken the name of the man she was about to marry.

Saba had forgotten that Nimra was the daughter of one of the bawdy aunts and she'd have to be careful, but she rolled her eyes anyway.

'That other guy you saw outside?' Saba asked, hoping to change the topic.

'Umm!' Nimra said. 'I wonder what his name is!'

Saba kept quiet. During the engagement, Nimra had been busy with her ICSE exams and hadn't attended so she had no idea that Uzair had been the boy who had barged into the room where the ladies had been sitting.

It suddenly seemed like Saba's room was the place where all the girls had decided to come and sit, because Saba was soon surrounded by all her female cousins who chattered on unmindful of the fact that Saba had her exams the following day. Saba wondered what was happening outside. She'd heard the truck leave, but one of the cousins said that the men from the bride's side were still in the house setting up the furniture in Zohaib's room, and so they'd been asked to go and sit in a room where they wouldn't be seen by them.

They were *all* talking about Uzair though. Ugh.

Saba receded into a corner of the room where she tried to study amid all the banter, when one of the girls spotted her ring.

'Allah! What a pretty ring, Api!' she said, picking up Saba's hand and turned it around so that the stones caught the light. 'Where did you get it?'

'Rabia Api gave it to me for my birthday,' Saba improvized, thankful that Rabia hadn't come yet. Hopefully by the time she did turn up, these girls would have gone.

The interest around her ring died slowly, but Saba was reminded of the time she'd put it on her finger and how the thought of being away from Shahid had seemed like the end of the world. Since then, she hadn't met Shahid at all apart from that brief moment they'd shared on the day her parents had left for Chennai. He hadn't seen the ring on her finger as yet. She smiled.

That was when her father came inside, a thunderous expression on his face.

'This Uzair says that he knows you. Is that true?' he bellowed.

49

Some of the girls in the room had stood up and were gawking at her father. Saba stood up slowly, letting her book slide down her lap but she retrieved it before it fell down.

'I. . .' she faltered.

Only then did her father realize that there were other people in the room and his face flushed before he stomped out, saying that he wanted to speak to her later.

'What was that all about?' Nimra asked as the girls settled down, although they were all talking rapidly. 'Who's Uzair?'

'Don't you know?' another young girl turned to her. 'He's the boy who came inside the women's room at Zohaib bhai's engagement! That gorgeous guy we all were just talking about now!'

Nimra turned to Saba. 'And you know him?' she asked her incredulously. 'And you didn't even tell me?'

Saba quashed her irritation with Nimra because she was more worried about how she would deal with Abbu later.

'Hardly. I opened the door once when he came after the engagement and he spoke a few words to me,' she said, knowing that she could get away by lying to these girls because they wouldn't be speaking to Uzair. She shuddered when she thought of what he would have told her father.

'Ooh! What did he say?' Nimra asked and the other girls crowded around her.

'Nothing!' Saba was assertive, but they refused to believe her.

'Okay, he said that his aunt, the bride's mother, sent him over to apologize but he had no plans of doing that. That's all!' Saba hoped the matter would end there, but the girls insisted that she give them proper details of what he said and *how* he said it.

'Do you know if he's single?' someone asked and Saba laughed shortly but she didn't answer. That much information about him and his life would surely incriminate her later on.

Finally it was time for lunch. It was a very late lunch because Abbu had insisted that the men from the girl's side also stay back and eat with them. Saba wondered how her father had managed to eat in Uzair's company because she was sure he wanted to strangle him. First asking about Rabia and now Saba!

'Mamu ordered from a restaurant,' a cousin said when Saba asked her about lunch. Saba nodded but her stomach was growling. Now would they do something idiotic like ask her to sit inside while everyone ate outside because Shahid was there?

She joined the girls leaving her room quietly. Nimra looked at her strangely, 'You're going out? Shahid bhai is there, na?'

Saba ignored her and headed straight for the kitchen. The atmosphere outside was very festive and she quickly spotted Shahid sitting among all the male members of the family, patiently answering questions.

'What are you doing here?' her mother asked her as she sidled into the kitchen.

Saba glared at her. 'I'm hungry.'

'Okay okay! You know that boy Uzair told your father that you met him for coffee? Thank God he didn't say it when the other uncles were around,' Ammi whispered looking around.

'Then why did Abbu come to my room and ask me about it when all the girls were there?' Saba asked, thoroughly irritated with her family by now. At this rate she was just going to have to run away somewhere.

'He did what?' Ammi asked, shocked.

'Okay, never mind! Give me food!' Saba muttered. She didn't want her parents fighting now. A few of the bawdy aunts barged in, and one of them gasped.

'Saba! What are you doing here? What if Shahid sees you? Go to your room!' she admonished. Saba pursed her lips and refused to answer. She picked up a plate from the stand and served herself and stood near the sink, eating.

One of the aunts shook her head. 'She's very headstrong,' she told Ammi as though Saba weren't standing there. 'Good you got this proposal for her, or it would have become difficult. I heard Rabia went back to her husband? What was the problem?' The aunt changed tracks swiftly and Saba spotted Ammi flushing uncomfortably.

'What problem?' she blustered. 'She's expecting, no? She wanted some rest here. That's all.'

'But I heard. . .'

'What did you hear?' Ammi asked in a high pitched voice and left the kitchen.

'It's okay. I just needed water. I can get it myself!' Shahid spoke as he walked inside the kitchen and stopped when he saw Saba.

'No, no! Saba is there inside, beta!' Ammi protested and then *she* blushed when she saw the two of them staring at each other. Saba refused to turn away and hide her face from him. Let everyone think whatever they wanted to.

'Saba!' Ammi admonished her and led Shahid outside, who looked amused. Saba felt like upending the plate of biryani on his head. She was back in her room studying by the time everyone sat down for lunch and was so angry with everyone that she didn't even speak when some of the aunts came to pick up their burkhas from her room where they'd kept it.

Ammi was concerned that Rabia hadn't come yet. She still had her doubts about Rafiq bhaijan and Saba didn't quite know how to tell her that her elder daughter had an active imagination and a tendency to run away from problems. Like her son. It seemed like she was the only person in her family with a sense of decency. She was also feeling bad for this other girl whom Zohaib bhai had been involved with. Whoever she was, she'd fallen hard for her brother and she was finding it difficult to let go. But she had to!

She didn't have much time to ponder over that as Abbu and Ammi came inside her room and Abbu sat down on the bed. She looked at him feeling concerned because of the lines around his eyes and the way he was rubbing the side of his neck, but she was also a bit afraid. How much more could she lie to him?

'Why didn't you tell me that Uzair was troubling you?' Abbu asked.

Huh?

'Shahid told me all about how he was pestering you after Zohaib's engagement and somehow managed to get your number. And you didn't know how to tell us so you told Shahid to speak to him to stay away from you,' Abbu explained. Saba briefly wondered how much more she and Shahid could lie before getting caught. Someone just had to speak to Uzair properly and the whole story would come tumbling out, about how *she* had got his number and *she* had called him for coffee.

'Umm. . .I. . .'

'I don't know whether to be pleased or angry with you that you went to Shahid and spoke about this personal matter,' Abbu continued. 'That Uzair needs to be whipped! First he was after Rabia and then you! The girl's side should be ashamed of having someone like him in their house.'

'You could have told me, no?' Ammi interrupted his tirade, looking at Saba squarely.

'But you both don't have any time for me!' Saba said finally and both her parents seemed surprised.

'I know you weren't planning to have a baby after Rabia, but here I am, okay? Twenty years old. Either you're worried over Zohaib bhai and his wedding or about Rabia and her married life! No one even remembered my birthday last month!' Saba said. Her father got up uncertainly.

'You just want to get rid of me and now you've found a convenient place to do that!' Saba ranted. She had started it merely as a way to detract attention from herself but found that she was unable to stop. Everything that had been bottled up inside her for so long was finding its way out.

'How could I have come to you for anything?' she turned to her mother. 'You *never* listen to me! You don't hear anything that I say! I have an exam tomorrow and here I am justifying myself to you. I asked Shahid, because I knew he cared about me.'

Okay, stop already, her mind protested. Saba was panting heavily with the effort of expressing all this all of a sudden and went to stand near the window. Her mother and father were both stunned by this sudden display of emotion from their practical, no-nonsense daughter.

'Saba. . .I. . .' Abbu started, but Saba turned around.

'I'd like to get back to studying, please,' she said and went to pick up her books. She wanted her parents to go away, because she didn't want to answer more questions about Uzair but also because this outburst had hurt her too. It was a swift moment of realization when she knew that even her own family wouldn't love her as much as Shahid did.

'But. . .' Ammi started, looking nervously at Abbu.

'Ammi, it's okay. I'm fine now. You know now that there's nothing to fear from Uzair, especially since Shahid already knows everything there is.'

Ammi was silent. Abbu came towards Saba and rested his hand on her shoulder heavily.

'Whatever you think, whatever you've thought so far, it's not true,' he explained. Saba didn't respond. 'I'm sorry if that's the impression we gave you but we really do care about you too. About your birthday. . .'

'It's okay, Abbu,' Saba stopped him, momentarily feeling a little petulant for having brought that up.

'We've just been worried about Zohaib and Rabia and you were our only anchor. The only thing in our life that has been so stable these past few months! Those two have got by life purely through charm and their good looks, but not you. You're hardworking and strong and you have a sense of balance that comes from inside,' he said. Saba nodded, opening her book. She hadn't thought of it that way but she didn't say anything. Her throat felt clogged and she bit her lower lip.

Her father seemed to wait for her to say something, to affirm that everything was all right but she couldn't speak. Sighing, he left the room.

Ammi watched him go and then she shook her head in a way that made Saba feel guilty all of a sudden. Then she too turned on her heels and left.

50

On Tuesday, Shahid parked his car in one of the lanes and walked up to the tall building where Zohaib's office was located. Last night he'd received a frantic call from Zohaib, who wanted to know how his colleagues had come to know that he was getting married.

'I'll kill that Saba!' Zohaib raged when he found out that Saba had been behind it. Shahid had tried to placate him and tell him that it was all going to be fine, but Zohaib was too distressed. This was the first time that Zohaib had called him since he'd gone to France and Shahid felt a little uneasy as he wondered what he'd thought of the news that he and Saba would be getting married.

Had he got suspicious? Had he been able to put two and two together? Or was he merely absorbed in his own problems?

'She'll surely come to the wedding now, dude! I'm getting really psyched.'

Shahid scratched his forehead briefly as he pondered over a solution to the problem. 'You're still coming, right?' he asked Zohaib. After staying silent for ten seconds, Zohaib spoke, 'Yes!'

'Well, thank God! We'll work something out!' Shahid assured him.

'I'm not so sure,' Zohaib had countered. That was when he asked Shahid for the favour. Shahid had refused at first but Zohaib cajoled him and pleaded and Shahid finally agreed. And here he was, standing outside Zohaib's office.

Inside, the receptionist called up someone and then took his contact details before giving him a visitor badge which he had to wear around his neck.

'You can go to the fifth floor and ask for Meenakshi,' she said.

Nodding, he took the lift observing the lax levels of security in Zohaib's office. Fiddling with the 'visitor' badge that hung around his neck from a strap, he was wondering exactly what he could possibly say to Meenakshi. Back off? Stay away? We'll call the police? He was just going to have to wing it.

The lift stopped at the fifth floor. Shahid stepped out of the lift and saw a glass-fronted facàde behind which many people sat working. He felt slightly self-conscious as he walked inside and a couple of people looked at him curiously.

Glad that the office was air conditioned, he loosened his collar and stepped towards the person sitting nearest to him.

'Excuse me, could you please tell me where Meenakshi is?' he asked.

The man looked up at him and removed his glasses. 'She's in a meeting right now,' he said.

'Oh okay. Can I wait for her here?' he asked, looking around for a place to sit.

'Find yourself a chair,' he said, and went back to his work. He looked around and saw an empty chair not far from where he was standing. Determined to finish the job he'd come to do, he walked purposefully towards it when a young chap smiled at him.

'New to work? Waiting while they set up your workstation?' he asked, rolling his chair back.

'Uh no. I'm here to meet Meenakshi,' Shahid explained and the other man nodded his head.

For some reason, Shahid felt compelled to explain further.

'Actually, I'm Zohaib's cousin,' he said. The other man who had gone back to his work whipped his head to look at him.

'What?' he asked. Shahid was surprised at the man's reaction because he'd nudged the guy sitting next to him, a very fat man, and told him almost conspiratorially, 'This is Zohaib's cousin,' emphasizing the word 'cousin'.

'You mean. . .' the fat guy asked and the first man rolled his chair towards him. Shahid bunched his eyebrows together. Suddenly the first guy was looking nervous when the other fat guy pulled up next to him. 'Go on!' he whispered.

'I just had to ask you, if you're T,' the man spoke quickly.

'T?' Shahid asked, surprised. 'What's that?'

'From the blog?' he asked.

Shahid shook his head. 'You're?' he asked.

'I'm Kunal. And this is Deepak,' he said, pointing to the fat guy. 'And that's Sampath,' he said pointing to another man a little far away who waved at them. 'We're avid readers of the blog, by the way. We think it's so cool she's doing that. And although she tried to hide all the names and everything, I actually figured out everything a few days ago.'

Shahid stopped him. 'Wait a minute. You have to explain to me from the beginning. What are you talking about?'

'Oh, come on! Don't be so modest!' Kunal said, smiling. 'You can tell her that we've figured out who she is too.'

'Could you explain properly?' Shahid asked, his heart thudding. Who was this 'she' they were referring to?

Deepak looked a bit flustered. 'Oh shucks, guys! Maybe he doesn't know about it,' he said to Sampath who had walked over to them. Kunal shook his head.

'Impossible. Why would she have hidden the blog from him?' Kunal asked. Shahid's eyes grew round.

'What?' he asked.

'*My Brother's Wedding*. The blog. We're all reading it here in office.'

'*My Brother's Wedding*?' Shahid asked, feeling his stomach drop. 'There's a blog by that name?'

'And who's writing it?' he asked in a strangled voice.

'Y's sister T,' he explained.

'Who is Y and who is T?' Shahid asked impatiently although he could feel the back of his neck growing hot.

Deepak slapped his forehead dramatically, but Kunal still went on, looking pleased with himself.

'It was easy to figure it out once we got a few details. Y is Zohaib, T is his sister.'

'Rabia?' Shahid asked, swallowing.

'No, no! That's Q. She's that bitchy type,na? How we all loved to hate her man! Too bad she's becoming kind of nice now that she's pregnant and all!'

Shahid put out his hand to stop the other man. 'You mean T is Saba?' he asked.

'Yes! That's her name! I keep forgetting! And she so sweetly invited us all for the wedding too!' Kunal continued.

'Okay. First of all, I have no idea what you're talking about,' Shahid repeated, but he was beginning to feel worried. These guys sounded like they knew everything that had been going on at Saba's home. From a blog?

'Would you mind showing me this blog?' he asked.

'Not at all! Come on in right here!' Kunal said, leading him towards his workstation. 'Sit down, sit down!' Shahid sat down uncertainly on a chair and looked around at the group of people now surrounding him.

'All you people have read this blog?' he asked, breathing heavily, wondering if Meenakshi had been one of those people too. What had she thought of it once Kunal had figured out that it was about Zohaib's wedding?

'No, not all of us!' Kunal explained. 'Just the few of us here.'

'And Meenakshi?' Shahid asked anxiously.

'No. She just joined our team and we're not really sure we like her,' Sampath said. 'Last year she was with us for a few months before she got posted to Mumbai. And now she's back as our team lead and that's not sitting well with any of us.'

Shahid looked at him wondering why he was telling him all this.

'Is she the girl who had an affair with Zohaib?' a stunning girl who had been at the periphery of the group asked, looking down at her shoes, however.

'What?' Shahid was really shocked. Saba had blogged about *that* as well?

'Well, we kind of figured that one out from the last post,' she replied, looking up. 'I'm Maya, by the way,' she continued.

Shahid shook his head. What was going on here?

'Does Meenakshi know about the wedding this Sunday?' he asked suddenly. 'Did she also get the email invitation from Saba?'

The group of people looked at each other and shook their heads. 'She's a bit weird. She's installed this tracker kind of software on our computers so she knows which websites we're surfing. She doesn't want us to goof up and all so we usually check the blog on our phones. I don't think she knows about the wedding or the blog,' Kunal spoke.

Shahid thought for a moment before turning to them again. 'Could you try and keep it a secret till Sunday?' he asked suddenly. Maybe they could still pull it off and once Zohaib was married, there was nothing she could do.

'I think that's manageable,' Deepak rumbled. 'Half the time she doesn't know what she's doing and despite that tracker software she still doesn't know what *we're* doing,' he smirked.

'How did you guys stumble across the blog in the first place?' he asked.

Kunal sighed. 'Sometimes it gets so boring with all the work we have to do, that we are usually dying for some kind of excitement. Facebook is not allowed inside the office and we started reading the blog a month before *she* came back here. Someone came across it and sent the link and we started following it. You know how it goes, right?' he asked. Shahid shook his head. He *didn't* know how these things go.

Maya leaned forward and spoke suddenly. 'I'm SO glad that she fell for you and not that other guy!

Shahid's eyes popped out, but he couldn't reply because someone handed him their large screen smartphone with the blog page open on it.

51

Saba gulped down a glass of milk and wiped her mouth with the back of her hand.

'I can't eat anything! No, no, I don't want keema and roti!' she protested before one of the many aunts who had come to their house and was going to be there until the wedding. This aunt, her mother's cousin, was sleeping in her room with two other aunts. Saba had had to move to Rabia's room temporarily and she hated being away from her desk and her computer. But apparently, all the aunts snored and Saba usually studied late into the night. She wondered what she would do the following day, however, because Rabia was coming to stay till the wedding.

I'll just have to run off to Riya's house and study, Saba thought as she left the house. She waited for an auto, wishing her exams were over already. She'd just finished two and the third one today was rather gruelling. There was one more on Friday. She fiddled with her pouch where she kept all her pens and she pulled out her crumpled hall ticket and straightened it. But just as an auto stopped near her, she saw Shahid walking towards her.

'I'll drop you,' he said and Saba looked at him amazed. What was he doing here?

'But. . .' she turned around to see if anyone in the house could spot them. No idea.

'Come!' he said and, pulling her along by the hand, he led her towards his car. She sat down and closed the door and turned towards him, her heart feeling full. It had been so long since she'd been with him in such close proximity. But he didn't look at her. He started the car and drove out quietly towards her college.

'What's the matter?' she asked after some time as they neared her college. He hadn't looked at her even once. He turned to her briefly and pursed his lips. Then he stopped the car at their usual place where he'd always drop her off in the early days. She leaned forward to kiss him, when he stopped her.

'What?' she asked.

'What time is your exam?' he asked.

'In another hour,' she replied, wishing he'd say what was wrong.

'Okay,' he said, nodding. He turned to look at her and Saba squirmed under the intensity of his stare.

'I read your blog,' he said finally and Saba felt the blood rush to her face.

'Why did you hide it from me?' he asked.

'I. . .I didn't know you this way when I started it,' she said.

'And later?'

'And later, how could I show it to you? You were one of the people I wrote about so much in it,' Saba whispered. God! Had he read all the posts?

Shahid's face contorted with emotion and he pulled her to him and, cupping her face in his hands, he kissed her. Saba leaned into him and put her arms around his neck and groaned when his lips left hers.

'Don't. Write. About. This,' he said, punctuating each word with a nip on her lips. Saba blushed furiously.

'Did you read everything?' she asked, moving away from him.

He took her hand in his and squeezed it gently. And looked down in surprise when the ring she was wearing poked into his palm.

'You're wearing it?' he asked, surprised, lifting her hand in wonder.

She nodded. 'I wore it on the night of my birthday itself. Once I put it on my finger it didn't look so garish,' she joked. He lifted her hand and kissed her fingers, lightly grazing one of her fingers with his teeth until she pulled her hand back.

'Don't look at me like that, or you won't be able to write your exam today,' he warned her. She batted his hands as they strayed towards her.

'How did you find out about the blog?' she asked him.

He rubbed the stubble on his jaw absently with his thumb and turned to her.

'Zohaib bhai called me on Monday night. Apparently some of his colleagues informed him that they were coming for the wedding. He was furious when he found out that they all knew about the wedding.'

Saba winced when she heard that.

'Then he wanted me to go to Meenakshi and speak to her.'

'Why? Why should you go?' Saba asked immediately. 'Why should you do *his* dirty work?'

'Sometimes your sense of loyalty is so warped,' Shahid said, smiling at her.

'So, did you go?'

Shahid nodded. 'I did. I went there yesterday.'

'Did you meet her?' she asked, feeling very curious.

Shahid's fingers walked across Saba's arm but she caught his hand and curled it into a fist that she held, 'Stop and answer me,' He shook his head.

'I didn't have to,' he said. 'The moment I said I was Zohaib's cousin, they wanted to know if I was T.'

'What?' Saba was shocked.

'You mean all of them have been reading my blog?' she asked, surprised.

'Don't look so pleased with yourself,' he said, pulling her hands into his and rubbing circles on her palm with his thumb. 'I can't tell you how embarrassed I was to read all that stuff.'

'What's embarrassing about it?' Saba asked, slightly annoyed. 'It's not like I *described* anything.'

'Yes, but they were behaving like they knew more about me and you than we did ourselves. And you have to admit, it was quite embarrassing when they started referring to our love story.'

Saba shook her head, looking thoroughly befuddled. 'I still don't get it. What does this have to do with bhai's wedding and Meenakshi?'

'Well, it so happened that you thankfully didn't send the email to Meenakshi and she hasn't read your blog. So she has no idea he's getting married.'

'But *someone* will tell her!' Saba protested.

'I've asked them to try and keep it a secret from her. There are about seven people in his office who know that the Zohaib who works with them is the same person as this Y. And they've all said that they'll keep her away from the wedding.'

Saba didn't look too convinced. 'Maybe you should have spoken to her. I mean, today is Wednesday and bhai is coming this evening. What if someone tells Meenakshi about the wedding? Anything can go wrong in four days!'

'As long as you don't blog about it, I think it's fine,' Shahid smiled and Saba looked out of the window.

'I started the blog so I could give a proper account of bhai's wedding, but it became something else,' she said.

'You know what would be a good think to do now? Make the blog private so no one will read it or pass it on to Meenakshi,' Shahid suggested.

Saba looked mutinous. 'But. . .'

'Bring it back *after* the wedding?'

She agreed reluctantly. It would be quite foolhardy to have the blog out on cyberspace, especially when her brother's colleagues were reading it.

Since she still looked upset over it, Shahid smiled deviously. 'You are *such* a bad girl,' he admonished her, yanking her braid lightly.

'I laughed like crazy when I read about Rabia! And did she actually think that Rafiq bhaijan was a jinn?' Shahid was laughing now. 'Did someone tell her that *she's* the witch actually?'

Saba slapped his hands and he stopped. 'And she saw us kissing that day?'

She nodded. 'Were you angry when you read the blog?' she asked.

Shahid was smirking. 'Uh no. Not since I read about your adventures with the Idiot.' When Saba glared at him, he amended quickly, 'And what you feel for me. After reading about us, I *had* to meet you,' he tugged the end of her dupatta to draw her closer to him.

'Well then I'm glad I wrote it. At least your highness decided to meet me in person after that,' Saba said, making a face at him, even as he leaned towards her, resting his hands on her nape.

'Don't you have an exam in half an hour?' he asked, but he didn't let her speak.

When they separated, Saba was breathing heavily and her face was flushed. 'Exam? What exam?' she whispered.

'Go on now!' Shahid was laughing at her expression.

'Oh well,' Saba said as she pulled her bag from the back seat. 'Will you be meeting me again or do I have to wait for two years?'

Shahid shook his head and smiled.

52

A little later that day, Rabia sat before her mirror brushing her hair. There was a little dip in her stomach and she looked down. They were both hungry.

Rafiq had hired a cook and a full-time maid to make sure that Rabia didn't have to exert herself for anything, but at the moment, she didn't feel like calling either of them. She thought of the amazing turn her life had taken since she'd come back and she knew it had been the right decision. Rafiq was more loving (if that was possible) and any aggressive behaviour that he'd begun to show before she got pregnant had disappeared.

In fact, some of his attitude was beginning to annoy her even though she had enjoyed it greatly in the beginning. His attitude towards her almost bordered on reverence, and Rabia wondered what he would do if he knew the reason why she'd actually stayed away for so long. At night, he didn't snuggle next to her like before. He slept far away from her and she wished for that easy intimacy that they'd shared earlier.

He kept her at arm's length now, almost as though he was afraid she would go back if he did something she didn't want him to do. Each day as he got up and padded towards the bathroom for his shower, Rabia would watch him over the growing mound of her stomach. He really, truly, loved her. And she knew now that he didn't have any special or supernatural powers. He was a very persuasive man, given to convincing people of what he wanted them to do, and yet making them think it was all their own idea.

Those were the times she thought that she loved him. Maybe she did. She couldn't define it even after two and a half years of marriage. And Saba! She and Shahid had been together for not even two months and she proclaimed her love for him so easily. She wished she could be so sure of what love was supposed to be like.

Sighing, she got up to go to the kitchen to pour some juice for herself, when she heard the front door bang. Who was it at this time of the day? Rafiq didn't come for lunch and usually came back only in the evenings. When he walked into the kitchen, his eyes were glowering and Rabia felt a momentary pang of fear. The kind that had sent her straight to her mother's home two months before.

'What's the matt. . .' Rabia broke off because he rounded the table and came to her and held her shoulders.

'You thought I was a jinn?' he asked her harshly, and Rabia gasped. Who had told him? Only her parents and Saba knew. Had she blabbed it to Shahid? Even so, why would he tell her husband? They were hardly well acquainted with each other.

'What? What are you talking about?' she asked, her voice cracking.

Rafiq controlled his breathing with difficulty and then pulled out his laptop and placed it on the table. He opened it, plugged a Tata Photon Plus USB stick on one side, tapped a few keys and turned the laptop towards Rabia.

Rabia was still puzzled. She sat down on the chair uncertainly and pulled the laptop towards her and looked at the website that had opened up. It looked like a personal blog. Then she started reading and looked away from the laptop after a few minutes.

'I don't understand. What's this?'

'You still don't get it?' he asked her, his nostrils flaring. Rabia felt a little scared when she saw that he was absolutely serious. Where was the doting man of this morning?

He sighed impatiently when she shook her head. 'Read again. You're Q, and Y is Zohaib and T is for both Shahid and Saba.'

'What?' Rabia turned back to the blog, shocked. 'Who wrote it?'

'Who's the writer in your family?' he sneered.

Saba! Rabia read with horrified fascination. 'But where does it say that I thought you were. . .' She couldn't complete the sentence because Rafiq turned red.

'Read the next post,' he said.

'Wait a minute. Y, as in Zohaib, had an affair with some girl in his office?' she asked, shocked.

'The next post, Rabia,' he said impatiently, and Rabia clicked on it with trembling hands. 'No need to read everything. I'm sure you'll have lots of time for it later. Scroll down and read,' he ordered.

Rabia swallowed and read one paragraph: *With a sigh she went on to explain how she'd come across the website and how the biggest proof that he was human was the baby growing inside her body. (I haven't mentioned it before, but Q was under the notion that her husband was a jinn. Yes.)*

Rabia felt her face grow hot as Rafiq pulled the laptop away from her and shut it loudly. She winced, but couldn't bring herself to look at him.

'Explain,' he said, folding his arms across his chest. He looked formidable and Rabia didn't know how she could voice what she'd thought without sounding foolish. Damn that Saba!

'How do you know it's Saba's blog?' she asked instead.

A vein throbbed furiously in his forehead. 'Google for "Indian Muslim Wedding" and her blog shows up as the third or fourth entry. One of my cousins found it and sent me the link, saying that the description of the events sounded a lot like what I had been going through.'

'Meaning?' Rabia looked blank.

'You leaving me and going to your parents' house. Zohaib's engagement, my insisting that you don't wear your pink ghagra. . .it's all there,' he said, counting off the items on his fingers.

'But. . .how does your cousin. . .know?' Rabia asked, although her heart was thumping crazily.

'I don't know! He came across it this morning and sent me the link. I thought it was some kind of joke at first but then. . .'

Rabia looked at him uncertainly.

'Everyone warned me against marrying you, Rabia,' he shook his head. 'They thought I was being foolish, marrying someone I didn't even know, but I knew I was in love with you the moment I saw you.'

Rabia experienced a sinking feeling in her stomach and the baby chose that moment to turn over. She gasped and clutched her stomach. 'What is it?' he asked, looking up.

This morning, Rabia would have said that the baby moved or turned and she would have seen a glow come over his face, his eyes shining with emotion. But now. . .she didn't want to risk him thinking that she was using the baby to distract him.

'Nothing,' she said.

He shrugged. 'He's been reading the blog for a while now and although he did think it was odd how the events there matched those that happened in my life, he sent me the link when he read that you thought I was a jinn.'

Rabia winced again. 'How could an educated girl like you think of such a thing?' he asked.

'I. . .'

'No, tell me!' he thumped his hand on the table. 'I've done more than any other husband would do for you and you. . .' He shook his head as he got up and packed the laptop in his bag.

'Aren't you staying for. . .' the words broke away when Rafiq gave her a withering look.

'You were going to your mother's house tomorrow, right?' he asked and Rabia was afraid to even nod her head.

'Go there today and don't come back.'

Rabia looked at him shocked. 'No! I. . .Rafiq, it was a mistake!' Rabia got up slowly and went towards him, clutching his hand but he shook her off.

'I managed two months without you, and I can do it again.' When Rabia touched him again, he backed off. 'I'm very, very angry now. Don't make me say something I'll regret later.'

Rabia stepped back, her eyes brimming. She had no idea when the tears started. 'Rafiq, please! Don't do this! It was a mistake!'

'Do you know how much *pain* I was in during those two months? Thinking that I'd hurt you somehow? And all the time you were avoiding me because you thought I was. . .'

He shook his head. 'I'm going to office now and I'll be back late at night. I'd prefer it if you moved to your parents' place before I came.'

'Rafiq!' Rabia called out horrified. He couldn't mean it.

'But. . .the wedding?' she called out as he moved towards the door.

'What wedding?' he snorted and left the house, shutting the door behind him loudly.

53

Friday evening

If Saba had thought that the engagement had been chaotic, she had no idea what the wedding would do to her sanity. There were people everywhere, chatting, laughing and gossiping and since her exams were over, she was expected to work with everyone. Thankfully, they didn't have to do any cooking because Ammi had hired a cook for a week and it made Saba wonder why they couldn't hire someone permanently. Imagine! No need to make tea every ten minutes when a new guest came or no need to worry about how to feed everyone.

Saba's room had been taken up by all the aunts and other relatives and she had no choice but to move to Rabia's room. Rabia was supposed to have come home the previous day but she hadn't. Ammi was expecting her to come today because the functions were supposed to start in about an hour. Saba had deactivated the blog from public viewing but she was still nervous that something would go wrong before Sunday.

She brushed her hair and pulled out a simple green shalwar kameez, edged with gold lace—her outfit for the evening. As she tied up her hair into a braid, she wondered if she would be able to see Shahid today. He hadn't texted her since Wednesday when he'd dropped her to college.

Zohaib bhai was back and Saba thought that he looked nervous and edgy, as though he was waiting for some boulder to fall on top of him. She hadn't seen much of him because he'd been busy finishing his own shopping.

Saba looked at the clock. It was 7 p.m. and most of the guests had started arriving. It was a private family function today, meant to be informal and fun. But where was Rabia? She hadn't even called Ammi the whole day. Saba picked up her mobile and contemplated calling her. Things between them had changed imperceptibly; although they could never be close sisters, Saba acknowledged that there was some kind of bond between them.

She dialled Rabia's number and it rang but she didn't answer. Anxious, she redialled her number and the same thing happened. She was extremely apprehensive now and she called Rafiq bhaijan. Her stomach heaved and she got up from the chair when he too didn't answer. What could have happened?

Her phone rang and she answered it quickly. It was him.

'Bhaijan! Where's Api? Where were you? Why didn't you guys pick up the phone?' she asked breathlessly.

'We. . .we. . .' his voice broke and Saba knew that something was seriously wrong.

'This morning, we had a fight and. . .I walked away and she followed me in the other car and. . .slammed it against a tree,' he said and, to Saba's horror, he started crying.

'B-but. . .is she okay?' Saba asked, trying to subdue the panic that was ballooning in her chest.

'She wasn't even wearing her seatbelt, Saba. Her head banged into the windshield and she's got some bad injuries on her chest from the glass splinters.'

'Oh my God! Why didn't you call us?' Saba asked, her voice high-pitched. 'How is she now?'

'She's in the ICU and I'm waiting outside. It's all my fault,' he cried again.

'The baby?' Saba asked quietly. 'Is. . .the baby fine?'

He started crying louder and Saba knew that all was not well.

'The baby has stopped moving. Its heart is beating only slightly and if that stops, they're going to have to operate on her to take it out.'

Saba swallowed and she sat down on the bed. 'When did this happen?' she asked.

'This morning. Rabia and I have been fighting for the past two days, ever since I confronted her about your blog and that she thought I was a jinn. Allah! I'm worse than a jinn! I'm a monster to have brought this upon my own family!' he cried out.

Saba covered her mouth with her hands to stop herself from gasping. Oh no! Why had she even started that stupid blog?

'Which hospital? I'll come there with Abbu and Ammi,' Saba said getting up, feeling the world crash around her.

He gave the name of the hospital to her and Saba dashed downstairs, her heart beating wildly, and when she reached her father it seemed that her lungs did not have any air at all. Abbu was talking to a group of uncles and didn't look too pleased at being interrupted.

'Rabia's been in an accident. She's in the ICU!' Saba gasped, and her mother, who was coming out from the kitchen, let out a shriek. Everyone left for the hospital, including Zohaib and Shahid who had just come back from shopping.

In the hospital, the nurses refused to let everyone through and in the end, only Abbu, Ammi and Zohaib were allowed to go inside. Saba pleaded with the nurses and they relented finally and said that she could go when one of the others came out.

Shahid walked over and stood next to her, ignoring all the looks that the aunts were giving him. Saba turned to him and put her head on his shoulders and started crying. Some of the aunts looked at them curiously, but Saba honestly didn't care.

'It's all my fault!' she whispered brokenly as Shahid caressed her hair.

'What do you mean?' he asked, stopping and resting his hand on her neck. Saba lifted her head and told him what bhaijan had said. Shahid looked grim but he shook his head.

'It's not your fault. No, that blog may have caused the fight, but what happened between the two of them was not because of you. Shh!' he consoled her as she started crying again.

Saba snuggled closer and Shahid shut his eyes to the censorious glances that everyone was giving them. They stayed that way, Saba's sobs wetting his shirt, and then Zohaib came out. He saw them locked in the embrace but didn't say anything.

'Go,' he said hoarsely to Saba who extricated herself from Shahid's arms and ran inside, wiping her tears with the back of her hand. Inside, there was a long corridor where Ammi sat on a plastic chair outside a room. Abbu was consoling Rafiq bhaijan who couldn't stop crying.

Saba walked faster, a sickening feeling telling her that maybe things were ten times worse than she thought they were. What if. . .what if Rabia or the baby died?

She covered the last few steps in a brisk run and stood panting outside the door.

'How's she?' she asked Rafiq bhaijan who controlled himself with great difficulty.

'The doctor said that she needs to be in the ICU for another day and that her condition needs to improve before they can say anything positive.' Saba glanced at the circle of glass on the door that showed the nurses and doctors moving around inside.

'Can't we go inside and see her?' she croaked.

He shook his head. 'They've just taken some kind of monitor inside to check the status of the baby and they want us to wait outside before they. . .they decide what to do.'

Saba bit her knuckle in despair. They waited for ten more

minutes before a doctor stepped outside. He looked serious and Saba's heart sank.

'Mr Rafiq,' he started and then noticed Abbu and Ammi who were looking at him anxiously. 'Who are all these people?'

'They're my wife's parents and sister,' he said. The doctor shook his head irritably.

'I keep telling you people not to get so many visitors. Anyway, what I came to say was that we did an ultrasound of the baby. Amazingly, it's looking fine and has started moving again.'

'Ya Allah!' Ammi cried in relief and the doctor looked at her over his spectacles and with a grunt, he continued, 'But your wife. . .'

Everyone looked at him, fear tantamount on their faces.

'Your wife has got a bad head wound and we did an MRI. Thankfully, she doesn't have any internal injuries. She's just regained consciousness and is in a lot of pain. You can see her if you want, but only one person at a time.'

Rafiq bhaijan pushed open the door and went inside. He came out in less than five minutes, and crumpled on the floor.

'I can't see her like this! I can't,' and he hunched down and put his head on his knees and cried.

Ammi, who had been crying silently, went inside and she too came out looking white. She was mumbling duas under her breath. Abbu went inside and he came out wiping tears from his eyes.

Saba looked at everyone and felt nauseated. She didn't want to go inside and see her, but how could she not go? Inside, the nurses carried on with their regular work because this was not a new occurrence to them. They saw injured people and dead bodies every day.

Saba inched forward, looking at an old man who lay groaning on one side of the ICU. Towards the centre, Rabia lay under a mangled net of tubes and her eyes were puffy. Her head was bandaged and her arm was in a sling. It was worse than any movie depiction she'd ever seen, Saba thought as she came to stand beside her.

Rabia opened her eyes and through bloated lips, she spoke. 'Saba.'

Saba nodded her head. 'I'm so sorry, Api! This is all my fault. I'm really sorry.'

Rabia blinked. 'Not your fault,' she lisped.

Saba shut her eyes and tears fell from them rapidly which she wiped away with the back of her hand.

'I should never have written that blog. I'm so sorry for being the cause of the fight between the two of you.'

Saba wondered if it was okay to hold Rabia's hand. Both were covered with IV tubes though. 'We fought,' Rabia seemed determined to speak. A nurse came and stood near Saba and stared disapprovingly. 'Why you letting patient talk so much, ma? Go. Go,' she said and she shooed Saba out. Rabia lifted her finger weakly to beckon Saba but the nurse wouldn't let her stay.

'I'll come back later,' she promised and left.

Only Rafiq bhaijan was sitting on a chair, his head in his hands in the ICU waiting room. Saba sat down next to him uncertainly.

'Where did Abbu and Ammi go?' she asked.

He looked up at her voice and shook his head. 'I don't know. They were saying something about cancelling the wedding.'

Saba was shocked but she nodded her head. She'd forgotten about the wedding that was to take place in two days.

'Bhaijan,' she started. 'I'm so sorry about the. . .blog.'

He shook his head. 'I was so angry that day that I told her to go to her parents' place and never come back. But she didn't leave. How much she pleaded with me when I came back home and I was such a proud jerk that I refused to listen to her. This morning, I told her to go away again and I took one of the cars and I didn't know she had decided to follow me in the other one. I saw it happen from the rear view mirror.'

Saba nodded her head. 'She can't drive. She must have been crazy to take the car when she was so upset.'

'In all our married life, she has never told me that she loves me. I've told her about fifty times a day, each day, hoping that one day she too would feel the way I feel for her. But when this jinn thing happened, something snapped inside me. I decided I couldn't wait any longer for her to meet me halfway. I couldn't go on loving her unconditionally while she merely tolerated me. I was so angry,' he whispered.

'This morning, just as I left the house in anger, she called out that she loved me, and I stopped. How I wished I'd turned back and gone inside,' he said, and pressed the corners of his eyes with his thumbs, trying not to cry again.

'I turned around and told her that it was too late and I just walked away.'

Saba felt the corners of her mouth turn down as she tried not to cry. Had Rabia been trying to tell her this?

'If something happens to her, I. . .'

Saba put her hand on his arm and pressed lightly. 'Nothing is going to happen to her,' she said in a voice that wavered. 'In no time she'll be all right, bossing over you and that little fellow who's inside her.'

Rafiq looked at her through watery eyes and tried to smile but it ended up looking like a grimace.

'Why didn't you call anyone from your family? Why didn't you call us?' Saba asked. Imagine sitting alone all day in the hospital, not knowing what had happened to Rabia!

'I couldn't,' he said. Everyone in your house was busy with

the wedding and I didn't want to call anyone from my family. I think. . .I wanted to punish myself by sitting here alone.'

Saba nodded, not really understanding, but there was little she could say to him. When she went outside, she noticed that most of the extended family had left. Only a few close family members were present, including Shahid. But she went and stood near Ammi who was talking to someone on the phone, sniffling.

Abbu had also been talking on the phone and he ended the call and looked at everyone grimly.

'We can't cancel the wedding. The bride's father says it's too late.'

'But how will we go with Rabia. . .' Ammi started as she put her phone away.

'No. He's saying that we have the nikah for Zohaib in the masjid and the nikah for the bride in her house. We can bring her to our house in the evening. He's willing to cancel the wedding booking even though it's going to be a huge loss for him.'

Ammi nodded.

Abbu continued, 'He said it's not a good idea to cancel the wedding. And he says that they'll inform the guests about the change in plans and has asked us to do the same for our guests too.'

Saba looked at them and wondered how they could talk of normal things like weddings when Rabia was in the ICU. But then, somebody had to be practical too.

Further into the night, almost everyone had left except for Ammi, Abbu, Zohaib, Shahid and Saba.

'We have a big job ahead of us, informing everyone that the daawat is cancelled,' Abbu said grimly.

'We'll take care of it,' Shahid spoke and Abbu looked at him gratefully.

'We'll hold a valima daawat when Rabia is well,' Abbu said, his voice breaking down a little.

Abbu and Ammi had been inside to see Rafiq bhaijan again. They had been allowed to see Rabia again but she'd been sleeping.

'Shahid, drop Saba and your aunty home. We'll stay here,' Abbu told Shahid and Ammi shook her head.

'I'm not leaving my bachchi, my daughter, and going anywhere!' she said tremulously. Abbu looked perplexed.

'Why do I have to go?' Saba asked. 'I want to stay here with you.'

'Saba, we have guests at home who are wondering what's happening. Please, you have to go home, and take care of them. Inform them about the change in wedding plans. I want Zohaib to be here with me in case there's some running around to do. Go with Shahid,' Abbu said.

Saba nodded her head and Ammi only momentarily looked uneasy at sending Saba with Shahid. Abbu saw her look and shook his head. 'He's not just your damaad. He's your other son now. Go, beta,' he said to Shahid who nodded without saying anything.

Together, Shahid and Saba walked back to the car park and Saba sat inside, heavily. This was not like any of the times she'd sat in the car with Shahid. Not before they became a couple, or after. But this was part of life and she had to accept that life would have both tears and joy.

'Why so thoughtful?' Shahid asked as he reversed the car. Saba shook her head. She didn't want to voice her thoughts and fears. She didn't want to think of the dreadful image of Rabia wrapped in bandages and how mean she'd been to her in the blog.

They were silent throughout the way and, at the signal, Shahid clasped Saba's hand tightly.

'She'll be fine. Really,' he said and then moved his hand back to the gears. Saba felt a heaviness in her chest as she nodded.

'And it's not your fault. Stop thinking that it is,' he said a little later when he saw that she was still staring at the road ahead morosely.

When they reached the house, Saba noted that it was still packed with all the relatives. The thought of facing them again, explaining everything to them suddenly seemed too much for her. She couldn't bring herself to get out of the car at all.

'Saba,' Shahid looked at her as he got out. 'Are you all right?'

She shook her head, her hand trembling a bit. 'I can't go in there. I can't go and sleep when Rabia is in the hospital.'

'Then. . .what will you do?' he asked uncertainly.

'Take me to your house. Please?' she asked and he looked at her surprised and shook his head.

'Please, Shahid! I don't want to face anyone. I just want to sleep in a room without the babble of voices over my head,' Saba said, her lips quivering.

'But won't these people get worried when no one comes from the hospital?' Shahid asked, turning to look at the house.

'Then you go and explain the situation to them,' she turned away because she was on the verge of crying again.

Shahid nodded and left and came back a little while later.

He didn't say anything as he got into the car and drove quickly to his house. That night, Saba slept in Shahid's mother's room, who strangely comforted her better than Ammi could. In fact, Saba put her head in Nausheen Aunty's lap like a small child and fell asleep immediately.

Nausheen Aunty hadn't asked Shahid why Saba was here and not in her own house. She'd quietly accepted her and insisted she eat something before she slept.

Shahid stood at the door, watching his mother caress Saba's head gently and he smiled ruefully.

54

It was a wedding, the kind which no one had ever seen.

On Saturday evening, Rabia had been declared out of danger and had been moved to a private room. What had been Zohaib's haldi was now spent in the hospital, where people were allowed to sit with Rabia in turns. She still looked terrible but her eyes looked better and the scratches on her face seemed to have slightly faded.

The bride's parents had visited Rabia earlier that day. Abbu and the bride's father had spent an hour discussing how to proceed with the wedding. The bride's mother started crying when she saw Rabia's face and Ammi had to console her.

'That poor girl! She looked so beautiful on the day of the engagement! And now. . .look at her!'

Saba felt like kicking the woman's shins. Rabia was not just a patient. She was a *vain* patient who had insisted that a mirror be brought to her the moment she'd been moved to her room. What happened after she saw the mirror was anyone's guess, but it had taken Rafiq bhaijan all of half an hour to console her.

Saba wondered about the previous night when she'd slept in Shahid's house. In retrospect, it seemed like the best sleep she'd ever had in her life. Ammi had been shocked when she learnt that Saba hadn't gone back home at night but had gone to Shahid's house.

'What will everyone say?' she whispered to Saba when she came to the hospital with Shahid. 'The two of you are already behaving like you're married.'

Saba didn't answer her but then she began wondering about getting married. Maybe she didn't want to wait for two more years. Life was short and everything could change in an instant. Zohaib's fancy wedding had been reduced to a simple nikah. Who knew what could happen in the future? She turned to look at Shahid who was talking to Abbu earnestly and she felt her love for him so strongly that she actually told her mother, 'Maybe we will.' Her mother gasped, naturally.

On Sunday morning, Abbu, Shahid and Zohaib, along with some other men, left for the masjid. Some time later, Zohaib came back, a married man. When Abbu and Zohaib left for the hospital, Shahid drove Ammi and some other aunts to the bride's house. Saba also insisted on going because Rabia had told her that she wanted to know how it went.

In the bride's house, it seemed like a repeat of the engagement, only the atmosphere was not that festive. The bride had been seated on a long sofa dressed in the rich and ornate ghagra they had got for her.

The bride's permission had already been procured earlier by witnesses and she'd signed the nikahnama. There was a short ceremony in which Ammi garlanded her, and then put the necklace around her neck and the bangles on her arms. She then hugged the bride with tears in her eyes and she straightened up. What followed was a huge hugging session with all the women hugging each other and crying freely.

Saba took the opportunity to go up next to the bride and sit beside her.

'Hi!'

The bride turned her face uncertainly and smiled at her.

'I'm Saba, Zohaib bhai's younger sister,' she said. The bride nodded her head and whispered,

'I know.'

'You know?' Saba repeated, a little surprised.

'I'm surprised you don't know who I am,' the bride said and Saba felt a little jerk inside. What did she mean?

'Didn't you see the invitation card? Don't you know my name?' the bride whispered.

'I know. It's Ashrafa,' Saba replied.

'My full name is Seema Ashrafa,' she said. Saba still didn't understand. 'I'm the Seema who used to comment on your blog,' she added.

Saba was mortified.

The bride nodded her head and continued whispering, 'I wanted to tell you who I was, but at first I didn't know it was your blog. As in, I didn't know *you* were my future sister-in-law.'

Saba licked her dry lips. 'Then you. . .you know everything,' she said, feeling an odd combination of anxiety and relief.

'Yes. It. . .kind of hurt when I read about Zohaib. In fact, I wanted to talk to my parents about it. And I was horrified when I read that he wanted to call off the wedding. Because my parents would. . .would have been devastated.'

Saba winced and nodded. 'But I decided I'd wait and see what happens. Also, your whole love story with your cousin was so cute, I couldn't resist reading more. And you actually fell for my cousin Uzair?' she asked, giggling.

Saba couldn't answer as the women had surrounded the bride again. They shared a smile before someone led her away.

Ammi wiped the tears from her eyes and then beckoned Saba. 'Let's go. I want to go to the hospital.'

Saba nodded, wishing she could talk to her new sister-in-law for longer. She was amazed at the coincidence, but also glad, because Zohaib's wife knew everything about him.

In the car, she sat at the back with her mother as Shahid drove them to the hospital. Saba watched the back of Shahid's head but she was also listening to her mother speak.

'We have to make arrangements for bringing the bride home tonight. And even though my son's wedding didn't go as we planned, at least his first night with the bride should be the way it was meant to be. Shahid, you'll help in decorating his room, no?' Ammi asked.

Shahid looked at them in the rear view mirror, his eyes meeting Saba's briefly before he nodded. 'Of course, Aunty,' he said and he looked at Saba again. Saba averted her eyes and looked out trying not to laugh. Her mother. Asking her boyfriend/fiancé. To decorate her brother's room. For his first night with his bride. Riya would laugh like crazy when she got to hear about it.

Her mind was formulating one last blog post though.

An auto stopped outside a stately building and two girls stepped out.

'Are you sure this is the right place?' the first girl asked.

'Yes, it is,' the other girl assured her but she looked around nervously.

'Then why isn't anyone here?'

The other girl shrugged and they climbed up the few stairs that led to the entrance, but a man stopped them.

'Where are you going, madam?' he asked the first girl.

'Inside,' she said, making a move to go in.

'There's no one inside,' he said and the first girl glared at the second one.

'I told you this was the wrong place. Zohaib is not getting married here.'

'But Meenakshi, the guys said it was this same place! I had to somehow avoid coming with them so I could bring you along! See the number of times they called me and I didn't answer, because I was going to take you along!' Maya protested.

'Zohaib?' the man asked and Maya nodded eagerly.

'That wedding is over,' he said.

'When?' the girls asked stunned.

'There was some accident in the family so they cancelled the function here, but they proceeded with the wedding in the bride's house,' he explained.

Meenakshi fumed at Maya who looked shocked.

'Why didn't they cancel the wedding?' she asked the man.

The man shrugged philosophically and said, 'Who knows? *Rab ne banadi unki jodi.* Who are we to stop them?'

Meenakshi grit her teeth and Maya looked at her uncomfortably. 'Wait till he comes back to office,' she said and Maya bit her lower lip. This had definitely been a bad idea.

55

The Last Post

POSTED BY THE OTHER T, 30-06-12

As you can see, this is the last post on this blog. I'm sorry but things have been rather hectic at home. Q met with an accident and she almost died and Y's wedding was not a grand affair as we had thought it would be.

I wondered what B and Y would have spoken about on their first night. Or do these newly-weds who don't even know each other do *more* than just talking? Ahem. I wouldn't know.

T texted me the morning after the wedding, saying that Y had called him and told him that he had come clean with B on their first night.

'*And? What did she say?*' I sent back.

'*It's all okay, apparently,*' he replied.

I was a bit surprised. I mean, a woman could be tolerant, but a new bride being this tolerant was a little weird. Then T texted again. '*She's convinced him to look for another job though!*'

Aah! Now it made sense.

B looked radiant in the morning and when we sat down for breakfast, I noticed how Y couldn't stop looking at her. She grinned when she caught my eye.

What happened to Q? She had a terrible accident but thankfully, her baby is fine and so is she. On the day of the nikah, after we came back from B's house, I was describing the wedding to her, when she told me what happened. Her voice was hoarse and she spoke in small spurts. She'd read my blog and she felt bad about the way she'd always treated me, but she also saw how much I'd observed about her husband and the way he'd loved her. That was when she also knew that she loved him and she'd tried telling him that but the accident had happened.

'But I thought my blog was the cause of your accident!' I protested.

'This accident happened because of my foolishness,' Q said and I looked at her, shocked. Q would never have admitted to such a thing before. I leaned towards her bandaged head.

'What are you doing?' she asked.

'Checking if they changed your brain by any chance,' I said.

She made a face and then grimaced because even that hurt. Poor thing!

Abbu had got a permanent worry line on his forehead but Q's husband was looking much better. He would hold her hand the moment they were alone. Such devotion would have been wasted on her, had she been the old Q. But you just had to look at the way she smiled at him and you knew that what she felt for him was strong and true.

My wedding date will be fixed soon and although it's at least a year away, I wish I'd had more time. But, conversely, there are times when I don't want to be away from T any longer. Also, I'm pretty sure that I wouldn't be finished with college even then. Ammi couldn't seem to understand my problem, however.

'So?'

'But how will I go to college?'

'His house is closer to your college. Think of all the auto money you'll save!' she whispered conspiratorially. I didn't know what to say to that.

T is obviously thrilled with the new developments. He says he'll always support me in what I want to do, whether it's my studies or anything else and I know he means it. But hello? I'll be that *girl who got married when she was in college*.

Oh, and have I told you that T is amused that I write my posts as though they were stories?

'Hell! Even I'd fall in love with myself!' he said after re-reading one of my posts. I punched him in the arm and then asked him something I'd been meaning to, anyway.

'So you don't mind me doing this blog thingy, right? I mean, I love writing and all and I still don't know what I want to write. I'm waiting for it to hit me but till then I want to blog and if you say no. . .'

'If I say no?' he asked. We were at home. Abbu and Ammi had gone out to a relative's house with Y and B and there was no one else around. So we were sitting in my room and he was lounging on my bed, idly playing with my dupatta.

'I'm going to still write even if you say no,' I retorted.

'Then what's the point of asking me?' he raised his head.

'Just to make you feel important,' I smirked.

'Very funny,' he said and pulled me down. I could feel the smile on his face as he kissed me and I traced his hairline with my fingers. Then the bell rang and we had to spring apart and act like we didn't know the other existed.

Oh, are you disappointed that I'm going away? Did I not bore you enough with the details of my brother's wedding? No?

Well then, look out for my new blog. It's coming soon. And it's called, 'How we became T Squared'.

Acknowledgments

Thank you, Sidra, Junaid, Ayesha, Shikha, Revs, OT and Geetha for the appreciation and encouragement. Also, thank you Junaid for not freaking out when you heard the name of the book. Above all, thank you, Allah, for freeing the ink in my pen and making this book possible.

product-compliance

990